# DARK
## —OF—
# NIGHT

ALSO BY
RICHARD NEHRBASS

*A Perfect Death for Hollywood*

# DARK
## —OF—
# NIGHT

## RICHARD NEHRBASS

HarperCollins*Publishers*

HarperCollins books may be purchased for educational, business, or sales promotional use. For information, please write: Special Markets Department, HarperCollins Publishers, Inc., 10 East 53rd Street, New York, NY 10022.

FIRST EDITION

*Designed by George J. McKeon*

Library of Congress Cataloging-in-Publication Data
Nehrbass, Richard
  Dark of night / Richard Nehrbass.—1st ed.
      p.      cm.
    ISBN 0-06-016635-5
    I. Title
PS3564.E2645D37  1992
813.54—dc20                                                                        91-58338

92 93 94 95 96 ❖/HC 10 9 8 7 6 5 4 3 2 1

*For Marilynn*

# DARK
## —OF—
# NIGHT

# 1

I HAD BEEN COOLING MY HEELS IN MACKENZIE GORDON'S OFFICE AT Paramount for twenty minutes, flipping through old copies of *Variety*, wandering around touching the fake Mayan pottery, and watching his secretary cross and uncross her legs as she studied *Vogue* as if there were going to be an exam later.

Finally I strode over to a window and stared out at a hangar-like soundstage thirty yards away. A group of men in German World War II army uniforms was walking by in a very unmilitary fashion, smoking cigarettes and joking with one another. Goering would have had them shot, I thought, as one of them flicked a cigarette in a high, long arc into the shrubbery. Gordon would probably only have them whipped.

A soft female voice drifted up behind me, interrupting my reverie. "It won't do any good, you know."

I turned around. Gordon's secretary was staring at me over the magazine, large dark eyes appraising me with studied nonchalance. She was Asian—Vietnamese, I thought—and in her mid-twenties. Very cool. Very professional. And very pretty.

"What won't?" I asked impatiently.

"Seeing Mr. Gordon. He's not accepting screenplays."

"No screenplay," I said wearily and checked my watch. "But there are other ways I could be wasting my time. If this meeting of his is going to drag on much longer . . . " Screw it, I thought; I'm going for a beer.

But the phone buzzed loudly on her desk, and she put the magazine down and picked up the receiver. Even without the phone I could hear Gordon's deafening roar coming through the walls as if he were in the same room. "Is that goddamn Eton here yet?"

Her eyes went back to me as she dredged up her professional-secretary's voice. "Yes, Mr. Gordon. He just . . . "

"Well, send him in, goddamn it," he bellowed and hung up.

She held the phone for just a second, staring at it before putting it down as gently as if it were made of fine china. The room seemed suddenly very quiet. Then she looked at me and smiled beautifully and without the slightest trace of emotion said, "You can go in now, goddamn it."

I smiled back. A sense of humor in Hollywood! Something to treasure in this never-never land of very little people who take themselves very very seriously. As I headed toward Gordon's door, she settled back in her chair and looked at me knowingly. "Anyway, I don't believe you. Everyone has a screenplay. Everyone!"

I wagged my head at her. "I investigate crimes," I said. "I don't commit them," and opened the door in time to hear a whiny male voice say, "But I don't think . . . " only to be interrupted by the same angry growl I had heard through the walls. "Goddamn it, Stiles, when I want your opinion I'll fucking *ask* for it. Do you understand? Until then, keep your mouth shut."

Brandon Stiles, whom I recognized vaguely from the trades, turned pale and then red and stole a look at the young woman seated next to him on the couch before glaring angrily at me as if it were I who had just snapped at him.

Mackenzie Gordon glanced abruptly at me from behind his big-as-a-Buick desk. He seemed wound past the breaking point, and he gave me only a split-second look. "Come on in, Eton. Find a seat. I'll get to you in a minute."

He turned his attention to the other two as Stiles said, "Mackenzie, it's all cliché! Christ, now that we can make some changes let's do it," but Gordon cut him off abruptly. "This isn't Burger King, Brandon! We're doing it my way. You *comprende?* My fucking way! This is last-chance time for you, buddy-boy. I mean it; you make trouble for me, and you'll be doing tire ads for Sears." He turned suddenly toward the young woman.

"And I expect you to keep *wunderkind* here away from *all* artificial stimulants. At least on the set. He wants to snort his brains away at home it's OK with me as long as he's back on the lot by 5:00 A.M."

I sat down in a wing chair between Stiles and Gordon and smiled my happy-to-be-here smile, but no one was paying attention.

Brandon Stiles looked as if he were going to start breaking things, but the young woman gave him a look that said, Relax, we've been through this before, and then turned calmly to Gordon.

"Don't you think you're being a bit harsh on him, Mackenzie?"

"We're two weeks behind schedule already, Kerry! I'm not putting up with any more delays. Now get out of here, both of you. I've got to talk to the shamus, here. And get working on that script."

Stiles and the woman came to their feet and moved in tandem toward the office door, a pair of whipped puppies dashing from under their master's feet. Gordon also stood, looking as though he didn't trust them to leave on their own, and strode brusquely over to the door, shutting it firmly behind them.

"Christ, I'm fucking going down the tubes here, and dipshit out there wants to be *auteur*." He came over and shook hands perfunctorily, introducing himself and flopping down on the couch where the young woman had been sitting.

"Brandon Stiles," I said. "I remember his early work. It was pretty good—sort of a cut-rate American Bergman."

"Well, he's going to be a cut-rate American shoe salesman if this picture doesn't turn a profit. He's had four straight bombs and he's not even thirty. Christ, even in Hollywood that's a record worth noting. I'm his last fucking hope; no one in this town will touch him anymore. The only reason he's working now's because I've got him back-ended: the picture goes in the black, and he gets his cut; if not, he sucks air. I'm saving the little creep's life, and he wants to *argue* with me about clichés! We're not doing *Wild Strawberries*, for Christ's sakes, we're not doing art. We're doing a *commercial* fucking film that people pay money to see. What's this *cliché* shit?"

"The younger generation," I said with a shake of my head. "They never have their priorities straight."

Mackenzie Gordon looked at me as if he suddenly realized who I was. Then he sagged back on the couch and wiped a thin film of perspiration from his head with the back of his hand. He was a heavyset and rough-looking man close to fifty, going bald and paunchy but with an intimidating air about him as if he were used to hand-to-hand combat. He had appeared in town suddenly from Canada thirty years ago with a small reputation as a TV writer/producer/director. Now he was one of the biggest film producers in Hollywood, an independent who only rented the office space we were in from Paramount. I had never met him before. He came suddenly to his feet as if yanked by invisible wires and began to prowl the large room. When he spoke again his voice was strangely subdued. "I talked to studio security about a problem I've got, and they recommended you. They said you know the community, Hollywood—" He waved a thick, hairy arm toward the window and the world that loomed vaguely outside and then looked at me.

I was being sized up and didn't particularly like it: prove your worth in thirty seconds or less. But there was no point in getting riled, I knew; it was just Gordon's producer's mind-set: Three decades of giving writers and agents ten minutes to pitch as many projects as they could had reduced his decision process to a consideration of quick sound bites. I gave him what he wanted. "My office is a block down Bronson. I'm on retainer to three studios, things their own staffs can't do or don't have the time for or don't want to do. I have a lot of contacts in the industry. I know what I'm doing. I charge a lot of money. And I get it." Not a bad spiel, I thought: three-movie deals had been made on less.

Gordon stopped prowling and looked at me. "Discreet?"

"You'd never heard of me," I reminded him. "You had to ask."

"Yeah, OK. Christ." He sat down again on the couch and looked at me. "It's my daughter. She's gone. Fourteen years old."

"Sorry," I said. "I don't do runaways. Or divorces. I'll recommend someone who specializes in that sort of thing." I took out a card and started to write the names of a couple of guys I know.

Gordon impatiently waved a large hand in the air. He had thick blunt fingers, with clumps of dark, wiry hair between the knuckles. Strangler's hands, I thought, hands made for breaking things. "It's not just a runaway. Listen to me, Christ, I wish that's all it was. Laural—Laurie—she's fourteen, cute as a bug, brown hair, big brown eyes, and a smile you'd kill for. Look—" He leaned toward the desk and turned a picture frame around so I could see it. He was right—

she was darling, grinning at the photographer, a playful look dancing in her eyes. A doll.

"She's mentally retarded. Nobody knows why, she just is. She's like a four- or five-year-old. She left three days ago, and I haven't any idea how she's taking care of herself. It's not like she's shacking up in Hollywood Boulevard crash pads like most runaways around here. She's like a little kid; she got mad because I wouldn't let her stay up one night and watch a video, and she snuck out of the house when I was asleep. How's she eating? Where's she staying? This city's crazy at night, like a war zone. I don't want her running around out there—all the fucking creeps and weirdos."

"Did you call the police?"

He shook his head slowly and stared at the floor. "No. No cops. Not for a few days, anyway. I don't want her mother worrying for nothing. She's in England doing a film for Lucas. Laurie's just upset. I figured she'd get scared out there and come back. When she didn't, I started looking around the neighborhood. Christ, I spent the whole weekend knocking on doors, driving around, asking people—" He sank back against the couch and closed his eyes, sounding defeated.

"When she left she took some things—some candy bars, a little stuffed unicorn she sleeps with. Then she came in the den and took the cartoon video I wouldn't let her watch. But what's killing me is she grabbed an envelope off my desk—one of those big accordion things. It's all pre-production material for the film we're working on—shooting script, storyboards, crap like that. It's important and I need it back."

"You don't have copies of all that?" I asked.

"Not the storyboards; it's only for the director—you only *need* one. That's what boy-wonder was in here crying about. I make directors stick to plan: I don't go for that 'artistic freedom' and 'fix it in editing' shit. It's just their way of getting a blank check. You don't keep tight reins on these assholes, they come back with eight million feet of film and spend two years cutting and pasting, making it 'perfect.' Meanwhile, all the money you invested isn't returning diddly. I don't work that way. I've got every goddamn shot worked out ahead of time—*every* shot—and then before filming, we go over it frame by frame, combining scenes and setting up schedules for everyone on both sides of the cameras. Everyone gets a firm schedule for the entire shoot broken down in fifteen-minute segments: where they're supposed to be, what costumes, and so on. None of this hurry-up-and-wait crap and playing pinochle on the set. The bankers don't wait and I don't wait. We're shooting this film out in Agoura beginning the ninth of next month; twenty days later we're done. Bam. Without the storyboards I can't do that, and I sure as hell don't have the time to plan it all over again."

"The girl's mother?" I asked. "Catherine Wilbourne, isn't it?" Ex–child actress and current star of more-than-modest proportions and more-than-massive fortune, much of it based on a treacly Christmas film done when she was eight years old and now resurrected each December with the regularity of sing-along *Messiah*s and second-rate *Nutcracker*s.

Mackenzie Gordon nodded and ran a hand through his thinning hair. "She's supposed to be in England for two more weeks, maybe three. I don't want to upset her if we don't have to. You find Laurie and *then* I'll tell her."

"I haven't decided to take the case," I reminded him.

He stiffened for a minute and looked at me. "Look, Eton . . . Vic. I called the people at City Federal Bank who put up the front money on this film—or half of it anyway: nine million bucks. Every day I lose money, they lose money. They've authorized me to pay you fifty thousand dollars if we get the script material and storyboards back in seven days. That's a lot of money for a week's work. I've got a contract all drawn up." He began to head toward the desk.

"You want your daughter back, too? Or just the storyboards?"

He stopped halfway to his desk, and for a moment he looked as if he were going to hit me as color rose in his face. Then he took a breath and forced himself to calm down. "Of *course* I want my daughter back. But she has the goddamn script material."

"*Had*," I said. "There's no telling if she still has it."

"Jesus Christ," he said heatedly. "Are you going to do it or not? I'll find someone else if you won't."

I sat back in the chair and stared at his flushed middle-aged face and thought for a moment. I'd already seen enough of Gordon not to want to have anything to do with him—but I sympathized with his concern for his daughter. With its legions of predators—sexual and otherwise—Hollywood was no place for a runaway—especially an attractive and retarded fourteen-year-old girl. If she wasn't found soon there was no telling what would happen to her. And any way I looked at it, fifty thousand was a hell of a lot of money for a week's work. Still, the "legendary" Mackenzie wasn't the sort of person I enjoyed working for, with his offhand rudeness and bullyboy mannerisms. So . . .

What the hell, compromise, make everyone happy.

"If I find the script material it'll cost you the fifty thousand; if I don't come up with it within a week, I get five thousand a week plus expenses for as long as you want me to keep at it. I'll look for Laurie for nothing."

He eyed me with relief, if not quite gratitude, his fat arms hanging loosely at his sides. "Thank God." His face softened suddenly, and he sank down on the couch looking almost lifeless and seemed for a moment to be stripped naked, a man facing the world without defenses, a father worried sick about his daughter. "Look, I'm sorry for yelling at you but, Jesus, this is killing me. Ulcers . . . " He shoved a hand into a shirt pocket and came up with two tablets the size of quarters, which he threw in his mouth and began to chew with obvious distaste. "Security told me you got a daughter, too. You must know how it is. And Laurie, being special . . . I mean she can do some things OK, feed herself and take the bus and watch TV— but not sleeping on the streets. Your wife's dead, I heard. You raising your kid yourself? It must be tough."

"We're raising each other," I said. "It works out. When did Laurie leave?"

"Thursday night, Friday morning; I'm not sure. I went in her room at six, she wasn't there. She usually takes the bus to the Holstead Special Day School about two miles away. I could drive her, but the teachers want her to do it herself to teach her independence. I wonder what they'd think of her fucking independence now?"

"Can I have that picture?" I said and pointed at the desk.

"Sure." He walked over and extricated it from the silver frame.

"Any friends she might be staying with?"

He handed the photo over and sat down again behind his desk. "Most of her friends are kids she only sees at the school. She wouldn't have any way of knowing where they live. Except for a girl she sees on the bus. Sometimes she goes over to the kid's house to play after school. Stephanie something . . . Stephanie Chauk, I think. They live about a mile from us, on Chester." He yanked an address book from the top drawer of the desk. "Twenty-three twenty Chester Circle. Her dad's name's Gregory; he's a professor at UCLA. Chemistry, something like that. Laurie and Stephanie see each other once a week at most. She's not always easy to play with." He looked up at me. "There aren't any others—" and left the sentence hanging.

"Has she ever done this before?"

"No, not overnight, anyway. Sometimes she'd run as far as the house next door. Usually when she gets mad she just goes to her room and slams the door."

"Is there any chance she's still at your place? Maybe hiding out in the back yard?"

"Christ, I don't see how," he said with annoyance. "I've gone through the house and grounds three times. She isn't there."

"Maybe I should check it out, anyway," I said. "I could do it this morning."

"Look, Eton, she's *not there*. I checked! Why would she take all that crap if she wasn't really planning to leave? I want you on the streets, not wasting your time doing what I've already done."

I stood up and sighed, already half-regretting that I'd promised a week to Mackenzie Gordon; as an employer he was going to be argumentative and domineering, traits I had expected to leave behind when I quit the Department five years ago. But hell, I reminded myself needlessly: fifty thousand. For that I could put up with just about anybody. For a week, anyway. "You better give me your home phone number," I said. "And any other place you might be this week in case I have to get you in a hurry."

He snatched a gold ballpoint off the desk and scrawled three numbers on an engraved memo sheet and shoved it over to me. "The first one's the Beverly Hills house and the second's my beach place at Malibu. The other's this number. Christ, I'll probably be here twenty hours a day. Find my girl, Eton. I miss her."

I left Mackenzie Gordon sitting at his desk staring at a pile of papers, and retreated to the outer office where the receptionist glanced up from her reading and gave me an I-told-you-so look. "No luck, huh?"

I nodded at the magazine that seemed to constitute the whole of her work. "Pretty boring job?"

"I'm a temp; this is my second day. Be honest with me—did he look at your script?"

I gave her an enigmatic smile—something to think about—and put Gordon's phone numbers in my pocket. "What kind of story are *you* working on?"

"A nuclear accident at a power plant in Mexico. And don't look at me like that. Everyone's got a screenplay. No matter what you say. If you didn't leave it with Gordon it's in the right-hand bottom drawer of your desk at home. You're just waiting for the right time to send it in. Or hoping you'll meet an assistant director or story editor at a party. I'm right, aren't I?"

"You've spent too much time in Hollywood," I said and shook my head sadly. "It's corrupted and tainted you, robbed you of your innocence, and put a giant zit on your nose. Who's the woman with Brandon Stiles?"

Her hand started to rise to her face but she restrained it in mid-air. "Kerry Daniels. She's an assistant producer."

"Is her office in this building?"

"Last door on the right before you get to the exit. But it won't do any good; she hasn't got script approval."

I found the office a minute later, Stiles's now-familiar whine drawing me to it like a radio beacon. I walked up to the open door and knocked. "Do you folks mind if I ask you a couple of questions?"

Kerry Daniels was sitting behind a cluttered desk with Stiles across from her, folded rigidly into a metal director's chair. He was dressed in the accepted boy-director's uniform of black work pants, checked shirt, skinny black tie, and Day-Glo suspenders. He glared at me with hostility, but Kerry smiled half-heartedly and waved me toward another identical director's chair next to Stiles. He seemed to cringe as I sat down, as if my physical presence were an affront to his sense of propriety or artistic integrity.

"It's about Laurie, isn't it?" Kerry asked.

I nodded. "We didn't get a chance to introduce ourselves," I said and shook hands with both of them. Stiles had offered his small, soft hand reluctantly, as if he weren't sure he'd get it back, but Kerry seemed unaffected by his obvious animosity; used to it, probably. She looked to be about thirty, trim, athletic, with a nice tomboyish body. Pretty but not Hollywood-beautiful. In front of the cameras she would have been best friend or comic relief, not the star. I wasn't sure what her status was here. Or how much she knew about Laurie.

"Did Gordon tell you what happened?" I asked her.

"Of course. I know Laurie quite well. She's a sweet kid, a lot of fun. Sometimes she gets a little moody, though. I guess it's difficult for Mackenzie with Catherine on location somewhere half the time. You're going to be looking for her, I hope. You took the job?"

I nodded and turned to Stiles. "Did you know her, too?"

He stared at me through thick tortoiseshell glasses, worry marks etched prematurely and permanently in his face—the onetime superstar director in decline but still haughty and proud, as only deposed royalty and the Hollywood elite can be. "Of course I know her. Now if you don't mind we've got a script to work on. . . ."

I turned back to Kerry. "You're working on the material Laurie took?"

She nodded and looked at me with a haggard expression that hinted at overwork and a lack of sleep. "We can reconstruct everything but the storyboards. Even without them we can go ahead with the shooting next month; it'll just mean more time, more film shot. And more money, of course."

"And a once-in-a-lifetime opportunity for some real creativity in a Gordon film forever down the drain," Brandon Stiles snapped. "It'd be our chance to do something authentic and meaningful instead of another one of those over-controlled monstrosities the great Mackenzie is so fond of. Did you know he's got every goddamn frame planned out ahead of time? It's paint-by-numbers. What the hell does he need me for? He could use a gaffer off the set and save another seven dollars."

I turned to look at him, keeping my face blank but just a little put off by his manner. "I guess I don't understand," I said. "Someone's forcing you to work on this film? You can't walk away if you don't like it?"

Stiles came suddenly out of his chair, all 140 pounds of him, and looked as if he were going to kick me in the shins, then stalked off to the far end of the office.

Kerry's pretty face smiled uncomfortably at me. "We've got a lot of work to do, so . . . "

"Do you have any idea where Laurie might be?"

"No—"

"Or why she took the script material?"

"I really don't think she planned that, Mr. Eton. She wouldn't even know what it was. I think she just grabbed a few things in a hurry and left. The things she took aren't of any value to her. Just us."

"Does she like you?"

"Very much. We get along fine, have a lot of fun."

"Would she try to contact you?"

She looked at me with uncertainty, thinking about it. "I don't know. I don't know if she would know how to get to my house. Or even call me. She can use a phone, but I don't think she could find my number; it's unlisted."

Brandon Stiles's sarcasm-laden voice tweaked up from behind me. "Oh, I think our little Laurie would find a way if she really wanted to."

"What does that mean?" I asked, turning around and looking at him.

"It means maybe she isn't as incapacitated as Gordon makes out. Maybe she knew exactly what she was doing when she walked out with that stuff."

I turned back to Kerry. "Can you think of anything that might help me find her? Some place she might go, some friends maybe?"

She shrugged helplessly. "No, I'm afraid not. Nothing."

Stiles was making impatient noises behind me and Kerry obviously didn't want to prolong our meeting. No sense irritating everyone right off the bat, I thought: I had a week to accomplish that. I stood up and took out a business card and put it down on the desk directly in front of her. "If you do think of anything, give me a call. If I'm not in just leave a message on the machine. I'd better get your home number, too, in case I need to talk to you again."

She hesitated a minute, then scribbled a number on a piece of paper. I didn't look at it until I was outside. It was the same as Mackenzie Gordon's beach house.

# 2

I WALKED THE SHORT BLOCK FROM PARAMOUNT TO MY OFFICE building on Bronson and picked up my Buick for the trip to Hollywood Station on Wilcox. It was chilly for November, and I shivered as I left the car in the gated rear lot with its BMWs and Porsches and crossed the fifty yards or so to the station house, a squat, unimaginative, boxy-looking building from the 1950s when architects seemed determined to cover all of California with squat, unimaginative, boxy-looking buildings. I found Rudy Cruz in the cavernous squad room upstairs at the desk he had worked at for a dozen years; the adjacent desk where I had frittered away four mostly dreary years was piled high with papers and empty coffee cups and soda cans, but no one was seated there. "Where's Fernandez?" I asked as I dropped down in the uncomfortable visitor's chair.

Rudy didn't look up from the departmental form he was writing on. "Kicking in doors, depriving people of their civil rights. Same old shit." He was forty-four but looked younger, only some receding around the hairline hinting at encroaching middle age. And a few stray gray hairs. "Premature gray," I had told him once, and he had said, "All gray is premature, one of God's little jokes on the human race, like brussels sprouts." I had known him eight years and figured I'd seen him smile maybe twice. He glanced at his watch and continued his neat, precise writing. "Shouldn't you be doing lunch at Spago?"

"Lunch is out. Now it's conceptual breakfasts: avocado and shad roe omelets, fresh guava juice from Surinam, tofu salad."

"Yum yum." He put his pen down and plucked a half-eaten candy bar from under the mounds of litter on the desk and offered it to me like a maître d' brandishing a bottle of Lafite Mouton. "Want some of my Kit Kat?"

"You're too kind. But I'd rather have some information."

"Information? Hell, yeah! Why not?" He tilted back suddenly in his swivel chair, the tips of his black bandido mustache curling with studied menace over the ends of his mouth; he looked like a half-mad Pancho Villa, a revolutionary in a sport coat. "Information is what we do best, my son. What is it you wish to know? The order of battle in the Crimean War? The vote breakdown in the 1960 presidential election? The proper wine for ragout?"

I plucked a witness-interview form off his desk and scribbled some names on the back before handing it to him. "Ask your computer for its innermost secrets."

He looked at the list, dark eyes narrowing with interest. "Mackenzie Gordon. A movie guy, right? And married to Catherine Wilbourne? That his real name?"

"I imagine," I said. "It's the name he came to Hollywood with. He's a Canadian by birth, may not be a citizen."

"Brandon Stiles. Last year's Steven Spielberg, this year's nothing. Such interesting friends you have. Kerry Daniels. Male or female?"

"Very female. I think Gordon and she are what the gossip columnists used to call 'an item.' Maybe you should run Gordon's daughter past someone in Juvie, too. Her name's Laurie, a runaway but not reported so far."

"That what you're looking for? The daughter? Catherine Wilbourne's daughter?"

I nodded.

"I thought you didn't do runaways." He stared at me without expression, curious now, wondering what I was up to, wondering if I was going to tell him.

"The girl's retarded, Rudy. Fourteen years old but the mind of a child. I look at her picture, and I think, what if that were Tracy? What if she were handicapped like that and lost somewhere in Hollywood? I want to get her home before some street punk rapes her or carves a swastika on her face. Her old man doesn't seem as concerned with that as he is with getting back some script material she took. It's costing him big bucks, he says." If I was right, I thought, if Gordon was really more concerned about his film than his daughter, would Laurie sense that? Or was she too disabled to tell? I didn't have any experience with kids like that, but I had to think she'd know. She'd realize what her mom and dad thought about her. And if she were unloved, she'd just be that much more determined to stay hidden.

Rudy put the list in his shirt pocket and shook his head. "This'll take a while; our new management-information philosophy stresses bilateral interfacing and sequenced terminal interdependence."

"What does that mean?"

"We wait in line. I'll call you tonight. How's Tracy?"

"A mystery. She's getting C's in the courses she likes and A's in the ones she hates. You figure it."

"I've got three in high school at the same time; I don't try to make sense of anything. Where are you going to start looking for the kid?"

"Gordon lives in Beverly Hills. The girl knows how to ride the bus. I guess I'll follow the bus line first; that would take me to the beach or Hollywood. This time of year she probably wouldn't head for the beach."

"So Hollywood. Do you know how many runaways end up here every year? Ten thousand, Juvie says. Maybe more. What do you think your chances are of finding this one?"

"I've got to find her, Rudy. It's been colder than hell at night, she's vulnerable and confused, and she's going to end up in pretty bad shape if she doesn't turn up soon."

I got to my feet, stretched, and glanced around at the squad room; it was going through the early afternoon doldrums: half-empty; cops in shirt sleeves sitting in clumps of two and three, feet up on desktops and talking, drinking coffee; other cops typing, speaking on the phone, or hunched over, writing reports. A radio tuned to a rock station. All very relaxed, getting ready for shift change and the madness of night. I looked down at Rudy, 240 pounds of hardened bulk taking up the ancient wooden swivel chair, and a thought moved in my mind, but I decided, No, it couldn't be:

It was just a cliché, a sort of running gag around the studios. But maybe I'd ask anyway. Just to see.

Keeping my voice light, I said, "You working on a screenplay?"

Rudy blinked dark eyes at me, his face going blank. Then his gaze darted quickly around the room as if he had become suddenly conscious of assassins lurking nearby, before coming again to rest on me. "Why do you ask that?" Sounding a little strained.

I gave a silent, rueful sigh. Eight years I had known Rudy: homicide partners, fishing buddies, drinking companions, seekers after truth, adventurers in Hollywood high- and low-life. We had been through it all, I thought: attacked by a crazed kung fu expert in front of the Pantages who broke the window of our car with his foot and my arm with his hand; shot at by a psycho on Las Palmas who turned his AK-47 on his wife and then us, getting off 150 rounds before Rudy calmly put a bullet in his thigh; rushed at by a peace-and-love hippie who slashed Rudy's face with a straight razor when we tried to question him about a shooting. I'd never seen Rudy scared, never seen him squirm. His expression was frozen into icy impassivity now but he was definitely squirming behind those moist dark eyes.

It was sort of fun to watch.

"I'm doing an arts survey," I explained calmly.

No response.

I shoved my hands in my jacket pockets. "I thought working in Hollywood here maybe you'd give it a shot, be creative on something other than your expense report."

He made a small offhand gesture to indicate our conversation was becoming remarkably silly and then glanced casually around the office again and took a little breath. "Well . . . I figure Joe Wambaugh, all the dough he made from writing up station house scuttlebutt . . . " His eyes came tentatively back to me. "I thought I could maybe do a little too, work in some of the weird shit we run into. You know, a day in the life of a homicide dick . . . " He began to show a little life. "Look, who told you? Julie?"

"Is it in your desk? Bottom right-hand drawer?"

His eyes darted to the desk. "No, no. Hey!" He leaned forward, suddenly struck by a great idea. "You think, uh . . . maybe if you run into a director or script editor over at Paramount you could let them see it? I know! I'll make you a copy. Maybe we could work together on this—"

I left Rudy musing on fantasies of the good life after his first sale—Aston-Martin automobiles, eel-skin boots, brunch with Madonna—and trotted down to the lobby where I used a pay phone to call Eddy Baskerville and ask him to meet me in an hour at Sid's on Gower. Eddy said sure; he didn't even ask why: a free meal, Eddy figured, was a free meal.

Sid himself met me when I came in the door. He's a bald-headed skinny little guy about fifty with a perpetually worried look on his face. He greeted me like the wagon trains used to greet the Seventh Cavalry in Republic films. "I was about to call your office. You really send Available Eddy over here? He's wolfing down lasagna and wine like a mule. He says you're paying."

We were standing by the little reservation table where the hostess, a striking six-foot-two blonde, was greeting a group of Japanese businessmen with "Smoking or non smoking?" a choice that seemed to fill them with unrestrained glee at odd American ways.

"How long's he been here?" I asked.

"Thirty-four dollars."

"Put it on the monthly. What room's he in?"

Sid gestured impatiently toward the next room. "Twinkies. I shoulda put him in Locals so he don't scare the Dubuques. Get him outta here soon as you can."

Sid's whole life is a series of simple dichotomies: good-bad, night-day, black-white. Dubuques to Sid are the out-of-towners who make up the bulk of his considerable business as opposed to the locals who hang out in the dreary back room and guzzle beer and poke indifferently at pasta and pizza. Twinkies is the large brightly lit front room where Dubuques come to stare at Stars but settle for their chalked caricatures strewn around the walls as if they were regular customers.

Eddy was sitting regally in the middle of it all at a table for four with two bottles of wine and a half-dozen plates of food.

He gave me a cursory look as I sat down, and said, "I ordered for you," before reattacking a plate of spaghetti.

"You might have asked me what I wanted," I replied as I carefully pushed dirty plates aside to give me some room of my own.

"It don't matter; I'm eating it. Have some bread."

A waitress came by and rolled her eyes at me.

"Just coffee," I told her, and she nodded her head and said, "It figures."

Available Eddy was a generally unemployed 270-pound actor in his forties who did odd jobs for people. I used him for legwork I didn't have the time or inclination for. He poured out the last of the wine and said, "So what's up?"

I picked up the Chianti bottle and looked at the label, trying to guess its price. "Disappeared teenager."

"Yuk."

"I know. But $250 a day will make it more palatable."

He finished off his wine, wiped his mouth with the napkin, and leaned back in the chair with a satisfied look on his face. "Hey, that was pretty good, wasn't it? Let's have some dessert."

The waitress came by with my coffee, and Eddy ordered apple pie.

"You want a piece or the whole pie?" she asked him curtly.

"Hey, back off, hon. Just two pieces would be fine. OK? What do you want, Vic?"

I said nothing for me, and she wandered off, muttering under her breath.

Eddy burped silently, then said, "These two Dubuques came over to the table and asked for my autograph. Elmer and Rose something-or-other from Knoxville. They're sitting over in the corner behind a potted palm staring at us. See 'em?"

I glanced in the direction he indicated and saw a sixtyish couple ogling us and whispering excitedly. All that way and they end up staring at Available Eddy, I thought to myself.

"I didn't know who the hell they thought I was," he went on. "So I said what picture of mine did you like best? No *picture*, they said; they liked watching me wrestle on the cable every Saturday. The Marauding Marvel or some shit like that. So I took the paper they gave me and scrawled a big fucking X on it and sent 'em away happy."

Elmer and Rose seemed happy, sure enough. Rose was fiddling in her purse for her Kodak, and Eddy gave her a big toothy smile and wiggled his fingers in a wave, then turned to me and said, "Let's trash the place for them."

"Do you ever wonder why you don't get more parts?" I asked him.

"Hell, no," he grinned at me. "I'm harder than hell to be around. I know that! Why the hell are we looking for a kid?"

"She's Mackenzie Gordon and Catherine Wilbourne's," I said and then told him the whole story.

He looked at me reproachfully. "Catherine Wilbourne! Christ, I remember her from thirty years ago: Like Elizabeth Taylor—always a star. But a fourteen-year-old retarded girl in Hollywoodland, Vic. This is definitely not going to be fun. You got a picture?"

I shoved the picture Gordon had given me across the table. Eddy picked it up gingerly in his massive hand and grunted. "Cute little thing. About Tracy's age, isn't she? Not someone you want wandering the streets."

"That's what I figure," I said. "I'll get the picture reproduced, and you can hand it out; it'll be another day or two, though, so you'll have to start without it." I glanced over Eddy's head and saw Sid flitting nervously from table to table, throwing anxious glances in our direction as if he expected Eddy to set the tablecloth on fire or start chasing the kitchen help with a meat cleaver. Eddy's reputation seemed to be taking on mythic proportions.

"How do you want to handle it?" he grunted as he wiggled his fingers happily again at Rose.

So we talked it out a while. I decided to handle the main east-west streets—Hollywood and Sunset, maybe Santa Monica—and Eddy would do the cross streets. He'd done this sort of thing enough to know the likely places to look: abandoned apartment buildings, alleys, city parks, and the newest crash pads of choice—tucked up underneath freeway overpasses. Eddy was pretty good at this and seemed to have decent rapport with street people, maybe because of his obvious disdain for the bourgeois life-style.

"This might take a while," he said when I finished.

"Well, we gotta find her. She won't last long if we don't." We agreed to a fifty-fifty split if he turned up the script material. "But don't bet the mortgage on it," he said. "She probably dumped it in the first trash can."

Just then the waitress came up to the table and dropped an entire apple pie, pan and all, in front of Eddy from a height of three feet; it hit the table with a metallic thud, letting loose little rivulets of apple juice that overflowed and ran down the edge of the pan and onto the table cloth. Everyone in the room was watching now, and Rose was nervously fiddling with her camera as Elmer bent over the table and whispered frantically at her.

"I figured, what-the-hell, Eddy," the waitress said. "Two pieces! I mean, it isn't going to hold you until dinner, is it? So why not have the whole thing?"

Eddy looked up at her and beamed. "Hey! Thanks a lot, hon! That's really sweet of you. I think we should leave you a little extra for that." He leaned across the table and patted my hand. "Hey, Vic. Double the tip, OK? She's a sweet kid."

Rose had scurried over to our table and began snapping pictures as Available Eddy attacked his pie with a fork, eating from the center outward.

I wanted to get on the streets before dark, so I left Eddy with Rose and Elmer and drove over to La Brea, where I dropped my car in a lot near A & M Records after retrieving my suede jacket from the trunk. Winter, or what passes for winter in LA, had arrived with authority, sneaking over the Tehachapis from the northern end of the state, chill winds slicing through steep mountain passes that wouldn't be here after the next major quake. The Big One, they kept calling it on TV, as civic officials incessantly harangued an uncaring populace to hoard bottled water and other necessities, force-feeding scenes of certain death and destruction. But how, I always wondered, was bottled water supposed to escape this massive devastation?

As I came out onto Hollywood Boulevard and into a stream of pedestrians I pondered how best to start. All I had to work with was the single picture of Laurie that Gordon had given me, and the knowledge that most kids head for the lights, which meant downtown Hollywood or West Hollywood, and that she either walked or took the bus. Assuming that the second notion made more sense in Laurie's case, I stationed myself at the nearest bus stop, struck a this-is-an-official-investigation pose, and started flashing the picture to the elderly men and women huddled in the three-sided shelter or climbing unsteadily off the buses. They looked at it, looked at me, and wordlessly shook their heads. Bus drivers hissed the door shut in my face unless I got on, then snarled in a half-dozen languages that I was making them late. The teenage hangers-on at the corner wouldn't even go that far, staring with blank, sullen faces or expressing their view of society in general with the stock phrase of a generation: "Get fucked," mumbled under their breath while looking through me as though I were invisible.

After three hours I began to work my way east on Hollywood, shivering in the icy wind, stopping at the shops and bus stops and flashing the picture. The air was clear and smogless, the temperature dropping rapidly; it was obvious that it was going to be near freezing tonight—no weather for sleeping on the streets or in a park.

By four o'clock I had worked my way down to Western, probably as far east as Laurie would have been likely to go, and several blocks beyond the superficial glitz and glitter of central Hollywood. I stopped at a photocopy shop and left Laurie's picture with instructions to print a thousand fliers with my office number and "Reward" prominently displayed. Then I went home.

At dinner Tracy told me I was going about it all wrong.

"Most little kids don't really run away, Dad. They just want their parents to think they did. If Laurie thinks like a five-year-old she'll do what I did."

"What did you do?" I asked.

"You don't remember? Before Mom died?"

There was a vague recollection rattling around somewhere in the back of my mind. But it wasn't clear.

Tracy seemed crushed. "I thought you and Mom were so worried. I ran away and left a note that said I'd never come back. Then I went to Christy's house and told her mom that it was OK if I stayed overnight. But her mom called you, and you came and got me and stuck me in my room for two days.

"Five-year-olds don't run away," she went on. "They don't know how to run away. You ought to check her friends' houses."

But the only friend her father could think of had been . . . I took the slip of paper from my pocket. Stephanie Chauk, 2320 Chester Circle. No phone number. But surely Gordon would already have checked with them. It would have been one of the first places to call.

I dialed directory assistance and was surprised to find that the number was listed. A moment later I was talking to Gregory Chauk. Yes, he knew about young Laurie's disappearance. Mr. Gordon—he hadn't actually ever met the man even though their daughters were friends—had phoned him the morning he had discovered Laurie missing. No, he hadn't seen her in two or three weeks but, of course, he'd jot down my number and call me if anything turned up.

"Then she's still in the neighborhood," Tracy said. "Probably close enough so she can see her house. Or even sleeping in her own backyard at night. Or she's at her school."

Of course, the school. I had forgotten about that. There wouldn't be anybody there this late, so I would have to wait to check it out. But I called Mackenzie Gordon at his office number and asked him to check out his backyard once more after he got home and again early in the morning. It was possible she had never actually run away at all, I told him. He didn't expect to be home for hours, he said, but of course he'd check the yard when he did.

I started thinking again about the Chauks. Maybe that did make the most sense at this point. Where else was Laurie likely to turn up? Who else was she likely to turn to? At any rate, it was worth checking out.

I told Tracy to get to her homework, then took a thermos of coffee and a flight bag I keep prepared for stakeouts, and drove out to the Chester Circle address where the Hollywood Hills segue into more upscale Beverly Hills. Gregory Chauk's house, like its neighbors, was an unprepossessing Spanish-style stucco home in a middle-class neighborhood that had been caught suddenly in the midst of the local real estate feeding frenzy. UCLA professors could no longer afford to buy into an area like this, where homes now cost ten or twenty times what he and most of his neighbors made in a year. Those who had gotten in early enough generally hung on until retirement, then sold out to record company executives or MD's and left for the Oregon coast, where they could live like royalty on the profits.

I cruised slowly past the Chauks' address, noting the seven-year-old Toyota in the driveway, then U-turned at the corner and parked a hundred yards up the street, behind a motor home, facing the house. It was eight o'clock and already cold; if Laurie were looking for a warm place to hide out she'd be doing it by now. I turned the radio to the Lakers game, poured a cup of coffee, and waited.

For two hours cars rolled by and pulled into driveways; lights snapped on and off in houses. I took a Chesterton paperback from the flight bag and read a couple of Father Brown stories in the cool, vaporish light from a street lamp. A patrol car prowled by around ten o'clock, and the uniformed policeman looked at me without interest and kept going.

Lights remained on in the Chauk house, but there was no discernible movement. Then shortly after ten-thirty a middle-aged man with glasses and a beard came out in a bathrobe and yelled something. Moments later a gray cat padded up silently behind him and disappeared through the partly open door into the house. The man retreated inside. I started the car up and ran the heater. Lakers 122, Celts 118 . . . No more coffee. I found a candy bar in the bag and ate it. The porch light went out at the house but lights remained on inside.

I was verging on sleep shortly after eleven, when a Mercedes sedan crawled down the street and turned into the Chauks' short driveway; the driver got out and walked around to the front door. As he passed into the moist light of a street lamp I thought I recognized him but couldn't be sure. I sat up and watched. After a moment someone let him in. Fifteen minutes later the man emerged and hurried to his car. I started up the Buick, and when he left I slipped into gear and pulled forward, keeping his taillights in view as he drove through Beverly Hills. Five minutes later he drew into the circular driveway of his Atherton Drive estate. I pulled over to the side of the road and walked back to the driveway entrance, the only place from which the mansion was visible from behind the ten-foot hedge that lined the street, and wondered if Gordon was going to check the grounds for his daughter. I waited for an hour but he didn't come outside again.

# 3

AT EIGHT THE NEXT MORNING I WAS BACK AT GREGORY CHAUK'S. I wondered what the hell Mackenzie Gordon, a man Chauk claimed not to know, was doing here last night. And why Gordon didn't mention anything about planning to come out to the Chauks' when I'd talked to him earlier in the evening. But the Toyota was gone from the driveway and no one answered the bell.

I left my card wedged in the door and drove to my office at the McKay Building on Bronson, just off Melrose. From my second-story window I can see a bit of Paramount studios, and if I were to stretch far enough out I could probably catch a glimpse of the low-slung building on the far side of the lot where Mackenzie Gordon rented space. I took the phone from the desk and wandered over to the window as I dialed the number Gordon had given me; when his receptionist asked who was calling I said "F. Scott Fitzgerald" as pleasantly as I could, and she "Ohh-ed" excitedly and said she *knew* I was working on a script, then put me through to Gordon.

"You come up with anything yet?" he growled impatiently; I could hear a jumble of other voices in the background and wondered who he was browbeating today.

"Not yet," I told him. "What about you?"

"Christ, no. I was here half the night trying to get this goddamn script straightened out. I checked the grounds when I got home but she wasn't there. What the hell have you been up to?"

I told him about my wanderings along Hollywood Boulevard and said I'd probably work my way the other direction today. I said nothing about staking out the Chauks' house or seeing him there. He wasn't happy, but I had yet to see him happy about anything, and after a couple of minutes of desultory conversation I hung up.

Then I remembered what Tracy had said about Laurie perhaps being somewhere near her school. It was worth a try. I wanted to talk to her teachers at any rate to learn what I could about her. I dialed directory assistance and got the number for the Holstead Special Day School. Two minutes later I was speaking to the principal's secretary. Yes, she supposed I could have an appointment as soon as possible since this was so important. How about tomorrow at four? The principal would be tied up in meetings off campus all day today. I wasn't happy about it, but there didn't seem to be any alternative. Tomorrow would have to do, I said.

After hanging up I remained standing at the window, staring out at the sea of treetops on the Paramount lot. Some teenagers in a white Mustang convertible at the stoplight just below me were listening to rap music, the sound thumping up through the closed window. An ambulance was screaming down Melrose, heading east, honking at the intersections. A noisy morning. I wondered what Laurie was doing right now. What a strange father you have, I thought: more worried about his storyboards than his child. What the hell was he up to? The light turned green, the convertible screeched suddenly onto Melrose, and I turned from the window and decided to walk down to Moses Handleman's. Moses is an ex–UCLA professor who runs a small antiquarian bookstore on the first floor of my office building: show business memorabilia primarily—books, scripts, Disney cels, and such. Most of his business is mail order rather than off the street, and he welcomes my two- or three-times-a-week visits as a break in what he calls "the quotidian tedium." We sit by the window in ancient armchairs, our feet up on the sill, sipping wine and watching the city outside sink into chaos and madness.

As I entered the shop Moses was smilingly but determinedly showing an obese and pimply teenager through the door to the street. "Maybe next year," he cried cheerfully, but the teenager slouched away wordlessly, merging with the tourists hunting desperately for a star on Bronson, or heading for Paramount where they were going to find the famous gates barred by armed security personnel.

"A difficult encounter," Moses said with a shake of his head as he came back inside. "The young man's words seemed not to correspond to any known language. Finally I deciphered 'Comics, dude!' Comics! Really *old* stuff, he said—from the seventies! I thought at first perhaps he was interested in animation art, so I showed him some very nice work from just after the war—classic Disney. I could let him have it quite reasonably—a sort of promotion to introduce a new art lover to my little shop. No, he said, he wanted comic *books*—something called Bonecrusher. Or anything with close-up sex, lots of body parts in detail. If poor old Walt were still alive . . . "

Shaking his large bearded head he patted me into one of the chairs and flicked open the venetian blinds so we could watch the pedestrian world outside. "Too early for wine, Victor, so what's up? The cold weather getting you down? You should live in New York. Or maybe you finally want to start your own little collection of memorabilia? About time. I could fix you up quite well in detective-film fiction. How about *The Falcon?* Do you remember him? A great series. George Sanders and Tom Conway solving murders while dressed in top hat and tails. Rather different from today, wouldn't you say?" and he glanced reproachfully at my jeans and sport coat.

"Actually, I need a little of your professional knowledge, Moses. What do you know about Mackenzie Gordon?"

He looked at me and shrugged as if the topic were of no interest. "Mackenzie Gordon. Not antiquarian, Victor, not rare, certainly he'll never be considered important. He's the film business's equivalent of what we in the book trade call 'ephemera.' Even the egregious Ted Turner won't want his movies in ten years. But they make money, don't they? At least for Gordon; I don't know about others associated with him."

"Like directors?"

"I don't much follow the day-to-day machinations of the modern industry, Victor. But Mackenzie Gordon, I hear, usually works percentage deals with both stars and directors, what the industry so amusingly calls *talent*. But it's always a percentage of net, not gross; then his bookkeepers sharpen their pencils and get creative, and the profit mysteriously starts to disappear behind a fog of obfuscation. *Vietnam Journal* grossed eighty million, and the accountants allege it ended up three million in the red because of promotion and distribution expenses. Who knows?"

"Brandon Stiles?" I asked.

"Very talented, they say. Perhaps too talented for Hollywood. A Matisse among the barbarians. But no head for money—his or his bosses. They yanked him off his last film at Columbia when the shooting had been completed for two years and he couldn't get out of post-production; it was thirty million over budget when it finally came out. Great reviews, puny box office, end of young Brandon. The pencil pushers think he's a nothing so he must be talented."

"Kerry Daniels?"

"Zero." He shook his great hairy head in a show of ignorance.

"She works for Gordon, maybe more."

"Still a zero."

"Catherine Wilbourne?"

This time Moses smiled with all his body, if that's possible, and sighed deeply, an unexpected display of emotion from the normally laconic bookman. "Ah, the lovely Mrs. Gordon . . . " He closed his eyes and mused aloud. "Imagine what life has been, lo these forty years, for the exquisite Catherine: in the public eye since childhood; private schools in Switzerland; the possessor of untold wealth; half the men in the world lusting after her voluptuous body with its promise of unearthly delights. And a business mind like J. P. Morgan."

"The singer?"

"The financier, you boob. The lovely Catherine is a millionaire many times over, a good deal of it from real estate."

"You're doing pretty good," I said, "for someone who stays away from the modern industry."

He gave me a little-boy look from behind his beard and made a brief flicking motion with his fingers. "Poof, Victor. 'Tis nothing."

"Have you heard any rumors about Mackenzie Gordon's latest film being in trouble?"

"I hear no rumors at all except about book auctions. I could, however, ask around if you like. Is it important? I'll ask my friend Winston at the University—he's the Aaron Spelling Professor of American Culture. He's very up-to-date."

"Tell me you're joking,"

Just then the front door squeaked open, and an elderly couple came in, looking around uncertainly and clutching two brown paper bags as if they had just been grocery shopping. Moses leaned over and whispered confidentially. "Treasure-trove time, Victor. It happens once or twice a week. Someone cleans out an attic or garage or goes through grandpa's box of books and then trots in here breathless with anticipation, grasping the family riches. It breaks my heart because none of it's worth a sou—old school books and the like. But then they get mad at me as if it's my fault grandpa didn't buy any James Joyce first editions. I'll call you after I ask around about your friends."

I got to my feet.

"By the way," he added confidentially, after standing and waving a greeting to his customers. "Would it be inappropriate to mention that I haven't seen the remarkable Judith Chen around lately?"

I felt a little bubble of unease growing somewhere within me. Judy Chen was a five-foot-seven dynamo with a knockout body and the skin of a cosmetics model, which she had been since age fifteen. "Judy? Well . . . no, she hasn't been around for a few weeks. I guess we're on hold for a while."

"Ah."

"What the hell does ah mean?" I snapped.

He clasped his hands. "It means you're becoming emotional about something. Are you likely to become loud and abusive? If so, I'll ask you to go upstairs. The book business is refined and sedate and filled with meaningful ahs."

"I'm not upset!" I hissed as the elderly couple started walking in our direction. "I'm just not sure Jude and I are on the same wavelength anymore. It happens."

"Wavelength," he mused. "It's a question of physics, then?"

"Chemistry. Or philosophy. She said she didn't like my ethos, whatever that means. And don't say ah!"

"A moral issue, perhaps?"

"Food, diets—a model's favorite fantasy. It used to be something called macrobiotics. Then carbohydrate-loading. Now she claims her dietary rules come from Paul McCartney: Never eat anything with a face. That kind of lets out most of what human beings enjoy, doesn't it? Like beef and veal and fish. She got upset when I brought home a bucket of Colonel Sanders. I told her chickens don't have faces. Anyway, my own dietary rules are evolutionary: I only eat Cenozoic-era food; if it doesn't have a backbone I leave it alone. It's an ethos, I told her. She said our relationship had become dysfunctional and left. She comes over and talks to Tracy, though. Sometimes she mentions my childishness."

"Astute," Moses replied thoughtfully and headed toward his customers. I went outside and back up to my office, where I found two messages on my phone machine: Rudy Cruz and Eddy Baskerville. I called Rudy at the station house.

"There's not a thing on any of those names you gave me. I congratulate you."

"For what?"

"For having such normal people as clients. It happens so seldom."

"They may not have a record," I said, "but I don't think there's anything normal about any of them."

Eddy didn't have anything tangible either. "Kinda hard without a picture," he said. "But no one's seen her, far as I can tell. I'll try again tonight."

I told him to stop by after dinner for the fliers. If I wasn't in, Tracy could let him have them. Then, on an impulse, I dialed the main Paramount switchboard and had the call switched to Kerry Daniels. When she picked up the phone I asked if I was interrupting anything important.

"Everything's important this week. Have you turned up anything on Laurie yet?"

"No, I'm still working on it. Have you given any thought to anywhere else she might go—maybe some place you've heard her talk about—the zoo or a park or shopping mall? Anything at all?"

"No, I'm really sorry, Mr. Eton, but you know what it's been like here since she left. I've been working with Brandon on the script all day, and I just haven't had the time to think of anything else. If I do, I'll give you a call. Laurie's such a sweet kid—"

So nothing. I grabbed my coat and drove over to the photocopy store and picked up the fliers and started tramping west on Hollywood Boulevard, leaving them in stores and at bus stops and stapled to telephone poles next to pictures of other missing kids. By three o'clock I was numb with cold, and tired and depressed from both the lack of concern and the determined ennui in the faces I had encountered: so a kid's missing? So what? Not my problem, man.

Maybe Gregory Chauk would offer a more humane response to another human being's tragedy. After all, he was a father and presumably a friend of Laurie's. This time the Toyota was in the driveway, and I drew up behind it. Chauk himself answered the door and remembered my name.

"Yes, of course, come in. We've all been terribly worried about Laurie. Such a nice child."

He brought me into the den, a masculine-looking room with rich wood paneling and bookshelves crammed every which way with what looked to be scientific monographs and books. A journal called *Inorganic Chemistry* lay open on the small coffee table in front of us. He saw me glancing at it. "I'm doing some research with the medical school. When I hit a dead end I bring my work home and hope the change of environment helps my thinking." He waved me to a chair. "I haven't told Stephanie yet that Laurie's missing. It would just upset her. And sometimes it's hard to explain things so she'll understand."

"Do you know Laurie very well?"

Chauk leaned back in his armchair and considered the question. He was a large man, which surprised me for some reason—perhaps violating my stereotype of what a scientist should look like—about six-feet-four and 240 pounds, with an out-of-control black beard and unruly hair. But not academic-looking like Moses: more northwoods lumberjack than scientist. A man who should be working with his muscles, not lifting test tubes. After a moment he bent forward, his voice as precise as his carefully chosen words.

"Perhaps 'well' is not the right word. I'm not sure one can ever know a girl like Laurie well since her world is so different from ours. But she's one of Stephanie's friends from the Holstead School, and she would sometimes take the bus over here. Steph has never been invited to their home, however, a fact that's always annoyed me somewhat. I realize both her parents work and that it's difficult to arrange play time, but I manage, and I'm raising Stephanie by myself. Sometimes I've felt they were using me as a babysitter."

"You're a widower?" I asked.

He nodded. "Stephanie's mother died in childbirth. Stephanie is moderately brain-damaged as a result of complications of the birth. She's not as handicapped as Laurie, but she'll never be able to live effectively on her own without supervision, even as an adult."

"Is Laurie also brain-damaged?" Gordon had been vague as to the exact nature of his daughter's problem, I realized. Perhaps purposely so.

Chauk looked thoughtful. "I've wondered that myself. She doesn't appear to be, but there's not always any obvious physical manifestation in these cases. She sometimes exhibits behavior typical of fetal alcohol syndrome. But from her rather willful behavior I've always assumed it's most likely an emotional problem."

"Willful?"

He scratched at his beard as he formed his answer. "Laurie is perhaps the most angelic child I have ever seen, Mr. Eton. Almost ethereal at times. And the loveliest, too; a real heartbreaker. And beginning to be a woman. I suppose I should worry about that if I were her father; I know I will with Stephanie. But, yes, sometimes willful, too, when she doesn't get her way. I saw her pull a doll out of Stephanie's hands once and rip it apart because she didn't want Stephanie to have it. How does Gordon know she ran away, by the way? Perhaps she was abducted. It happens enough in Los Angeles—part of our unlovely urban milieu."

"He doesn't know for sure. He just assumes. She took some personal items, some food, some film material he was working on."

"Yes, the film material. He came by here last night, you know—the only time I've ever met him. An unpleasant man, I thought, driving up in an eighty-thousand-dollar car and going on about how much money he's losing because Laurie took off, as he phrased it. He almost made it sound as though she had committed a crime. He thought she might be here, and when I told him that that was ridiculous, he wanted to question Stephanie. At almost midnight! I told him I wasn't going to wake her, but if I heard anything I'd certainly call him. He left upset, I'm afraid. He's a wheeler-dealer in the movies or something, isn't he? That probably explains his arrogance."

"A producer," I said.

"I'm afraid I don't keep up," he said with a half-smile. "The last movie I saw was *The Sound of Music.*"

Just then a door opened and slammed shut somewhere in the house.

"That would be Stephanie," Gregory Chauk said. His face brightened, and he looked like any proud parent happy to see his child safely home from school. "I didn't question her this morning; we can do it now." He raised his voice. "In here, Stephanie."

A moment later she came in, still clutching a school lunch box with Smurfs pictured on the side—a freckle-faced girl about twelve, in glasses, smallish for her age, with brown hair combed forward in bangs and falling almost to her shoulders behind. She looked at me curiously as she came to her dad, and he smiled and slipped his large hand around her waist, giving her a hug. "How was school?"

"OK." She smiled at him and gave me another wary look.

"Were any friends there today?"

"Friends," she agreed and nodded. Her voice had a strange toneless quality, as if she were reading meaningless words off a page.

Chauk gave her another big smile and squeezed her again. "How about Laurie?"

She didn't answer, and looked confused by the question. Or perhaps alarmed. Patiently, Chauk repeated it. "Was your friend Laurie at school today, Stephanie?"

"Mrs. Stevens *said!*" Stephanie told him. There was a trace of something—defiance?—in her voice, and she put her hands on her hips.

He looked over at me. "Mrs. Stevens is the teacher. Mrs. Stevens said what, dear?"

"Laurie's not at school."

"*Was* Laurie at school?" he repeated.

"Laurie stayed away. Laurie's bad! Mrs. Stevens said if I know where Laurie went. She was *mad* at me!"

Chauk's eyes went back to me. "I guess Gordon was asking the teacher for help, too. He seems to have a lot of persistence, doesn't he, coming over here, getting the teacher involved, sending you and the young lady—"

"What young lady?"

Chauk lifted Stephanie up to his lap and looked a bit like a black-bearded Santa Claus listening to a Christmas list.

"Some woman he works with, I gathered. I came home between

classes today, and she was at the front door waiting for me with the same questions Gordon asked last night. I gave her the same answers, of course."

"Was her name Kerry Daniels?" I asked.

He nodded agreement. "Daniels. Attractive. Another movie person, I suppose."

"What time was that?"

"Oh, ten-twenty or so, I suppose. Does it matter?"

Ten-twenty. An hour later she was telling me what a busy day she had been having with the script and Brandon Stiles. I got up to leave and handed Chauk a card. "I'd appreciate it if you'd give me a call if you hear or see anything. Or if Gordon pays you another visit."

He looked at me curiously. "I thought you were working for him."

"I'm not sure," I told him.

They both walked me out to the car, then Stephanie spied her cat and began to chase after it, racing toward the backyard and squealing happily.

"Sad, isn't it?" Chauk said as I opened the door to the Buick. "Gordon and that Daniels woman seem more concerned about their movie than about Laurie. And Ms. Stevens is probably more concerned about the reputation of her fancy school than about any of its students. Even Stephanie doesn't seem concerned."

# 4

AFTER DINNER TRACY WENT OFF WITH THIS MONTH'S BOYFRIEND—A lanky, happy-looking fifteen-year-old named Jason—allegedly to study together in the school library. I called my office to see if there were any messages on the machine, hoping to find a response to the fliers I had distributed, but there was only one call, an anxious-sounding ten seconds from Brandon Stiles who wanted me to call him as soon as possible. Surprise, surprise, I thought. I dialed the number he left on the tape, which I recognized as belonging to Paramount, but there was no answer. I tried Kerry Daniels's number but no one answered it either. So I called Mackenzie Gordon. He was his usual pleasant self.

"What the fuck you been doing the last two days? I thought you were supposed to be good."

I sighed and thought to myself, Mackenzie, you prick, but instead asked, "You ready to call in the police?"

"Christ, no, we wait until the end of the week like I said. So what the hell you been doing?"

I told him about the fliers and Available Eddy and my several hours of trudging through the post-nuclear landscape of West Hollywood, talking to street people. And this time I told him I'd been to Chauk's, without mentioning that I knew about his late-night visit. I wondered what his reaction would be. I should have guessed.

"What the hell are you going out there for?" he shouted. "Laurie's not there, she's in Hollywood somewhere. Christ, Eton, you stick to the fucking streets or parks or something. She's not at Chauk's."

"Your last film," I said matter-of-factly. "You were using the wrong kind of lighting on all of the interior scenes; everything was too bright, too many hard-edged shadows; it looked like a soap opera. And the costumes weren't right, too flashy—"

"All right, all right!" he bellowed. "I won't tell you how to do your job. But I want my kid found. *Soon!*"

When Tracy got home at ten I was brewing up five cups of coffee. She knew what that meant.

She rolled her eyes and gave me a motherly look. "Most parents are going to bed about now. Mine's going out to peer through windows. Why don't you get a normal job?"

"Normal jobs are for normal people."

"Yeah. Forget it. Are you going back to Laurie's friend's house?"

"Not this time," I said, thinking aloud. "There's something funny going on; has been since I took this on. Since no one wants to tell me what it is, I think I'll check out my slightly odd employer, see what he's up to. It might be fun."

Tracy shook her head in warning. "Don't bite the hand that pays for my braces."

After Tracy went to bed I took the flight bag and thermos and drove through Hollywood to Beverly Hills. Up in the remotest hilltops where Mackenzie Gordon lived the neighborhoods are determinedly rural in aspect if not in reality; it's hard to be "hunt club country" when you're surrounded by several million people. But money—if you have it in sufficient multi-million-dollar quantities—can buy you an "English country house" and an acre or two, heavily wooded so you can't actually see your neighbors and only infrequently hear them. On quiet nights you can close your eyes and try to imagine yourself in Surrey or Devon or wherever, riding to the hounds with Surtees.

Mackenzie Gordon's house, like its neighbors, was completely obscured from the road unless you happened to be standing at the electric gate which guarded the driveway. I drove up the twisting two-lane road, past the gate and grounds, and fifty yards or so up the street where I U-turned, pulled into a narrow turnout, and cut the engine and lights. Patience is one of the small virtues an enigmatic Providence has blessed me with; I dialed the radio to an oldies station, put the seat back into a reclining position, and waited.

In two hours only seven cars came past me up the hill and just one went down. And nothing at all came from Gordon's house. I drank a cup of coffee, then took the Chesterton from the flight bag and read a couple of stories before putting it down with a yawn. The quiet was beginning to get to me. I rested my head against the seat back and closed my eyes. Hollywood was never this quiet, even at four in the morning. It was so damn peaceful I couldn't keep awake. Then I heard the sudden angry growl of tires skidding noisily on gravel, and glanced into the rearview mirror to see red and blue flashes lighting up the darkness with a carnival-like intensity; almost instantly a high-powered spotlight completely illuminated the interior of my car, and an amplified voice said, "Very slowly . . . get out of the car . . . and put your hands on top of your head."

In the mirror I saw the two front doors of the police car already open and knew there were cops crouched behind each door with guns drawn. *Jesus* . . .

I flicked on the interior light and held my hands up to show them they were empty, then opened the car door and climbed gingerly out into the moist night air, the spotlight following my movements as if I were the star of a one-man show: Vic Eton, dancing with his hands on his head. Silently, I waited as a thirtyish, heavy-set Beverly Hills policeman advanced on me from the darkness, gun drawn.

"I'm a private detective," I said as he approached. The spotlight hit me in the eyes, and I blinked them half-shut. I could hardly see who I was talking to. "I'm working on a case. Would you mind turning your flasher and radio off?"

"Turn around and face the car," he ordered in a quiet voice as if I had not spoken.

I did as I was told, spreading my legs and bracing against the car as he frisked me.

"You know the drill," he said tonelessly. "How many times you been arrested?"

I put my arms down and turned to face him. Out of the corner of

my eye I saw the other cop approach from the darkness at my rear. "I
want to take my wallet out of my pocket," I said. "I want to show
you my ID. I'm a licensed PI."

The other cop shone a five-cell flashlight in my car and saw the
thermos and book. "You planning to spend the night here? You one
of the homeless?" He said it as if he had never actually seen a homeless person.

"I'm a private detective," I repeated. "I'm ex-LAPD. I'm working
a stakeout. I want to show you my ID. It's in my left rear pocket."

"Loitering is illegal in Beverly Hills," the first cop said. "Even
*walking* is illegal on most streets. We like to keep things moving."

I looked at him. "Do you want to discuss the difference between
working and loitering? Is that it?"

"I'm ex-LAPD too," the second cop said. He was smaller, younger,
with the requisite cop mustache, neatly trimmed and brushed and
fussed over. He switched off his flashlight, came over to join his
partner, and looked me over. "Everyone's ex-LAPD. Only the assholes stay. Who'd you work for?"

"Reddig in Hollywood. You want to turn down your radio and
turn off the flasher before the whole neighborhood knows we're
here?"

He squinted his light brown eyes at me. "Never heard of him."

I started to reach for my wallet but he said, "I didn't ask for no
ID. Keep your hands where I can see 'em. You know Captain
Millington in Ramparts?"

I said no, and he grinned stupidly, like a child who had just
tricked the grown-ups. "Good, I made the name up. I worked Auto
Theft downtown. Shit detail. You know how many goddamn cars are
stolen in downtown LA every day? And they expected us to *find*
'em? Christ, the one's that aren't set on fire end up in Tijuana. Two
years of that horse pucky and I was outta there, come over here
where the rich assholes pay us to keep the poor assholes away from
their mansions. From the looks of it, you're one of poor assholes.
Who you staking out?"

I pointed down the hill.

"I didn't ask you to fuckin' *point* at a house. My dog could do
that. I said who the fuck are you *watching*?"

I could have made something up but there was no point in being coy, especially since there was only one piece of property actually in view. And the sooner they satisfied themselves with what I was doing the sooner they'd leave. I said, "Mackenzie Gordon."

They looked at each other. The first cop said, "You think he's dickin' some guy's old lady, and you're going to get some dirty pictures? A little of the old in-and-out on your Nikon? Divorce work appeal to you?"

"It's a private matter," I said. "Confidential."

The first cop put his gun away and stuck out his hand as if he was going to hit me. "Well, *confidentially*, let's see that hotshot ID of yours."

He took it back to the car and made a call, keeping both doors open and the flasher lighting up the road, the radio still on full-blast just in case anyone was still asleep. Meanwhile the second cop wanted to BS about the LAPD; two years of hassles and horse pucky, he said. Maybe you gotta watch yourself a little more in Beverly Hills, don't roust some guy who plays golf with the President or owns a chain of TV stations. But no gangs, either; no drive-bys and crack sellers on the corners. No punks shooting into parked cars.

A few minutes later his partner came back from the car and handed me my ID as if it were a dead ferret he was holding by the tail. "You check out OK, Eton, but we got our funny little Beverly Hills laws here like I said, and one of 'em is no private dicks sitting in parked cars at 1:00 A.M. staring at folks' houses. So you hop back in your vehicle and drive across the line to LA where all the fairies and gang-bangers are. If we catch you here on our next pass we'll drag you in for vagrancy."

Thirty seconds later they left in a spray of gravel and a blast of two-way radio. I climbed back in the Buick, started it up and ran the heater for five minutes to warm my frigid toes. Then I retrieved the Father Brown volume and transported myself again to the simple pleasures of Edwardian England. No drive-by shootings there either, I thought. No gangs or crack sellers or punks shooting into parked cars. No hard-ass Beverly Hills cops.

After twenty minutes I was half-asleep; I yawned, put the book down, and flipped on the radio. A DJ on a terminally hip rock station was interviewing a young woman who played an MD on a popular TV series, asking her how much jewelry was a turn-on when she looked at a man. "Would you date a guy who wore no jewelry?"

You could almost see her squint her eyes shut as she considered the weightiness of the question. "Well . . . maybe . . . if he was, like, going to the beach." She ended on an up note, as if she were asking a question: to the beach?

"How about a single gold chain around his neck?"

"Oh . . . I like that." Squeals of delight.

"Two chains?"

The questions were becoming more difficult, and she was faltering. I switched over to the oldies station. "Louie Louie." Something I could understand.

Half an hour later the coffee had gotten to me; I went out into the cold and stood on the road and urinated in the general direction of Mackenzie Gordon's house. Something symbolic there.

By two it had started to rain, at first lightly, then with more force. I was verging on the edge of sleep again, the monotonous sound of the rain dulling my brain, and rummaged in the bag for a box of NoDoz, shaking out two. The coffee was gone so I shoved them in my mouth, swallowed hard, and tried to ignore the taste. The rain drilled the hood. Every twenty or thirty minutes a car would come slowly up the mountain, its headlights arcing around the corner and reflecting off the wet asphalt; even fewer headed the opposite direction. Dead time. The rain continued. I yawned, and rested the book on my lap.

Then I sat up suddenly as I saw two cones of light flash past the hedge in front of Mackenzie Gordon's house and turn abruptly downhill. *Christ!* I tossed the book aside and pumped life into the car, slipping into gear and spinning out on the wet pavement as I started to follow. Gordon's lights were intermittently visible as he rounded a corner below me; they quickly vanished, then reappeared. Instinctively I checked my watch; 3:12 A.M. An odd outing for the odd Mackenzie Gordon.

I kept him barely in view, slipping precariously on the wet hairpin turns until we got to Sunset, where Gordon spun a wicked right and shot down the street as if he were late for an appointment. He hit a red light at the first corner, and I hung back until it turned green. Then we took off again down the broad, mostly empty street. We continued west for at least a mile, the rain slanting down heavily, until I saw his turn signal flashing as we approached the San Diego Freeway. He banked into the on-ramp and merged quickly into the sparse traffic heading south. Staying over in the right lane, I kept him in view as he continued south past the Santa Monica Freeway, past Culver City, then hit his blinkers again: Century Boulevard. The airport. Fly-away, fly-away, where are you heading, Mackenzie?

I stayed a block behind as he came off the freeway onto a deserted, surreal landscape of towering slab-sided office buildings and hotels, bisected by a single rain-slicked eight-lane road completely empty of traffic. We headed west toward the barren terrain of the airport and the inevitable oceanside fog bank, getting green lights all the way to the double-decked traffic circle, where Gordon slowed, as if searching for something. Then suddenly he swung an abrupt left into a multistory open-sided parking structure.

Damn! It would have been too obvious to pull in behind him. I could go around again—probably a three- or four-minute drive this time of night—or pull into the next parking area. I only had a second to decide and yanked the Buick sharply into the entrance of the adjacent structure, then skidded to a halt to grab a time-stamped slip from the machine and wait for the crossing arm to rise with painful slowness. Flicking off my lights, I headed toward the side adjacent to the building Gordon had pulled into. There were few cars and no one that I could see walking about. Driving slowly down the aisle, I stared across to the other structure. Nothing. Or nothing I could see. At the end of the aisle I turned quickly, sped up to the second floor and tried again, inching slowly down the left-hand aisle. Then I saw headlights flash on, off, on. I jerked into a parking slot, cut the engine, and gazed across the forty or fifty feet through the thickening veil of blowing rain and fog. Lights again flashed on, off, on. Gordon's car? I couldn't be sure. Then the car drew slowly forward, turned sideways, and halted. A blue Mercedes sedan; it was Gordon, all right. Another car, with its lights out, had drawn up on the opposite side, where it was obscured from view.

Gordon pushed open the car door and slowly lumbered out of the Mercedes, carrying something. A briefcase? Or a bag? The rain was pelting down in sheets, and I could only vaguely make him out as he walked around and climbed into the front seat of the other car.

I debated getting out and going over there on foot. But to what advantage? I would never get close enough to hear them. And what would I say if I ran into my slightly volatile employer? Better to keep my distance, I decided.

They sat together for at least five minutes; then Gordon's head reappeared, bobbing above the two cars as he walked rapidly back to his Mercedes, again carrying a bag or case, but a bigger one this time, I thought, and climbed inside. After a few seconds the other car—a nondescript blue Ford, I could now see—eased away, its tail-lights illuminating the dull bunker-like building with splashes of reflected red light. Leaving separately. Prudent. So who should I latch on to? Gordon's car started up also, a burst of exhaust shooting out from the rear. But he stayed where he was, idling. I decided to stick with my boss. The man's not done yet, I thought, he's up to something. The Mercedes remained where it was. I relaxed back and watched, wondering if the Ford was out on Century yet. Then Gordon stepped on the brakes, put the car in gear, and it exploded in a tremendous flash of light and sound that ricocheted horribly off the hard concrete walls and ceiling. The car had become a nightmarish jumble of twisted steel; pieces of metal and glass lay strewn everywhere, and part of the wreckage was burning with a bright white flame. Car alarms blared, and my ears hammered from the force of the explosion. Cursing loudly to myself, I slammed the Buick in reverse, then raced toward the exit. Sirens and alarms seemed suddenly to be everywhere, people were running confusedly through the rain, shouting to each other, waving their arms, pointing. The parking lot attendant had disappeared but the security arm still blocked the exit; I hit it at fifty miles an hour, and it flew free and I was on the street looking for the Ford. But all I could see through the rain was a fire engine heading toward me, its siren screaming, going the wrong way on a one-way street.

# 5

I PICKED UP THE FREEWAY AT CENTURY AND DROVE STRAIGHT TO Mackenzie Gordon's house. I wasn't sure what I expected to find, but I was certain I would find something. Something that would tell me why Gordon had gotten up at three o'clock in the morning and driven to the airport. Or why he had hired me in the first place, since he obviously didn't trust me with his secrets. Or if his daughter was even missing.

It was 4:35 and still dark when I approached Gordon's home. I swung a left off Atherton Drive and into the driveway, and was just through the gate when I had to swerve violently to keep from hitting a blue Corvette that barreled by me in the opposite direction; the driver lost control momentarily when he hit the rain-soaked road, and the car fishtailed wildly, completely spinning around before tearing off again down the hill. Man or woman? I asked myself, but it had been too dark to tell. I momentarily considered following, then thought better of it. I cut the headlights and drifted toward the house. Lights were on downstairs; I accelerated slowly onto the bumpy cobblestone driveway and sat for a moment with the engine running, watching as the rain drummed down. It was a massive 1930s Beverly Hills notion of what an English estate should look like—white stucco and exposed timbers and half a dozen chimneys, with a five-car garage off to the side disguised as a carriage house. A BMW sat in the open by the stone steps leading to the balustraded entry. I hadn't expected to find anyone home, if that's what the lights and car indicated. Or had Gordon simply left the lights on when he went to the airport? Of course he could also have live-in help; even live-in help with a BMW, I supposed. Then again, maybe the errant Corvette driver had left the lights on.

Might as well find out.

I got out of the car and trudged through the rain to the BMW and felt the hood: it was cold. Putting my head down, I ran over to the uncovered porch and rang the bell. After a moment I had the sense of someone watching me through the peephole. Then Kerry Daniels opened the door.

She looked at me wordlessly, a frown on her face.

"Aren't you going to invite me in?" I asked. Not that it mattered much; I wasn't going to stand there any longer with water dripping down my collar and along my spine.

She stepped aside, and I came in to a brightly lit marble-floored entrance. The heat was on full force, and I could smell coffee brewing. All very homey, very domestic. Kerry Daniels was wearing slacks and a blouse and looked as if she were on her way to work. I took off my jacket and shook the water from it before draping it on an old-fashioned clothes rack. "On your way to keep *wunderkind* from all artificial stimulants?" I guessed.

She smiled slightly in spite of herself. But she wanted me to know that she wasn't pleased to see me and gave her voice a sarcastic twist. "I was, in fact. I try to be there by five during both pre-production and shooting. Just to keep an eye on things."

"Very admirable. I like to see people happy in their work. And you stopped by here first to borrow a little Yuban?"

"Wrong. I spent the night. With Mackenzie. Do you want to watch our videos? He's very athletic."

I stared back to the hallway behind her where more lights burned. "Was anyone else here this morning?"

The idea seemed to please her. "The decadent Hollywood crowd! Yes indeed, two is never enough for us, is it? So we form our little ménage à trois. Last night it was the lovely Mae West who joined us. In spirit only, of course, but she adds so *much* to our evening."

"Someone drove out as I was coming in," I explained.

She was completely unfazed. "I can't imagine who. It wasn't

Mackenzie; he's not here. No one is here except me. What is all this?"

"Where is Gordon?" I asked and tried not to stare as she answered.

But she merely shrugged, showing her impatience. "Actually I thought he might be with you. He told me he had to meet someone this morning. Something to do with Laurie. He didn't go into it: all very hush-hush stuff. I thought it must be the mysterious shamus."

"Has Laurie turned up? Did Gordon get some information on her? Is that why he left?"

Kerry Daniels looked at me with widened eyes. "All these questions! I'd think you'd know more about all that than me. You're the one looking for her. Aren't you?"

I glanced around at the entrance hall—cold marble floor, mirrored walls, a crystal chandelier dangling pretentiously overhead, a double stairway rising behind Kerry. It tried to be elegant but had all the warmth and charm of a modern shopping center theater lobby. "Can we go someplace and sit down?" I nodded toward the interior of the house.

She gave me an uncertain look and hesitated. "Yes, of course. But I really don't have much time, I want to get to Paramount. And I don't expect Mackenzie to come back here this morning."

We were walking into a den: overstuffed couches and chairs, a large desk, awards and photographs on the walls. I said, "Mackenzie is dead."

She stood unmoving for a moment, staring dumbly at me with deep brown eyes that seemed to darken with disbelief. Then her body stiffened all the way through. "Is that supposed to be funny?"

"He was in a parking structure at the airport an hour ago. He met someone, and they talked a few minutes. Then his car blew up."

She looked at me as if she wanted to scream but no sound came out. Her mouth hung open, the muscles in her face stretched taut, and the skin tightening horribly around the eyes as she stared and stared at me. She seemed to age forty years as her mind struggled to grasp what I said. "*Killed* him? Killed him? Someone *killed . . .*"

Her body began to rock with a rigid back-and-forth motion, and I took hold of her elbow and steered her to a chair. She sat down heavily, in a daze, and when she began to cry a moment later, I found the kitchen and rummaged around for something to drink, finally discovering a half bottle of brandy among the cooking supplies; I splashed two ounces into a crystal water glass.

When I returned to the den, she was no longer crying but staring blindly straight ahead with the vacant, reddened eyes of an accident victim. I put the glass on the table next to her and said, "Take a drink," and when she ignored me I wrapped her fingers around it. "Drink!"

She brought the glass numbly to her lips, took a sip and grimaced. Again the stare into space, and a tiny shudder, as a chill raced through her body. I was watching her, reading what I could in her eyes and expression. What was she feeling? Shock? Loss? Disbelief? Who *was* Kerry Daniels to Mackenzie Gordon? Lover? Companion? One-night stand?

I pulled a chair around and sat across from her, our knees almost touching, and stared into her face. "The police are going to be here soon," I said, trying to keep any emotion from my voice, trying to make her understand what I was saying. But she gave no indication of hearing. "Do you want to be here when that happens?"

She twisted suddenly forward in her chair and glared at me, eyes blazing with fury. "You bastard! Why the hell—" then fell back and subsided into silent sobbing. After a moment her eyes focused on me again, her voice sounding soft and distant as her mind began to function once more. But there was no energy in it, a voice from a dream. "Maybe I'd better not. There's no point in upsetting poor Catherine, is there?"

"What does that mean?"

"Whatever you want it to mean," she snapped. "Let's get out of here." She started to push out of the chair.

I put my hand up. "We've got a few minutes. I want to get clear on a few things first. What did Gordon tell you about this meeting at the airport?"

She sank back into the chair, looking lifeless, and closed her eyes. "He didn't tell me anything. He got a call at the studio; he said it had something to do with the missing script material, and he had to meet a guy this morning."

"A guy?" I said. "Not 'a woman'; not 'a person.' A guy?"

"Yes! *No!* I don't know. He said he was meeting someone. I didn't pay attention."

"First you said it was about Laurie. Now you're saying it's about the missing script material."

"It is! But they're tied together. If he knew about one . . . "

The telephone rang on the desk and she jumped. It was probably the police, wondering if anyone was home at the deceased's residence. "Ignore it," I told her. "When did he get this call?"

"Yesterday about two o'clock. We were going over the shooting schedule in his office."

"Did you hear any of the conversation?"

Her voice hardened. "No!"

"How did he act? Excited? Upset? Like he had expected the call?"

"Mad. He acted mad. He slammed the phone down after talking to the . . . the person, whoever. Then he left—said he had to go out for a while. I came over here about eight, but he wouldn't talk about it except to say it was about Laurie. He said he had to meet someone at three-thirty who knew something about her disappearance; he didn't even say where."

Gordon's answering machine switched on and the caller immediately hung up. I checked my watch; it wouldn't be too long before Homicide showed up, now. I asked, "Who was in the office when he got the call?"

"Just me."

"Where was Brandon Stiles?"

"Brandon? I don't know. His office, I suppose."

Watching her face, her hands, I said, "What was Mackenzie Gordon to you?"

She held my eyes with hers, a cold steady stare. "A lover."

"A lover? Or *the* lover?"

Her eyes flashed angrily, and she started to say something but changed her mind. "We enjoyed each other. It was a mutually attractive relationship. I didn't *love* him, if that's what you mean. But I loved being with him."

Even that didn't sound too convincing but I let it go. "And his wife? Did she know?"

"It wasn't my problem, was it? He was the one married to the bitch. But as far as I know she didn't have a clue. She was never home, anyway, always off in such charming and exotic locales, lolling around with assistant directors or whatever. Frankly, I don't . . . "

". . . give a damn. Yeah, I know, I saw the film. Who did know?"

She sat upright and stared impassively at me. "You know something? I really don't care."

I came to my feet. "The cops are going to be here in a few minutes. What can you tell me that you haven't?"

"About what?"

"Laurie. Gordon's death."

She looked at me with a mixture of anger and helplessness. "Nothing! Honestly. I don't know anything. Mackenzie never really opened up to me about any of this. We were . . . friends. Not confidants. He let me know only what he wanted me to know. Which was never very much."

With nothing to base it on but my often imperfect intuition, I believed her, maybe partly because I wanted to. I liked Kerry: There was a steely bluntness and honesty to her that I saw all too rarely in Hollywood, and it was appealing, even if sometimes annoying. It wasn't going to serve her well in this land of obsequiousness and practiced ass-kissing, but it was a nice change. I said, "Did Gordon ever do any work at home? Did he have an office here?"

She gazed vacantly around at the room we were in. "Quite often. That's his desk." Her eyes began to water again. "He worked here almost every night, usually going over correspondence."

I checked my watch again. "I'm going to go through this room. Laurie's still missing, and I want to find her before something bad happens. You can help me if you want. If you want to leave now I'll understand. But I haven't got much time before the cops show up, and I want to see what's here."

She looked at me through red-lined eyes, unsure of what she wanted to do, probably sensing some disloyalty to her murdered lover in searching his house. For a moment I thought she was going to leave. But the appeal to Laurie's well-being evidently convinced her. Sounding resigned but willing, she gazed at me. "What do you want me to do?"

"Start with the bottom drawers of the desk. I'll start with the desktop and work down. If anything seems out of place or strange in any way or has Laurie's name on it, let me see it."

She sighed her assent, and we crossed over to Gordon's massive desk. Kerry dropped to one knee and began to rummage through a deep file drawer, while I stood next to her searching through the piles of paper littering the desktop. Screenplays were strewn everywhere, visual proof of his secretary's ominous declarations. Letters, bills, memos brought from the office. All very mundane. I picked up a letter and read the signature. "Who's Sam Weiss?"

"An agent. If you're looking for a suspect in Mackenzie's death, all agents would qualify. Would you like a list?"

In the top drawer I came across a leather-bound address book. I dropped it in my pocket to look at later. There was also an appointment book. I decided I'd better leave something for the police to find, so I quickly flipped through the appointments for the past three months or so. Most were for meetings in his office. Some weren't.

"What do you think 'Brk' means?"

"Probably Breakers. That's his Malibu house. There's nothing in this drawer except material on films from five, ten years ago." She closed the drawer and tried the next one.

"And Sharon Haynes? It says, Brk: Sharon Haynes."

Kerry looked up at me with a strained look. "An actress," she said after a moment. "Very pretty, very young. Mackenzie must have been meeting her at his Malibu house. What day was it?"

"Wednesday the nineteenth . . . Wednesday the twelfth. . . ." I was flipping backwards through the book. "Wednesday the fifth . . ."

She stood up and gave me a not-quite-angry look, perhaps more one of sudden recognition—or resignation. "His golf day at Hillside, he told me. I always thought he must be a hell of a player."

"I guess he was." I flipped to the next few days. For tomorrow night at seven he had jotted "Howie Wiltz" and a question mark. I felt a vague shudder of recognition.

"The porno magazine publisher," Kerry said, looking at it. "*Hollywood X-T-C*. I guess nothing about Mackenzie surprises me now."

"Did he ever mention him to you?"

"No. But I'm learning he didn't mention all his friends, aren't I?"

"Do you think they might have been planning a movie together?"

Kerry shrugged listlessly. "Mackenzie and sex movies? As an actor or producer? Yes, I suppose he could be thinking of something like that. Maybe something for cable. He'd been talking about television lately."

I jotted down Howie Wiltz's number on a piece of paper and dropped it in my pocket. As Kerry resumed rummaging through the desk I walked over to the bookcase, moving rows of books aside until I found the wall safe I had expected to find. No Beverly Hills den would be complete without it. The safe and the Erté to show that you've truly arrived.

"What's his wedding anniversary?" I asked Kerry.

She thought a minute. "March 31, 1975."

I spun the dial: Three, thirty-one, seventy-five. No luck.

"Birthday?"

"July 19, 1943."

Seven, nineteen, forty-three. Nothing.

"Do you know Laurie's birthday?"

"Sure. Christmas day, either thirteen or fourteen years ago. I'm not sure."

I tried fourteen and felt the tumblers fall. I gave the door a pull and it swung open easily.

I put my hand inside and came out with a thick stack of unbound sheets. I immediately sensed what they were. "Is this what you've been looking for?" I asked.

Her mouth dropped open as she rushed over to the bookshelves and took them. "The storyboards! But why? . . . In the *safe?*"

I stuck my hand inside again. There was nothing else.

Kerry was looking at me incredulously. "What the hell did he have us busting our asses on the script for if he had them all along? And what about Laurie? He said Laurie had them!"

I slammed the safe shut, spun the dial, and wiped my prints off with my handkerchief. "Who do you know who owns a blue Corvette?"

"A blue Corvette? Brandon. Why? Why the hell were we recreating the storyboards if Mackenzie had them all along? Why did he lie about it?"

"All these questions again! It'll give us something to think about."

I checked my watch; it was way past time to get out of here. "Put the desk back the way it was. And hurry it up; we've got to leave."

I shoved the storyboards in a large envelope and stuck it protectively under my arm.

"Hey! We need that," she protested.

"Not anymore," I said.

She sighed and blinked and looked at me. "Yeah. Maybe not. I guess I'm out of a job. So is Brandon. And you."

"Laurie's still missing," I reminded her. "I'm still looking for her." But I had been hired to find the storyboards. Which I did. And for which I now had a nice fee coming from the bank.

Five minutes later I was in my car, the lights were out in the house and the front door locked. Kerry left first in her BMW, heading for Paramount and a job she no longer had. I took off a minute later for my apartment. Halfway down the hill I passed an LAPD squad car, several miles outside its jurisdiction, heading uncertainly in the opposite direction and looking for house numbers on the curbs.

As I headed home I wondered what Kerry had said that had bothered me so much. Something about Gordon that hadn't made any sense.

# 6

I SLEPT UNTIL HALF PAST ONE WHEN TRACY GOT HOME. "HOW WAS
school?"

"Brutal. Part of the New Realism in California education, our
English teacher said. I have to write an essay tonight. We've never
had to do that before."

"Dare I ask the topic?"

"We've been watching 'My Mother the Car: The Lost Episodes,'
in class the last three weeks. We have to relate it to social conditions
in America today. And it has to be at least three hundred words!"

"Brutal," I agreed.

We were saved from further ruminations on the changing face of
California education by a call from Rudy Cruz.

"According to the departmental form now in front of me in tripli-
cate," the emotionless, bureaucratic voice said slowly and precisely,
"one of the names you asked me to check on just ended up splat-
tered on the walls and ceilings of a parking structure at LAX."

I said I had heard something about that. "And his daughter is still
missing," I added.

Rudy sighed heavily. "Well, since Daddy's no longer able, it's up
to you to put in a missing person's report, amigo. You can do it in
person since you'll be coming down here in a few minutes."

"I don't think so," I told him. "Tracy and I are discussing the new
realism tonight. Later there's a Lakers game. I thought you were

coming over to explain what they're doing wrong."

"I am. But the homicide team was out at your buddy's digs in Beverly Hills this morning, going through papers and belongings, sprinkling magic dust everywhere. You know how they are—a little messy, but thorough. Anyway, when they ran the latents through that new sixty-million-dollar computer of theirs guess whose name popped out?"

"Robin Leach? Darryl Zanuck? Dan Quayle? Help me out."

"You better get down here before they have to send someone, Vic. I don't think you want Captain Reddig any madder than he is."

I had known Oscar Reddig for years. He liked me about as much as he could like anyone who had quit the force and who now belonged to that great mass of unwashed known officially as citizens; unofficially all civilians to almost all cops are thought of collectively as "assholes," a quick typing that makes it unnecessary to worry about them as individual human beings and eases the psychic discomfort of having to manhandle and harass them as part of the daily routine of the job. As a gesture of these bonds of comradeship Oscar had brought me into his private office instead of an interrogation room, where he stared at me now like a massive black Buddha dispensing the wisdom and sagacity of the ages: "Fucked up again, huh, Victor?"

"Mackenzie Gordon was my employer, Oscar. You would expect to find my prints there."

Jaime "Don't-Call-Me-Geraldo" Rivera, newly promoted homicide lieutenant and longtime prick, said, "She-it."

Oscar glanced over at Rivera but didn't say anything. Evidently feeling the need to expand on his eloquence, Rivera added, "Christ, the asshole admits to breaking and entering the deceased's premises—"

"The asshole admits to entering, not breaking," I said. "I was invited."

Rivera gave another "She-it" and shifted angrily in his chair as if body language could convey what words alone couldn't.

Oscar said, "After the car blew up you should have waited for the black-and-white, Vic. You know that. What the hell did you leave for? That could be considered obstruction since you're a licensed investigator. You're supposed to know better."

"I wanted to follow the Ford, Oscar. There was no one else to do it."

"Then you should have come in here after you lost it."

"I'd been up all night staking out Gordon's house. I needed some sleep. I didn't have anything vital for you guys anyway. Someone I couldn't see, in a vehicle that was undoubtedly stolen, blew up Gordon. Anyway, I was on my way in when Rudy called."

I glanced over at Jaime Rivera to see if he was going to offer his third "She-it" but he snorted his disbelief more reverently instead. "Jesus Christ! You had enough time to run over to Gordon's house and leave your prints all over his den. What were you doing over there, having a seance? Looking for secret passages?"

"He hired me to find his daughter. I was hoping for something that might help me. Anything, a note maybe, I don't know. You guys know how it is when you start tossing a place: you don't know what you're looking for. And I had to get it done before the Beverly Hills cops sifted through everything. They don't even have a homicide team over there. God knows they'd screw things up." That was designed to cheer things up a bit; everyone hated Beverly Hills detectives—widely thought to be yuppie prima donnas in Dockers and Topsiders who couldn't make it in real-world urban America. Mostly they were right.

Oscar sat back in his chair and scrutinized me. "You remove anything from the premises?"

"That would be illegal, Oscar."

"Just checking." He stared at the water stains on the ceiling.

I asked, "You didn't happen to find a wall safe, did you? These Beverly Hills types usually have one but I couldn't find it."

Rivera crossed his arms and glared at me over his Groucho Marx mustache. "We found it all right, Sherlock. Took us all of fifteen minutes. Maybe you're not such a hotshot detective after all."

"Anything in it?"

"We got somebody from downtown coming out to open it. They're probably going to have to blow it. Don't expect revelations; Gordon probably kept his Rolex collection in it."

Oscar had resumed his Buddha expression, his eyes going from

Rivera to me as if watching a mildly interesting tennis match. But he remained silent.

"Does Gordon's wife know about all this, yet?" I asked.

"We got a call in to London," Oscar replied. "Movie folk are hard to get in touch with sometimes. They lead weird lives. As you know."

"I gave Missing Persons and Juvie a picture of the girl. Maybe they'll be able to turn something up before she gets here."

"You think there's some connection between her leaving and Gordon's death?" Oscar asked.

"Evidently. But it doesn't look like a snatch to me. She was upset at her dad and took off. It happens."

Oscar said, "But the script material she took with her—that's what Gordon seemed to be after?"

"Seemed to be," I said. "I thought he was more interested in that than getting his daughter back. Just a feeling I had." Another theory shot to hell, of course, now that I knew he evidently had the storyboards all along. But I wasn't about to tell Oscar that.

"One other thing," I added. "When I got there someone was leaving. I think it was Brandon Stiles, the director. He seemed to be in a hurry."

Jaime Rivera stood up suddenly and stalked over to the Plexiglas wall that separated Oscar's office from the bedlam of the squad room. Oscar tilted back in his chair and regarded me evenly from his impenetrable black eyes. "It *was* Stiles, Vic. He came to *us*. Doing the good citizen bit. In fact, he said he saw someone in a Buick or Oldsmobile coming in as he left."

"What was he doing there?"

"That's official business, Sherlock!" Rivera snapped from the window.

I looked at Oscar but his face showed no emotion. He kept his voice steady. "That's official business, Sherlock."

"If there's nothing else then . . . " I said and began to stand.

"Let's recap," Oscar said, settling his bulk back in his swivel chair and clasping his massive hands on his stomach. I happened to glance over at the squad room window as Rudy Cruz walked by, pantomiming a hook shot just like Kareem used to do in the glory years of the Lakers. Two points, I thought automatically, but Rudy determinedly did not look in my direction. It was hotter than hell in the tiny room, and I hadn't eaten in hours and wanted to get home. But I sat back and smiled at Oscar; our meeting would be over when he said it was over: the man was master of his domain. His voice was calm and reasoned as he reconstructed events:

"Mackenzie Gordon hired you to find his fourteen-year-old daughter. She ran away and took some script material he needed. But he didn't want the police involved."

"Not exactly, Oscar. He said he'd give it a week. If I couldn't come up with her he'd call Missing Persons. But he didn't want his wife alarmed."

Rivera said, "Why'd he think a private dick could do something the LAPD couldn't?"

"Experience?" I guessed. "Or common sense. I don't know. What do you think?"

Oscar shifted his weight a little, his eyes again going from Rivera to me. "Jaime's handling the case, Vic. That's why he's here. He's going to stay here until we're done. You two want, you can use the ring in the gym later, do your macho act in front of an audience. But try to keep it civil for now because my ulcer is beginning to hurt and that always makes me testy, as you may recall. So after Gordon hires you, he starts sneaking around behind your back, going out to that professor fella's house, sending his girl Friday out—"

"She's an assistant producer. She doesn't know any more about it than I do." Except that she had lied to me about going out to Chauk's, I thought. And I was still just a little pissed about that. What the hell had she been up to?

Oscar said to Rivera, "You been out to the professor's?"

"He's on our list. Probably tomorrow."

From the look on Oscar's face I figured it'd better be today. He said to me, "So the man hires you to find his daughter and the script material. Now he's dead. You're out of a job, the way I see it. I guess you'll be going back to investigating thefts off soundstages now and leave this to us." It wasn't a question or meant to sound like one. It was an order: Stay away from Gordon's, stay away from the case.

I came to my feet and put on my jacket. "I'm not working for anyone now, Oscar. But I am going to look for that girl. On my own. I don't need permission."

On the way out of the building I checked my watch: 2:40. If I hurried I'd have just enough time to break into Gordon's house before my appointment at the Holstead School.

There was something in the house.

Had to be.

When I'd been there in the morning I'd only had time to search the den. This time my goal was Laurie's room. I should have done it days ago, but Gordon didn't want me anywhere near his house. Or Chauk's house, either, for that matter. Stick to the fucking streets, in his typically charming instructions. It had bothered me then and it bothered me now. Of course, I had no idea now what the hell Gordon had been up to with that elaborate fantasy of the runaway daughter and the missing storyboards. There must be a reason why he didn't want me poking around his place. But why make it difficult for me to find the girl that I was supposed to be looking for? And why the hell offer me fifty thousand dollars to look for something that wasn't lost? And if the storyboards weren't lost, was Laurie? Maybe the answer was in her room.

I hurried along Sunset to Crescent Heights, then into the hills to Atherton and Gordon's house. I let the Buick idle for a moment just inside the iron gate as I stared around for signs that the police might still be poking around. But there was nothing. The house loomed darkly in front of me, evidently empty, the grounds deserted. Not even a security guard. The Beverly Hills cops would be dropping by periodically, though, until Rivera returned with the detonation team to blow the safe, so I wanted to get in and out as quickly as possible. Accelerating up to the house as if I belonged there, I climbed out into the chill afternoon air and shivered slightly. Sparrows chattered overhead; a covey of doves fluttered up from a clump of tall grass and disappeared behind me; dead leaves whistled across the lawn like bits of scrap paper. Glancing quickly around to make sure I was alone, I slipped under the yellow crime-scene tape and tried the front door. Locked, naturally. As were the side and rear doors.

The first-floor windows, all old-fashioned casements, were also locked. Time to put my Academy training to work. I hurried back to the Buick and took a rag and a thin, flat piece of hardened steel shaped like a loose S out of the trunk. Better choose one in the rear, I decided, and went around to the back of the house where a dozen identical windows offered themselves up for sacrifice. May as well try the first one. I quickly jammed one end of the pry between the frame and the sash, gave it a yank upwards and out, and watched as the window popped free of the cranking mechanism. Reaching up for a handhold, I braced myself with a foot against the wall, and pulled through. Working quickly, I reattached the crank, wiped off my fingerprints, and stared around. Where was I?

It looked like a storage room: a single wooden table with half a dozen sealed cardboard boxes sitting on top, two metal filing cabinets, a side chair, and an upholstered couch. No sign of recent use, everything covered with a thin sprinkling of dust. So find Laurie's room. It shouldn't be too difficult, even in this sprawling monument to early twentieth-century Hollywood excess. Three stories: The bedrooms would probably be on the second, then.

Going out into the hallway I'd walked down earlier in the day with Kerry, I hurried past Gordon's den, then stopped abruptly, retraced my steps, and peeked inside. The room was in mild disarray from the evidence team's morning visit. I stepped in and gazed around. The desktop had been swept empty, its contents checked and inventoried and then neatly packed in a cardboard carton on the floor. All the drawers had been removed and were stacked, still full, against a wall. The bookcase shelf that covered the wall safe had been cleared of books.

I'd love to get my hands on the evidence report, I thought, as I stared around, and considered asking Rudy, then decided against it. It wasn't wise to push the limits of friendship too far. Besides, if the techs had come up with something important, Oscar would have been hinting about it back in his office to see what I knew.

The phone from Gordon's desk sat nearby on the floor, still plugged in. The answering machine blinked a red "2." That meant calls received after the evidence team had left. Kneeling down, I pushed the button and waited as it rewound. Then, a beep and a woman's voice, sounding irritated:

"It's Sherry, Mac. Can't make it to lunch. Lenny wants to conference about the TV thing for NBC. I think we're going to have a major problem with it. Gimme a call and we'll reschedule."

Another beeping sound, and:

"Hey, Gordon: it's Wiltz. Don't forget our meeting tomorrow. Seven sharp. Don't be late, lover boy."

*Hollywood X-T-C,* again, I thought. What the hell was Mackenzie Gordon doing with a lowlife scuz like Howie Wiltz? Maybe Gordon's life was equally scuzzy. If so, I hadn't heard any rumors or seen anything in the trades. It was hard to believe, though; most producers try to stay clean so the banks don't turn up their noses when they come hat-in-hand looking for financing. But maybe Gordon was different. Or was different too mild a description for my odd ex-employer? You were a man with a million secrets, weren't you, Mackenzie, you little prick?

Casting a final hurried glance around, I went back into the hall and past a large, airy room with a grand piano, and finally to the front entranceway with its double stairway sweeping upward to the left and right. Feeling vaguely like Clark Gable at Tara, I mounted to the second-floor landing and a broad, high-ceilinged hallway that branched out in both directions. Turning left, I tried the first door I came to: Mackenzie and Catherine's bedroom, I thought, and immediately felt a stab of embarrassment for the lovely and—I had always assumed—classy Catherine Wilbourne. The room was almost as big as my apartment and expensively decorated, but in a hideously garish sort of way that seemed so unlike Catherine, or the picture we had had of her in films all these years. A gigantic specially made circular bed in the exact center of the room completely dominated everything, yards of rose-colored fabric flowing down to its frame from a single point fifteen feet overhead, turning it into an image cribbed from some kitschy Rudolph Valentino film from the twenties. It must have been twenty feet across and sat like a desert tent atop a three-foot-high platform of gray-and-white marble. The sheets were a pale blue satin and the pillows covered in white-and-gold silk. A dozen more pillows, large and small, decorated with intricate geometric designs, were balanced against the fabric-covered walls and strewn haphazardly on the Persian carpet and glossy marble floor. On the near side of the bed platform, a semi-circular tile pool, perhaps twenty feet long and two feet deep, reflected the blue of the ceiling; a gold fish's mouth at one end spewed out a thin, airy fountain of water. Exotic beaded lamps and gilt-edged mirrors were everywhere, and, directly across from me, where it couldn't be missed, an eight-foot-square oil painting of a wild, white horse leaping out of a whirlwind.

Everything but a lava lamp, I thought. It was all oddly depressing and unbelievably tacky, as if Elvis Presley's interior decorator had been pumped full of amphetamines, then set loose in here and told to *make it fancy!* I would have liked to have poked around— Mackenzie and Catherine probably had secret compartments and Captain Marvel decoder rings hidden in the walls—but I wasn't going to have time now. Closing the door, I tried the room across the hall. A guest bedroom, probably, and remarkably subdued by comparison. Another guest bedroom next to it, equally dull. Outsiders, evidently, weren't allowed to play sheik-and-slave-girl with the Gordons. At the far end of the hall was a "media room" with a wall-sized projection TV and a video recorder and stereo. But that was it in this wing. I retraced my steps, crossed the stairway landing, and tried the other half of the house. Another guest room. An empty, musty-smelling room across from it. And finally, Laurie's bedroom.

It was large for a child's room, perhaps twenty by thirty feet, with a double bed covered with a cheery yellow-and-blue Sesame Street bedspread. Another large-screen TV and video recorder along one wall; along the opposite wall, an attractive built-in desk and bookcase, with dozens of cartoon videos strewn along its laminated top. Laurie's electronic baby-sitter, I supposed, as I glanced through the cassettes: Disney, Sesame Street, Looney Tunes. A giant stuffed Pooh Bear rested against a wall with a dozen other stuffed animals, staring obediently toward the TV. And next to the bed, also on the floor, Ken and Barbie dolls, Ken and Barbie house and car, Ken and Barbie beach equipment. It reminded me of Tracy's room when she was seven.

What was I looking for? I wondered as I stared at it all. I still had no idea. But I knew next to nothing about the girl I had been hired to find. I had her picture, I had a few banal comments from Gordon who was obviously less interested in her than in getting back his missing script material. Or so it had seemed then. But there hadn't *been* any missing script material! Again it occurred to me that if Gordon had lied about that, he could have lied about Laurie running away, too. But if she hadn't run away, where the hell was she?

The whole thing was weird. And sad. And it didn't make the tiniest bit of sense to me. So get to know Laurie, I told myself: Root around in here and see what you can come up with. If you don't find anything, try the people who knew her; push a little, make something happen, as Rudy always says. *Make* it happen.

I stared around again: mild kid disarray, not police department disarray, this time. The police hadn't known about the missing daughter when they'd searched the house, and had left this room alone. I pulled open the top desk drawer. A wad of crumpled-up school papers: Laurie doing simple sums, tracing words, drawing pictures. No dates but it all looked recent. Some pencils, mostly broken; a few coins; a two-color pen. Gum wrappers. A half-dozen ragged five-by-seven color pictures of Disney characters, some of them "signed" in ink by the characters: Goofy, Donald, Scrooge. A Teenage Mutant Ninja Turtles figurine. A handful of publicity photos of actors who had appeared in Gordon's films. A couple of them had been signed, too, authentically, I supposed. *To Laurie* . . . A New Kids on the Block photo. Signed again. Interesting but not very exciting. Pretty much the same for the other drawers: school things, girl things, maybe more expensive than you'd find in most kid's rooms but, except for the studio photos, nothing unusual.

A double dresser was built-in next to the desk. Laurie obviously didn't want for clothes: shorts, pants, T-shirts, underwear. All of it new, much of it unworn. But nothing out of the ordinary here, either. And nothing very personal, it seemed—just things. Stuff. The bookcases held board games and a few simple puzzles. On top of one game I found an unframed photograph of a teenage boy with dark, deep-set, oval eyes and thick, curly hair. Good-looking kid. Written on the back was *To Laurie. Love. Richard.* I stared at it a moment. Not a publicity photo, was it? *Love* . . . and stuck it in my pocket: something to think about.

Against a wall there was a wooden easel with little bottles of poster paint on a shelf. A half-completed painting of a middle-aged woman was attached to the easel; she was sitting on a couch, smiling, petting a gray cat. Behind the painting there were a half-dozen others, mostly unfinished. They were pretty good. Laurie was not exceptionally talented but certainly far better than the typical fourteen-year-old. With some training she'd probably be pretty good. I wondered if her parents cared. Someone must—to have bought the easel.

I walked over to the large walk-in closet and looked inside; it was crammed with clothes: winter clothes, summer clothes, shoes, purses, all the normal appurtenances of any young teenage girl's life. But that was it. Still no personal items—no notes or letters or diary or—except for the photo—hints of a life elsewhere or any indication of a place she might want to run to.

The bathroom seemed oddly austere, cold and hospital-like. A single bottle of inexpensive perfume sat on a shelf; a tube of Crest, almost empty; fingernail polish. And sanitary napkins; Laurie was a young woman. I went back to the bedroom and looked at my watch: forty minutes I had spent here already. Not much to show for it but I'd better hurry; I didn't want to be around when the Beverly Hills cops came by. I took my shop rag and wiped away my prints and let myself into the hallway.

Two more rooms, both with locked doors, down the hallway. A final room at the end. I opened the deeply carved double doors and took a breath, feeling like Judy Garland must have when the world changed suddenly from black-and-white to a brilliant Technicolor.

The first thing I noticed was the room's immenseness, then the ocean of pale blue carpeting stretched out at my feet, and then, as my gaze drifted upward along painted white arches, the molded concave ceiling that rose at least thirty feet in concentric circles to a sort of star burst design with an amber glass bowl at its center, which caught the light from outside like a miniature sun. Across from me, an enormous tapestry with a delicately woven hunting scene hung along one wall, while eighteenth- and nineteenth-century landscapes in ornate gilt frames were spaced along the others. The far end of the room had been turned into a sleeping alcove, where a canopied bed rested in front of a carved altarpiece that had probably been removed from a medieval Italian church. Antique dressers and wardrobes and mirrors led to a music area where there was a harp and, next to it, an ancient harpsichord and pianoforte, and a grouping of chairs. Three tall windows on the south wall were stained glass—probably also from a church—and washed a rich, warm light over everything. I stared in fascination. A museum room, I thought,

as I stepped inside and gazed around. A dozen delicate seventeenth-
or eighteenth-century knickknacks—a small brass globe, an ivory
statuette, crystal eggs, a crystal pen-and-ink set—posed like art
objects on marble tabletops. A jeweled lamp, one of the few things
in the room less than two hundred years old, rested on a stand next
to the bed. The effect was dazzling, and elegant in a way that the
first bedroom definitely was not. Like night and day, I thought. I
picked up a gold letter opener, looked at it, put it down and did the
same for a slender silver vase with a likeness of Zeus etched on its
surface. It was as though two different families—or two different
cultures—had been forced to share one house. A carved door on a
side wall led to a walk-in closet, larger than my own bedroom,
crammed with dresses and skirts and shoes and sandals. Another
door led to a bathroom dominated by an elongated Roman tub with
gold fixtures, and probably big enough to accommodate all twelve
Caesars at the same time. Cabinets and shelves were stocked with
more unguents and creams and exotic perfumes than old Perc West-
more ever dreamed of; probably even frankincense and myrrh, I
thought, as I drank it all in.

I felt like a child lost in a palace, and inexplicably my spirits rose,
a sense of dreams reclaimed flooding over me. The lovely Catherine
was a classy lady after all, classy enough at least to have a bedroom
separate from Mackenzie Gordon and his tacky Arabian Nights fantasy.

There were a half-dozen bottles of prescription drugs from a phar-
macy on Canon in the medicine chest: antibiotics for Catherine;
pain pills; and a prescription for Laurie. Ritalin. A stimulant, if I
recalled correctly, sometimes prescribed to control the behavior of
hyperactive children. I put it back and returned to the bedroom. On
an antique dresser there were three framed pictures. One appeared
to be at least thirty or forty years old—a middle-aged woman grasping a young girl tightly by the hand. The girl I recognized immediately as the very famous, very young Catherine, the older woman
was probably her mother. The other two pictures were of Laurie:
one, a posed professional photo that looked recent, the other, Laurie
sitting in the sand at the beach, also recent. In both she was smiling
to break your heart.

There hadn't been any pictures of Laurie in Gordon's bedroom, had there? Yet Gordon said he loved her, acted like she was Daddy's special little girl. A funny way to show your love. Poor Laurie, I thought suddenly: almost invisible in this huge house except for two tiny pictures on Mom's dresser, and a bedroom full of possessions. It was sad, but it was also beginning to make me angry: It was almost as if she was a prop—". . . playing the role of the daughter is young Laurie Gordon"—and didn't in reality exist, wasn't really a part of anything. And now that she was missing even her mother didn't seem concerned enough to come home and help look for her.

Poor Laurie.


On the way out of the house I pushed the window shut from outside and wiped off my prints. Almost a quarter to four; I could probably still get to Laurie's school by four o'clock for my appointment with the principal. As I nosed the Buick through the gate and back onto Atherton I remembered the picture I had shoved into my pocket. *To Laurie. Love.*

Who was Richard?

And what the hell did Mackenzie Gordon want with Howie Wiltz and his sex-for-sale fantasies?

# 7

THE HOLSTEAD SCHOOL WAS ONLY A COUPLE OF MILES AWAY, ON WIS-
teria, a broad street lined with seventy-year-old elms in the flatlands
of Beverly Hills just off Wilshire, in a neighborhood of early movie-
era mansions thrown up with the first feverish outpourings of stu-
dio-generated wealth. Since the sudden, and mostly surprised,
mega-millionaires who erected these houses had no experience of
wealth, they modeled them after pictures seen in books—Italian vil-
las, English country houses, French châteaus—and plunked them
down on stately looking streets hastily staked out in the fields just
west of Hollywood. The Holstead School, evidently someone's mud-
dled notion of Italian or Spanish, was three stories of whitewashed
colonnades and arches, and had been erected—or posed—on a
slight promontory and surrounded by an acre or so of grass by an
architect with an eye for composition. It was an LA postcard view,
or—more accurately—a scene through a viewfinder. Industry people
obviously continued to think so, because I instantly recognized it as
an exterior location for numerous films and TV shows over the
years. With a Stutz or Reo out front it immediately became flapper-
era elegant; with a new Mercedes, a Mafia don's headquarters. An
eight-foot wrought iron fence with spikes at the top had long ago
been erected along the front of the property to keep the barbarians
at bay, but the barbarians were evidently welcomed now, as the
heavy double gates were pulled open. I drove through on a circular

cobblestone drive and left my year-old Buick feeling alone and shabby in a small parking area next to half a dozen Jags and Mercedes.

Rather than going immediately inside I decided to take a quick tour around the grounds. The more I thought about it, the more sense Tracy's notion made that Laurie might be hiding at her school. For a child like Laurie there were limited options, and school was probably a place where she felt comfortable. Most kids—even most severely retarded kids, I presumed—looked up to their teachers, sometimes even more so than they did to their parents. When faced with a crisis, what more logical choice than to come here?

I stood by my car a moment and stared around. A dozen oaks and elms dappled autumn sunlight over the broad expanse of lawn sloping down from the house. Beds of massed winter annuals—pink and yellow pansies, blue violas, soft pastel snapdragons—flowered in formal gardens bisected by rustic paths, with benches and stone statues nestled in cozy little nooks. Lily pads floated in a pond. Birds chirped overhead. Smell of wet leaves and wood smoke. All very idyllic, I thought: deliberately calm and sedate; soothing, like a drug. And not at all California. Old-line Connecticut, perhaps, or Long Island. Another image plucked from a book: Gatsby's East Egg.

I followed a meandering path around to the back of the house where even the mandatory California-style swimming pool and tennis courts were absent, and instead, a volleyball net and basketball backboard had been set up behind a tall chain link fence; both the net and backboard were only about five feet off the ground. Beyond this, in the rear of the large yard an animated young woman in slacks and a bulky cableknit sweater was attempting to teach a boy of about eight to throw a baseball. Each time he picked up the ball it slipped from his hand, and he mumbled something unintelligible and looked as if he would cry as the woman hugged him and encouraged him to try again.

The sides and rear of the yard were ringed with neatly trimmed bushes, none of them more than two or three feet high. Could Laurie have hidden there? It didn't seem likely. But if she had, there would have been no cover from rain, no protection from the frigid evening wind. I hoped she'd found something better. A small adobe building with a pitched roof sat against the side fence thirty yards from the house. I crossed over and pulled open the door: lawn equipment and gardening tools. Laurie could have spent the nights here, I supposed, but where would she have spent the days without being noticed? I shut the door and walked all the way around to the other side of the yard, out to the front of the house again and mounted the stone steps to the door marked OFFICE. A mahogany counter had been erected just inside, and behind it a slightly frazzled-looking middle-aged woman sat talking quietly on the phone while she typed on her word processor. I waited until she hung up, introduced myself, and asked for Ms. Ravich.

"Are you sure you have an appointment?" she asked, rummaging around the papers on her desk until she found her calendar. "Mrs. Ravich doesn't usually see parents in the afternoon. Oh, here it is— Eton, Vic, four o'clock." She glanced up at me over the tops of her half-glasses with obvious surprise. "You're on time, aren't you?"

"Odd for Beverly Hills," I agreed with a shrug, and felt a little foolish.

"Well don't let it become a habit, young man," she said with a smile as she picked up a telephone and pushed a button. "You'll never be a success in this town if it does. Perhaps we could find you a support group to counsel with. Every time you feel an urge to be on time you could call a producer or an attorney, someone who's never been tempted . . . oh, Mrs. Ravich, Mr. Eton is here. . . . Yes, of course."

She put the phone down. "She can see you right away. I'd better take you back. This is a rabbit warren."

She lifted a board in the counter, and I passed through and followed her back into the interior of the house, along a wide, wainscoted hallway smelling of the same red furniture polish I remembered from my childhood, and adorned with hundred-year-old sporting prints in neat black frames. I glanced quickly into one room as we passed, obviously a library with shelves of books and an ornate nineteenth-century billiards table. A sign on another door said SAUNA. Another was the MUSIC ROOM. A bit eccentric, I decided, and a bit weird for a school, but definitely the sort of house I could live in.

"How long has the Holstead School been located here?" I asked, as we rounded a corner and started down another, longer, corridor.

"About fifteen years," she said. "This used to be one of the

Zukor's homes, I think; someone from the silent days, anyway. Then it was a girls' school for a while. It's been a school for the learning handicapped since before I got here. Oh, here we are—"

She tapped lightly on an open doorway and sing-songed, "Mr. Eton, Mrs. Ravich—"

A thin, middle-aged woman at a large, ornately carved desk at the far end of the room rose slowly to her feet and greeted me with a distant, husky voice. "Mr. Eton? I'm pleased to meet you. I'm Anna Ravich."

She stood stiffly, holding out a hand as I advanced across the thick carpet, and again I had a sense of the non-California aura of the place. The room was massive and paneled and dark, the only light filtering in weakly from narrow small-paned windows, and from a brass lamp that threw a soft golden glow on the desk. Anna Ravich was dressed in an attractive, if somewhat severe, tweed suit and wore her glossy black hair pulled back from her face. There was a single strand of pearls at her throat; on her wrist a jeweled Piaget watch. She was smiling professionally, without much warmth, but as I took her hand and looked into her face I had to revise my estimate of her age—early thirties perhaps. And extraordinarily attractive beneath the passionless exterior. If I hadn't known we were in a school, I would have guessed her to be the president of an old-line European fashion or jewelry concern. Or an empress in training.

"And this," she said after we shook hands, "is Emily Stevens." She paused a moment and added, "Laurie's teacher."

I hadn't noticed the other woman, small and inconsequential in a large wing chair off to the side. She was at least forty, even more severe looking than Anna Ravich, with her long, thin face, extremely short brown hair, and steel-rimmed glasses. But Emily Stevens very definitely did remind me of school. A no-nonsense sort of woman, I thought, as I stepped over and shook hands; my mind drew up a dozen prototype Emily Stevens's from my childhood, shouting to me about lost hall passes and overdue library books, and always seeming to smell of paste and paints and mild disapproval.

I sat in the chair Mrs. Ravich waved me to in front of her; Emily Stevens remained off to the side in the periphery of my vision as if she didn't want to draw attention to herself or had been instructed to remain a respectful five paces removed from the imperial presence.

"We've all been quite worried about Laurie," Mrs. Ravich began, with an obvious but unidentifiable accent, as she took the chair behind the massive desk and seemed to shrink in comparison. "Everyone here likes her so much." She leaned slightly forward, looking into my face. "Have the police come up with anything yet? Do they have any idea where she might be?"

"Nothing," I said. "That's why I wanted to talk to you." I turned to look at Laurie's teacher. "And Mrs. Stevens. School seems to be such an important part of Laurie's life that I thought you could tell me about her—what kind of child she is, what she likes to do, and so on—things that might help me find her."

"Yes, of course." Anna Ravich sat back, the dull light from the narrow windows falling on her almost Asian features, shadowing her perfect dark eyes and smooth, unlined face. She looked as though she had just spent an hour being made up by studio professionals, but it didn't seem vain or ostentatious. Instead, it appeared as if she had done merely what nature had intended for her marvelous face, and not one iota more.

"Laurie—" she began after a thoughtful moment, and her eyes came to rest again on mine, unexpectedly sending a little frisson of excitement racing through my body. "Laurie is a wonderful young woman: very gentle and trusting; oftentimes quite serene, one might almost say spiritual. And quite attractive, of course. But severely handicapped."

"From what cause?" I interrupted.

There was a moment's hesitation as she glanced at Emily Stevens. "We cannot go into that, I'm afraid, Mr. Eton. I can tell you that Laurie's condition is medical rather than emotional in nature, but California law shields minors from outside inquiries into the exact nature of their disabilities. I feel free to tell you that she's retarded to the point where she'll never be able to work, though; she'll never be able to take care of herself. She will always be the ward of the state if not the responsibility of her parents—her mother, now, of course. But if her mother should die, Laurie would almost certainly have to be institutionalized for life."

I had a sudden thought. "If that were to happen, if her mother died and she became a ward of the state, could she inherit?" I was thinking of Catherine Wilbourne's multimillion-dollar wealth and who would come into it.

She looked startled. "I don't know. I've never been involved in anything of that nature. You'll have to ask a lawyer."

You bet I will, I thought. It raised some interesting possibilities. With one of Laurie's parents dead, most likely the other inherited. But what if both died? Or what if Laurie died? Presumably Gordon would have provided for her separately in his will—perhaps quite handsomely, given her need for professional care. But who would *her* heir be? Inheritances and wills could be complex, with multiple provisions and possibilities. But one thing I had learned from dealing with the super-rich the past few years was that when it came to estates, every possible outcome had been sketched out ahead of time and provided for by their attorneys. It was worth following up, anyway. I tried out something else on Mrs. Ravich that had been bothering me for days.

"Do you think it's likely Laurie could have run away on her own? Could she figure out where to go and how to get there, what bus to take, and so forth?"

Anna Ravich looked at me disbelievingly. "Do you mean she might *not* have run away? She might have been kidnapped?"

I shook my head. "I'm just wondering about her skills. Kidnapping is always a possibility, but so is getting lost."

"I see." Her eyes went again to Mrs. Stevens and she appeared uncomfortable. "Well . . . I think Laurie could have run away on her own. Emily?"

Emily Stevens's face was half hidden in shadows as I turned toward her. She was staring toward Anna Ravich, her voice calm but matter-of-factly authoritative in the way that teachers often seem to be. "Laurie takes the bus to and from school every day, of course. We insisted upon that. She understands how to pay, where to get off, and so on. But if she had to go somewhere new, someplace where she had not established and memorized a routine . . . I think she would have a great deal of difficulty."

"So she might get on a bus but not know where to get off? Just ride around randomly?"

"I think that is certainly likely. Until she panicked or followed someone off."

"Then she could be in downtown LA or Santa Monica or the Valley or anywhere the bus ended up," I said.

"That's true."

Anna Ravich said, "But why do you think she took the bus?"

"I don't," I admitted. "I don't know. She could have walked. She could have hitchhiked. . . . I'm trying everything." I turned back to Mrs. Stevens. "Both Laurie and Stephanie Chauk are in your class?"

"Yes."

"They're friends?"

"Yes. Or as much as they can be. Neither of them plays really well with other children."

"Did you ask the other kids if they had any idea where she might be?"

Emily Stevens's expression hardened into instant disapproval. "Her father came here the morning she disappeared—"

Anna Ravich interrupted, showing irritation either at the question or Mrs. Stevens's intended answer. "Mr. Gordon asked us to question the other students and of course we did. And this afternoon we had a visit from Social Services,"—she exchanged a quick glance with Emily Stevens—"a woman who insisted on doing the same thing. So we let her, naturally. But there was no point. The children obviously know nothing, and all these questions only upset them. They're all very concerned about Laurie. I'm sure some of them are going to have difficulty sleeping tonight."

"Is there some favorite place Laurie talked about, then? Someplace that excited her, where she might have liked to go? The beach perhaps? Or Disneyland? Something like that?"

Emily Stevens shifted uncomfortably in her chair. "I don't think she went places at all. I don't think her parents had much time for that sort of thing. They seemed too busy with their own lives."

Anna Ravich began to tap a gold pen impatiently on the polished desktop. "I really don't think we should be passing judgment on the parents of our children. Especially the dead."

"Better off dead, perhaps. For Laurie's sake," Mrs. Stevens said, and a tiny spark of electricity passed between the two women.

I looked at them both and wondered what was going on. Something unsaid hung in the air between them, something I would have to probe later, when I had each alone. To Emily Stevens I said,

"Does Laurie have any favorite toys? What does she like to play with? What entertains her?"

A smile appeared on her face. "Laurie loves playing with building blocks and Legos, designing and constructing things. She dearly loves Barbie dolls, and she's always talking to me about cartoons on television. I suppose watching TV was her main form of entertainment."

"How about video games?" I was wondering if perhaps she ended up at an arcade like so many other runaway kids.

"No, I'm afraid that would be far too taxing for her."

"In other words, there's nothing tangible for me to go on, nothing to point me in any direction?"

The two women were silent.

"Was she ever a disciplinary problem?"

"All of our children are disciplinary problems from time to time," Anna Ravich said.

Emily Stevens leaned forward, her face easing into the light. "Laurie loses her temper sometimes and starts screaming. I've been working on that with her and she's not as bad as she was. If she starts acting up I put her in 'time out,' a desk where she has to sit by herself and not talk to anyone until she calms down. I've seen tremendous improvement in the past few months."

Remembering the Ritalin, I asked, "Was she on medication?"

Anna Ravich said, "We can't answer that."

I sighed and repressed an annoyed frown. I wasn't learning anything tangible that I didn't already know and wasn't any closer to discovering where Laurie might be. I was still curious about this fancy school, however, and its role in her life.

"How many children do you have here?" I asked Anna Ravich.

"Thirty-six currently, in five different classes."

"Pretty expensive, I imagine," I said and stared around at the luxurious office with its fifteen-foot ceilings and paneled walls.

She smiled at me, the perfect executive, an answer already prepared for what was probably a common question. "It's all relative. People want the best for their children, of course, and we're the best."

"Did Laurie's mother or her father enroll her?"

"Her father. Mr. Gordon was very much admired by all the staff of the Holstead School and his death was a particular shock. Nothing like this has ever happened to one of our families. When Laurie is found—if she is all right—I'm afraid she is going to require a good deal of counseling. We've already discussed it with our staff psychologist; this is going to be a very difficult time for her. Do the police have any idea yet who did it?"

"Not as far as I know."

"You're not looking for the killer yourself?" Dark oval eyes stared at me.

I shook my head. "I'm looking for Laurie. But Gordon's death is probably linked with Laurie's disappearance. One will lead to the other."

"But not necessarily," she said.

"Not necessarily," I admitted. "But that's why I'm rummaging through Gordon's life—talking to friends, acquaintances, people he knew." I smiled weakly. "That's how it's done in real life: read people's mail, muck around in their lives, check out their friends and enemies and colleagues; muddle through, in other words, mess things around a bit, rattle cages. Pretty soon something turns up. It always does."

"Sounds interesting," Anna Ravich said while managing to convey that it didn't sound interesting at all.

"Mostly it's just tedious," I replied and stood up. "At any rate, I'd better go out and rattle a few more cages of my own. Thanks for your time."

They both came to their feet. Anna Ravich said, "Perhaps Emily could show you around the school before you leave, give you an idea of what Laurie's day was like. It might help." She managed to sound both optimistic and gently questioning at the same time, and I supposed it was a habit, the practiced sales pitch to prospective parents that concluded all interviews and preceded the signing of the tuition check: We do our best, but nothing is guaranteed. It was the way I felt, too.

"I'd like that," I said, glad to get Laurie's teacher alone for a while.

As Anna Ravich and I shook hands, I stared into her face, as hard and unlined as a Noh mask. But there was nothing there, nothing behind the dark eyes; no emotion at all. We said our good-byes, and I left with Emily Stevens.

"I'll show you my room first," Mrs. Stevens said softly as the door shut behind us, and we began walking down a long hallway, away from the building entrance. "I have eight students, most of them in their early teens."

"How long have you worked here?" I asked. She was about a head shorter than I, and away from the austere presence of Anna Ravich and her Prussian field marshal's office, seemed suddenly more human, not so much the Miss Grundy of Theodore Judah Elementary School a quarter-century ago. Or perhaps all the Miss Grundys of a quarter-century ago hadn't been so terrible after all.

"Just two years. I was in the Beverly Hills public schools before that. The Holstead School pays better, the classes are much smaller, and I think we accomplish more. Of course, we keep the children longer each day, too. Here we are."

We walked into what had probably once been a den, a large, high-ceilinged room with narrow leaded windows overlooking the rear yard. A half-dozen students were facing away from us, watching a video with a Hispanic man in his thirties. We stood just inside the door, whispering.

"That's Ernie, my assistant," she whispered. "We're doing a module on 'people in the neighborhood,'—policemen, letter carriers, newspaper deliverers, and so on. It helps the children adjust to people outside their families."

"Would it help if I asked the children about Laurie?" I tried again.

"Look, Mr. Eton. Mr. Gordon was here to ask before he died, a social worker has asked, we asked. We need to leave these children alone for a while. All of this is very upsetting to them."

Just then I noticed Stephanie Chauk twist around in her seat and stare at the two of us for a moment. I wasn't sure if she recognized me but she frowned and turned her attention again to the film.

"What did you think of Mackenzie Gordon?" I asked quietly, remembering the little spark of electricity in Anna Ravich's office.

"Not much."

"Meaning?"

"Laurie's father was in this classroom exactly once in all the time I've been here—and that was last week. Mr. Gordon was interested in his movies, not his child."

"And Mrs. Gordon?"

"She's been here a few times. But she's out of the city a good deal, I guess."

"You're disapproving."

She turned and led me back into the hall. "Yes. Disapproving. I'll show you the rest of the school."

She led us into three other classrooms and then into a small play room and eating area with an incongruous mixture of mahogany paneling and bright red-and-yellow plastic tables and chairs. "We're not big enough to have a cafeteria, of course, so we have lunch sent in."

"Catered meals," I said wistfully. "Only in Beverly Hills."

"It costs twenty-two thousand dollars to send a child here. Mrs. Ravich naturally tries to offer value for that."

"How do you like working for her?"

"She's very professional. Holstead School is quite successful."

We had reached a rear door of the building. Emily Stevens turned a deadbolt and pushed the door open, and we stepped into the chill autumn air.

"Is she the owner or just the administrator?"

"Mrs. Ravich and her husband own the Holstead School. She's originally from Russia and came to this country as a teenager, I believe." We began to follow a path to the edge of the expansive rear yard. "It's a little cool today, isn't it? That's Susan Bonares teaching coordination. She was in the Olympics a few years ago in gymnastics."

We stood on the path and watched the young woman trying to teach the boy with the ball. I marveled at her patience as the ball again and again slipped from his hand; working with these students clearly wasn't something all teachers could handle. After a moment, I said, "This seems like a wonderful environment for the children."

Emily Stevens smiled unexpectedly and stared at the boy. "It is. We do marvelous things."

"Was Laurie happy here?"

She thought a moment. "No. Not very."

"Do you know why?"

She hesitated a moment, still staring away from me as the wind blew leaves at our feet. "I can only guess. Her home life was not very supportive. She had no friends outside of the school that I know of. It's very sad . . . I like Laurie very much." She hesitated again, as if there were something she wanted to add but decided against it.

I gave her a little push. "The police are pretty worried. It's unusual for a child to be missing for this long. They're afraid something might have happened to her."

"I'm worried, too." She folded her arms as if she were cold, and shifted her weight from one foot to the other. But she added nothing.

The little boy started screaming happily. He had thrown the ball over the head of Susan Bonares, who stood where she was and clapped loudly. Mrs. Stevens smiled broadly and shouted, "Excellent, Eric."

AFTER LEAVING EMILY STEVENS, I CLIMBED BACK INTO THE BUICK AND was about to put the key in the ignition when I felt a strange sadness come over me almost physically, like an illness. I sat a moment, holding the steering wheel with two hands and staring sightlessly through the windshield when, with what seemed like a moment of complete clarity, I sensed that I would never find Laurie. I was up against something I could neither see nor understand, and I felt suddenly impotent and helpless. It was like fighting the fog: There was something out there just beyond my reach, beyond view, and always had been. I kept getting tantalizing little hints of it— Mackenzie's odd secrets, Kerry's lies, Brandon's hostility, Anna Ravich's glib defense of the inattentive and neglectful father—but no one was letting me get a complete picture. Glimpses only; tiny snatches inadvertently surfaced and then were quickly squashed down. Whatever it was they were hiding, it was more important to them than Laurie's disappearance.

Anna Ravich, I knew with an unyielding certainty, was hiding something. I wasn't sure yet what it was, but its edges had begun to appear from behind the less protective profile of Emily Stevens. Laurie's teacher was worth a follow-up in a day or so, I decided, but away from the looming Rasputin-like presence of her grim-faced employer. Perhaps Emily wasn't the prig I had assumed her to be, I reflected as I started the car. First impressions are often lasting but not necessarily accurate, and I was beginning to like her. Instinctively I began to cast the two in films, a habit picked up from lingering at too many industry parties. Anna Ravich as the first Queen Elizabeth. Or better, Catherine the Great of Russia. Anna Ravich as Frankenstein's bride. Or an Aztec priestess, standing triumphantly atop a pyramid, holding a beating heart in her bloodied hand. Emily Stevens as the befuddled secretary who turns out to know more than her boss, the pompous CEO of Mega Industries. Or starring in *Nine to Five*, tying her employer to a chair. . . .

But after a moment I began to feel like an idiot. Your B-movie imagination asserting itself, I thought, as I hit the gas and pointed the Buick out onto Wilshire, then headed east toward Hollywood. Stop fantasizing about the mysterious Anna and begin wondering about more immediate though mundane matters, like what to put together for dinner tonight. Tracy would be home, unless she was planning to go to the library again. What was this sudden fascination for libraries? Books or lanky young Jason? Perhaps we'd just have sandwiches. I didn't feel like cooking or going out. Maybe it was time to have a chat about Jason, too. He was fifteen and went to Hollywood High, while Tracy was still in middle school. He'd be driving next year then. I didn't know if I liked that. Jason would be sixteen and Tracy fourteen. I felt a shudder. Fourteen! Christ, was I really ready to face Tracy's high school years? It's tough being a teenager around here. No one knows that better than someone who'd been on the LAPD and seen what had happened to the "wonder years" in the last generation or so. I recalled the scraggly army of teenagers I'd seen ensconced on Hollywood Boulevard and their ritualistic "Get fucked . . . " If only Tracy's mother hadn't died. . . . I wasn't sure I wanted to handle this by myself. It must have been even worse for Gordon and Catherine Wilbourne, though. A teenager and a child together in one person. Maybe I had been too judgmental there. How did I know what they had been through with Laurie?

Maybe we won't have sandwiches, I decided suddenly. Maybe we ought to go out to dinner, a nice restaurant. Tracy and I hadn't spent much time together the past few days. It'd be fun for us. And I thought: Guilt, the Great Parental Motivator. As well as the restauranteur's best friend. Might as well wait and see what Tracy wants to do. Maybe she has other plans.

But five minutes later, dinner was pushed from my mind as I found myself trapped in the rapidly tightening grip of the daily drive-time bumper-to-bumper traffic on Wilshire, horns pounding noisily all around me, taxi drivers making obscene gestures, people yelling, pedestrians darting crazily across the street. The spaces between cars seemed to shrink and the buildings on either side of me grow taller and tilt inward toward each other. Like a German expressionist film from the twenties, I thought, as a headache began pounding behind my eyes; I winced and rubbed my neck and decided abruptly, To hell with it. And to hell with dinner. I'd buy Chinese take-out later; Tracy always liked Chinese. We could spend our "quality time" at home later. What I wanted now was a drink and a chance to relax and stop agonizing about Anna Ravich and Emily Stevens and Laurie and Kerry and all the rest of Mackenzie Gordon's not-so-merry bunch. What I wanted was thirty minutes of untroubled escape.

I ducked out of traffic and aimed for the first place I saw, Gables, a stylish-looking bar I'd been in once before, on the ground floor of a twelve-story office building on Bedford that catered primarily to stockbrokers and attorneys. I found a parking place on the street, locked the Buick, and went through the double glass doors, immediately experiencing the sense of relief customers were supposed to feel in this quiet and spacious shrine to Golden Age filmdom. Giant posters of Errol Flynn, Betty Grable, Tyrone Power, and the like hung from velvet-flocked walls; towering palms and banana plants sat in ceramic pots on the black-and-white tile floor; red leather semi-circular booths surrounded Formica-topped tables. There was an aura of studied calm and permanence in the air, as if Gables had been here through fifty years of slow time rather than the two months of its actual existence. I lowered myself onto a stool at the curved bar and said, "Gimme a Bud," to the middle-aged bartender who blinked as though he wasn't quite sure what I meant before disappearing, then coming back a minute later and setting a bottle down in front of me.

"American," he said and looked at me quizzically. "Don't get much call for it. Had to look in the back."

A six-foot TV screen in the rear of the room was showing a video of *Sunset Boulevard*, Gloria Swanson in marvelous black-and-white, rattling around the massive old Getty mansion down Wilshire that had been razed to make way for the Getty Oil Building when someone decided that what LA really needed just then was another office building.

The small TV over the bar was tuned to the local news, and with a sinking feeling I saw the smiling flat face of Mackenzie Gordon staring at me like an old friend. He and his pals had conspired to follow me even in here, I thought ruefully. *No further information on the Gordon killing,* the surprisingly boyish reporter was saying directly into the camera's eye just like they teach you in film school, but it took him two minutes standing in front of Gordon's house to say it. Milking it for all it's worth, I thought, as I sipped at my beer. Then Laurie's picture flashed on the screen, the one I had given the police earlier, and my head began to pound a little harder. Pretty fast work on the department's part. They must be worried. Good. At least someone is. Then a woman reporter appeared suddenly, standing in front of the Cinerama Dome on Sunset. The well-known producer's mentally retarded daughter was thought to be a runaway someplace in Hollywood, she said. Anyone who saw her should immediately call the Beverly Hills or Los Angeles police. The numbers flashed on the screen. End of story. Three minutes of commercials and I rubbed the back of my neck. Then Dr. George came on and acted out the weather report for the hearing-impaired, and the male and female news anchors giggled about something—war in the Middle East or whatever—and I called the bartender over and pointed at the TV. "Every minute you watch that channel you lose ten thousand brain cells. Put on 'Lucy.'"

"Hey, don't knock the news team," he said protectively and swiped at the bar with a rag. "You know what they say: Those are the ones that passed the audition. You shoulda seen the losers."

"Yeah, yeah," I said. "Now they're programming VPs. Come on, this is the network that used a witch a few years ago to pick its new shows. Get something else on."

He reached up and flipped to a "Magnum PI" rerun and I relaxed. Real life.

"You want another beer? You're not in a very good mood. Maybe it'd help you loosen up."

"How about some aspirin instead?"

"Sure, we're a yuppie bar, we're prepared for everything. Even The Big One; got cases of bottled Evian Water and frozen goat cheese out back to keep the bond traders alive. Like someone would want to!" He snatched a bottle from next to the cash register, shook two Anacin tablets onto a cocktail napkin, and put the bottle down. "You want some water?"

"Beer *is* water." As I swallowed the aspirin, my eyes drifted to the mirror behind the bar and the reflection of two guys three stools away, slugging back Bombay-rocks like mineral water. They were sitting sideways, facing each other, waving their arms and whining about the lack of loyalty everywhere they looked. "A totally fucked industry," they were saying loudly, as if they were alone in the bar. "Totally!"

"Entertainment attorneys," the bartender said and rolled his eyes as he wandered away.

They began to bad-mouth a trendy hunk-star who had evidently just split to a rival firm, screwing up the package they had put together and leaving them holding nothing, which really pissed them off because there's just no fucking loyalty anymore. They were in their twenties; they wore gold-and-white Rolex watches, eighteen-hundred-dollar suits, and called each other Dude.

I wondered if they'd be interested in a film about a nuclear accident in Mexico. Or a Hollywood homicide dick who didn't talk much. Or we could combine the two. We'd have to spice things up a little, of course: add some car chases and exploding bodies, lots of shattered glass. Hell, it had potential! But by the time the bartender returned I'd changed my mind and I handed him the bottle of aspirin. "Do the world a favor—drop this in their drinks."

"Dipshits, ain't they?" he said. "Always bitching about someone. They come in here every week while their BMWs are being detailed in the parking lot." He slapped his rag at the bar again. "You seem to have a discerning mind, young fella; not exactly the sort of customer the three dentists who own this place want to see around here, but OK with me. Have a beer on the house." He disappeared for a moment and brought back a St. Pauli Girl and poured it carefully into a clean glass. "It's all hops and barley but the orthodontists think nobody on the Westside wants American so they stock up on this foreign shit. Close your eyes and no one would know the difference."

"I'll keep my eyes open. I still won't know the difference."

He glanced down the bar, then leaned toward me on one forearm. "The two dinks, they're from New York originally. That's what I hate about this town—no one wants to be *from* LA. They just want to live here. Guys come in, I say, Hey, howdaya like them Dodgers? And they look at me and say, Dodgers? What about the Cubs? Or the Cowboys or Browns or Celts. New York and Detroit, they're the worst. Goddamn Tigers fans! Jesus, if it was so fuckin' great back there, why they out here cloggin' up the freeways?" He looked at me suddenly and straightened up. "And don't ask. I was born over at Cedar's the day World War II started. Used to hang out at old Gilmore Field in the Pacific Coast League days, before the Dodgers showed up. CBS Television City's there now. Gilmore for the Hollywood Stars, old Wrigley Field on 42nd for the LA Angels. Only city in the country with two minor league teams. Great times, my friend: the old DiMaggio brothers from San Francisco, Al Heist, Ted Williams, even Tommy Lasorda. Remember Chuck Connors, 'The Rifleman'? Played first base for the Angels. Gilmore had the stars, though, the ones in the stands: George and Gracie, Joe E. Brown, Slapsie Maxie, George Raft. Every night was like Oscar night. Hold on, I gotta refill zombies for those two women in the corner; they do PR for Armana Records when they're sober. Which ain't often."

A few minutes later he returned and stuck his hand in my face. "My name's Sal, by the way."

"Vic."

"Glad-ta and all that. You want some nuts? I gotta good mix here—less than half peanuts. I keep 'em under the bar so the dinks in red suspenders don't eat 'em."

I put my hand in the bowl as the phone jangled, and Sal walked over to the register to answer it, putting it down almost immediately. "Yo, Phil. Your car's ready."

One of the attorneys slid off the bar stool and walked over to where Sal was standing and handed him a hundred-dollar bill. Sal rang up eighty-five dollars and handed him three fives, one of which the guy slapped on the bar before leaving. When Sal got back I said, "The orthodontists own the detail business, too?"

"Nah. That's mine. They let me do it because it brings people in here. It takes a couple of hours to detail so the customers sit in here

and suck up drinks. I pay some high school kids seven bucks an hour
to do the cleaning and polishing. They love it—they get to crawl
around Corvettes and Aston-Martins and Jags and pretend they're
rich. So I clear maybe sixty bucks a car after materials. And what's
eighty-five, ninety bucks to the dinks? Hell, it costs them more than
that to do lunch at the Polo. So I'm happy, the owners are happy, the
kids out back are happy, and even the dinks are happy. I feel like I'm
doing some good in the world. You know what I mean? I'm a positive force in society. Have some more nuts."

"You're all right, Sal. Even if you do work in a 'concept' bar." A
sudden sinking feeling hit me. "You're not writing a screenplay, are
you?"

"You kiddin'? What would I wanna do that for? I got me a great
little racket here, got a nice apartment over on National, get to
watch classic flicks all day while I work. Why would I wanna write a
screenplay?"

I stuck my hand across the bar and we shook again. "Blood brothers."

I nibbled on nuts while Sal went off to concoct strawberry
daiquiris for two tourists from Idaho, where presumably there was
no baseball team to argue with him about. The hour must have
changed, because we were getting the news on this channel now
also. A woman was droning on about Mackenzie Gordon's unsolved
murder. The police were interviewing people who might have had
business dealings with him. They were also searching for Gordon's
daughter. The scene changed as they showed a brief interview with a
detective from Missing Persons. Yes, he said, they were doing everything they could to find the girl. They really needed the public to be
on the lookout, too. She was retarded and probably not able to take
care of herself. No, there didn't appear to be any connection
between the father's death and the girl's disappearance. But they
hoped she wouldn't find out about her father's death from strangers
or from TV. Then the film switched to a panoramic shot of the Holstead Special Day School, and suddenly there was Anna Ravich,
Queen of all the Russias, looking concerned and caring, and saying
how much they all missed Laurie.

I thought, Yeah, Anna, everyone misses Laurie.

So where is she?

If Laurie was a runaway she should have turned up by now. Everyone knew that. So maybe she's not a runaway: Maybe she was snatched. The cops hadn't mentioned that possibility. But if she was snatched, everything would suddenly become a hell of a lot clearer. *Cui bono?* in the trite jargon of the lawyers: who benefits? As easy as that. Who benefits from Laurie's disappearance? Or death? As much as I didn't want to, I had to face that likelihood: if she *had* been taken—unless it was a ransom kidnapping, and there was no indication of that—she would almost certainly have been killed by now. There wouldn't be any reason to take her and not kill her. But why? Who would benefit from Laurie's death?

It was likely that Laurie stood in line for a good chunk of Mackenzie Gordon's millions after he died. Of course, Gordon was killed after she disappeared. But maybe the timing's not relevant, only the result: Gordon dead, Laurie dead. Cui bono? Catherine? Her mother? No, I wasn't ready to accept that.

So who else benefits?

Brandon? Not in any way I could see.

Kerry?

One of Gordon's business partners?

As far as I could tell, no one benefited from Laurie's death.

Meaning what?

Meaning maybe she *was* just a runaway.

I suddenly remembered the photo in my pocket and took it out, putting it face down on the bar. *To Laurie. Love. Richard.* Sal had come back and was busying himself washing glasses.

*Love.*

After a moment I said, "What would you think if you saw this on the back of a picture in a girl's bedroom?"

He squinted at it briefly, then flipped it over. "Good looking boy. I'd say she had a boyfriend. You find this in your kid's room?"

I shook my head. "She's got a friend, though, doesn't she?" A friend. That had been the one thing missing from Laurie's life, probably the one thing the Gordons couldn't buy—although if Gregory Chauk was to be believed, they tried to force Laurie on Stephanie: if you can't buy a friend, coerce one. But a boyfriend? Laurie was retarded. Like a five-year-old, her father said. Five-year-olds don't have boyfriends. But in a teenager's body. A teenager's

hormones. I was tempted to call Emily Stevens: I just didn't know
enough about kids like Laurie. Did they have boyfriends? Maybe I'd
call Emily tomorrow. Or the odd Anna Ravich. Maybe push a little
this time, see what happened.

*Love. Richard.*

It was autographed. But Laurie had personally autographed pictures of Mickey Mouse and one of the New Kids and half a dozen
movie stars. Maybe it meant nothing. Maybe Kerry would know who
Richard was. If he was anyone.

Kerry. Anna Ravich. Brandon. Mackenzie Gordon. Even Emily
Stevens. . . . There seemed to be something horribly abstract about
their concern for Laurie—as if, of course, they'd be concerned about
any missing child, especially a retarded child. . . .

But nothing more than that, no *love*.

The most worried person appeared to be a Hollywood PI who had
never even seen Laurie. Only a picture.

Love . . . Richard.

I stared at the photo as Sal turned again to the news and the
weather report. Where the hell are you, Laurie? Three million people and no one has seen you? It doesn't make sense. Almost two
years older than Tracy. But playing with dolls and watching cartoons
alone in her room in that Gothic Beverly Hills mansion of theirs. An
updated *Sunset Boulevard*, perhaps. Maybe Gloria Swanson could
figure it out. Mad old Gloria—what was her character's name?—a
Hollywood Miss Havisham, living out her own B-movie fantasies.

For a moment I sipped my beer and let my mind play with the
notion that Laurie hadn't been snatched *or* run away, that she was
hiding somewhere in that massive house and slipping out at night to
eat and watch television and play with her toys. Then racing back
upstairs to the attic as the sun came up. Maybe a better analogy was
*Who's Afraid of Virginia Woolf?*—the child that doesn't exist, a bedroom made up for a phantom. Not very likely, I decided with a twist
of annoyance. Laurie was lost or kidnapped or dead, and I was sitting in a bar designed like a half-century-old Stork Club rather than
looking for her. Time to face reality again. Whatever the hell that
was. I reached for my wallet and slid some bills toward Sal. "Guess
I'd better be going."

"Yeah, well, come on back sometime," Sal said cheerfully, shifting his attention from the TV. "Leave your car with the kids out back and we'll detail it. Special discount for blood brothers."

I hopped off the bar stool and turned toward the giant TV screen, where Gloria Swanson was staring dumbly at a body floating face-down in her swimming pool.

I'd never liked the way that movie ended.


Rudy Cruz came over just as Tracy and I finished the last of our kung pao chicken and egg rolls. While I filled the dishwasher, he lined up six odd-looking greenish bottles on the kitchen table as if it were a demonstration of some sort.

"Genuine yuppie beer," he explained in his flat, gravelly voice. "Had to go out to Santa Monica to get it, but it's supposed to be worth the trip." He made it sound as if the journey was fraught with danger.

"What was it?" I asked. "Five miles out of your way? Four?"

He looked over at me and patiently shook his head. "Not the point, Vic. It's the time-warp: Everyone out there thinks it's still 1969. It gives me the creeps: record stores selling albums by Vanilla Fudge and the Tubes and the Kinks. People saying, 'outta sight,' 'groovy,' and 'right on.' Jane Fonda posters, Earth Day, Stop the War. It makes Hollywood look sane." He held a bottle up like an archaeologist with an unusual artifact and let the overhead light filter through the odd, dullish glass. "Granola Beer, handmade by middle-aged hippies on Ocean Boulevard: very healthful, all natural hops and grains, no cholesterol, no preservatives, recycled containers. It costs two bucks a bottle but five cents goes to Save the Whales. Where's the nachos and processed cheese spread?"

We sat in front of the large-screen TV and watched the Lakers and Warriors. Rudy passed me the nachos and asked, "You didn't blow up Gordon, did you?"

"Nope."

"Good," he said, his eyes riveted to the screen. "Oscar wanted me to ask. Just to be sure. What the hell'd you say to Don't-Call-Me-Geraldo, anyway? Man's pissed, even pissed at me." He turned a serious expression on me. "Guilt by association is an ugly thing, Vic. He won't even *talk* to me now. I am very sad. Gimme the chips again, grief makes me hungry."

"Remember Brandon Stiles?" I asked.

"The big-time director, seen leaving the premises of the deceased? You want to know why? That's why you're plying me with chemically preserved chips and overpriced beer?"

"You brought the beer. I only supplied the chemicals. And Oscar wouldn't tell me."

Rudy wiped all-natural foam from his mustache and yanked the recyclable cap off another bottle. "Don't let Oscar upset you. He's got to pull the Official Secrets Act around Rivera or he'll go bitching to Parker Center about civilians mucking up an investigation. Stiles was at Gordon's place for the oldest reason in the world, Vic. Nooky."

I put my beer down and looked at him; it couldn't be true.

Placidly, Rudy said, "Stiles thought Gordon would be out at his Malibu place so he got up early and dropped in on the missus for a . . . what do you call an early morning tête-à-tête? An A.M.er? Seems the two of them have been tooting each other's horns for a long time, even though he's young enough to be her third-cousin-once-removed, or whatever. Anyway, he saw the Daniels woman's car out front and got the hell out of there. Four's a crowd, you know, even in Hollywoodland." His broad shoulders gave a sudden shudder and he winced with apparent pain. "Christ, this beer *tastes* like whale shit." He picked up the bottle and squinted suspiciously at the contents list.

"I don't believe it," I told him. "Catherine Wilbourne is in Europe. There's no way Stiles expected to meet her."

Rudy sat back and shook his head. "She's not in Europe, Vic, or at least not on location in London. She didn't show up on the set two days ago; not a word to anyone—just didn't show up. And she doesn't seem to be in LA either. Kinda fouls things up, doesn't it? Mackenzie Gordon is dead, his daughter's run away, and his wife has disappeared."

After Rudy left I called Gregory Chauk.

"The police were out here already this evening. Of course I heard about it on the radio hours ago. I never did understand why they wanted to talk to me, though. Weren't they supposed to read me my rights or something before questioning me? It was a very unpleasant man, a Lieutenant Rivera."

Chauk seemed keyed up from talking to them; he'd probably never had the experience of a homicide investigation before. Some people react with morbid curiosity, others with fear or concern; Chauk seemed mostly irritated.

"They don't have to read you your rights unless you're a suspect or accused of something. I suppose they came out to see you because they're concerned about Laurie."

"But why me? Did you give them my name?"

He was beginning to remind me a little of Brandon Stiles with his determined whine. "I did, but they had it anyway. I suppose they found it on Gordon's appointment calendar. Or heard it from Kerry Daniels."

"That Daniels woman! She called here tonight, too, and wanted to know if Laurie had turned up. Or if I'd come across any of the script material Laurie had taken with her."

"Script material?"

"You know, the storyboards, that stuff she left with when she ran away."

"When was this?" I asked. "Today?"

"When she called? About an hour ago, I suppose. Why is everybody suddenly interested in me?"

I told him I didn't know. But it was a good question: why was everyone interested in Gregory Chauk? And what the hell script material was Kerry Daniels talking about?

After I hung up I sat back on the couch, thinking it out: Laurie was still missing, her father was dead, and her mother, instead of rushing home to help search for her daughter, disappears also.

And Kerry Daniels, one of the only two persons who seemed to tie all three together, was lying to me. Before Gordon was killed she lied about questioning Chauk. Now she was calling Chauk, looking for the storyboards we'd found this morning.

So what about the other pivotal player here: Brandon Stiles? Why should I believe what he said about going out to Mackenzie's at 4:30 in the morning? Young Brandon, I felt instinctively, was not to be trusted either.

But Kerry Daniels . . . lovely Kerry . . .

Lovely Kerry had lied to me for certain.

Kerry and Brandon. Anna Ravich and Emily Stevens. Mackenzie Gordon and Catherine Wilbourne.

Everyone with something to hide.

And now Catherine was missing. Millionaire-father dies, only child runs away, and mom disappears. What if they were dead, too? Who benefits? . . .

Stop speculating, I told myself: your B-movie imagination again! Laurie's a runaway. That's all. And we'll find her.

If Laurie was alive, everyone agreed, if she really was a runaway and wasn't snatched, she could only have walked or taken the bus.

If Laurie was alive, she was in Beverly Hills or Hollywood. Had to be!

I grabbed the phone again, punched out Eddy Baskerville's number, and left a message for him to meet me at Lee Wong's in an hour. We were going out together tonight; we were going to find Laurie.

# 9

LEE WONG'S IS A COP BAR A COUPLE OF BLOCKS FROM THE STATION
house. Eddie Darcy, a longtime patrolman, bought it from a Chinese
couple who had tried to operate it as a restaurant-nightclub. Darcy
kept the sign out front because he was cheap, dumped the dim sum
and egg rolls, put in topless dancers, and never looked back.

There were a dozen cars jammed haphazardly into the tiny pot-
holed lot out back where I left the Buick—belonging mostly to day-
shift cops who hadn't made it home yet or didn't have a home to go
to—and a scattering of mean-looking chopped Harleys from the
Satan's Patrons motorcycle gang, gleaming menacingly in the purple
vapor of the outdoor lights like futuristic instruments of torture. A
blast of heavy-metal music thundered momentarily from inside as
the rear door banged suddenly open, and a middle-aged Asian couple—tourists with cameras bouncing vigorously around their
necks—bustled out, gesturing and muttering angrily to each other
in Chinese and flipping through an outdated tour book.

Inside the door I stopped to let my eyes adjust to the darkness
and my ears adjust to the music pounding the building with the
incessant, jackhammer-like power of several hundred watts. A heavyset ex-cop sitting on a stool checking ID's looked up at me through
a fog of swirling cigarette smoke. "How y'doing, Vic? You run into
Available Eddie? He's been looking for you. He just left."

I moved aside as two college kids hurried in and flicked fake driver's licenses at the guard who waved them inside with a yawn. "I told him to meet me here. Did he say where he'd be?"

"Uh-uh. But he's coming back in half an hour or so. Said he had to eat first. He always has to eat first. How do you like the new girl?"

On the T-shaped stage, a large-breasted redhead had worked up a sweat dancing to "Jumpin' Jack Flash." "Nice," I said. "Keeping the classics alive."

"I told her she's too big to dance topless. Look at her boobs flying around like that. She's going to get a rupture or something."

"I think it's probably called something else. If Eddy comes in, point him in my direction." I walked past the stage seats where the motorcycle gang had settled in with territorial aggressiveness, stacking up beer bottles on the tiny tables and hooting at the dancers, and slipped into a deserted booth in the rear. Eddie Darcy came up and put a Bud in front of me with a glass. He was in his late fifties, fat, a Marine Corps haircut that hadn't changed since Parris Island thirty years ago, and Marine Corps insignias tattooed in red on each forearm. He stared down at me and wiped his hands on his bulbous stomach.

"Drinking alone now? That's a bad sign, bucko."

"Waiting," I said and pointed to the seat across from me. "Sit a spell."

"Can't. Got to watch the till. One of my barmen didn't show up; he called from Mexico and said he's taking a little vacation. What-daya think?"

"I think you better have your accountant look at your books."

"I hear ya. Is it true you're looking for that kid on TV?"

"Looking," I said. "But not very successfully."

"Available Eddy working for you?"

"Uh huh."

"That's what I figured. He was in here earlier. He sat at the stage, ate a couple of quarts of peanuts, and started bad-mouthing Harleys to one of the dancers, talking real loud, you know, calling 'em pussy bikes. I told him to get the hell out until he learns some manners."

"What brought the shitkickers in?" I asked, turning to look at the bikers. "This isn't their natural sort of prowling ground." Usually they hung out in biker bars where outsiders were as rare as Sinatra records.

"Showing us their balls. Someone told 'em this here's a cop bar, so they decided to come in and make a little noise, be tough guys." He rolled his eyes, a beat cop who had seen it all. "I don't give a shit as long as they don't start breaking things. I got my twelve-gauge over-and-under behind the bar. You hear me yell 'Freeze, fucker!' dive under the table. And if you see Eddy you keep the asshole quiet or I'll let the Satans have him for dinner."

Darcy waddled off, and the dancer retired backstage as a Bon Jovi record exploded over the speakers. Five seconds later, another dancer popped out as if she had been propelled by a slingshot; I'd never seen her before, either, but Lee Wong's wasn't exactly a career opportunity for the girls; two or three months and most of them were gone to wherever topless dancers go. Darcy came by again and dropped a bowl of popcorn on the table. "Better finish it before Eddy gets here."

I sat back and tossed popcorn in my mouth and nursed my beer. Was I imagining it or was the sound level higher each time I came in? And why did it only seem to bother me during songs that had become popular after I'd turned thirty?

Twenty minutes later, when Bruce Springsteen rumbled over the speakers, I decided to visit the restroom. The tiny room stank of urine and disinfectant, and I had to wait while two bearded Satans stood at the urinals, making a production out of peeing, spitting in the bowl, flexing their legs, and buttoning up their pants, all the while talking about what they'd like to do to that fat asshole that'd been putting down Harleys. When they were done, they glared at me suspiciously, as if I also might harbor doubts about the virility of their bikes, then pushed their way back to the bar. When I got back to my booth, Ellie and Elsa, dancers and twin sisters from New Zealand, were waiting with a pitcher of beer. They had their blond hair in pigtails and were wearing T-shirts about two sizes too small that said *Some Fun*.

"Only five minutes before our set," Ellie said in her cute accent. "If we work at it, the three of us can finish the pitcher."

"Free beer," I marveled. "What can the occasion be?"

"Our birthday," Elsa said. "Or close to it, anyway. It's actually next month. We'll be forty-four."

"Twenty-two each," Ellie explained, and they both giggled.

"Wanna help us celebrate?" Elsa asked, large blue eyes stretched open expectantly.

"Anything to further international understanding," I said and poured beer into my glass.

"Come over to our place when we get off tonight, then. We'll have a party," one of them said. I was beginning to lose track already; there was something about a mole but I couldn't remember what; anyway it would have been hidden from view at the moment.

"I don't think tonight's very good," I said. "I'm working, probably late."

"Oh, come on!" They giggled in unison. "We'll have something for you to eat. Then we'll both blow out the birthday candles." They giggled again in case I didn't pick up their meaning.

Their glasses went empty simultaneously, and they refilled them and quickly polished those off, too. Ellie, or Elsa, spilled a few drops on her shirt and rubbed at it with her finger tips. Her sister said, "Don't let the Satans see that or they'll want to lick it off right here."

They both glanced over to the dozen men sitting at the stage and shuddered. "Gimme the creeps, they do."

"Haven't got them that bad at home. . . . Oops—" the beer was gone again and they quickly refilled their glasses.

"Going to be embarrassing if we've got to tinkle while we're on stage."

"It'd be a lot easier to cut out the middleman," Elsa—I think—said thoughtfully. Maybe it wasn't Elsa. Maybe I was seeing double. "Just take it straight from the bar," she went on, "and pour it down the toilet."

The record that had been playing came to an end, then Prince came on, and the girls shrieked together and said, "Ohh—that's us," and quickly pulled off their T-shirts. They left them on the table— "Watch these, love"—and rushed for the stage, dressed only in sequined G-strings, wobbling precariously in high-heeled boots. When Darcy wandered by, I told him to bring me a microwaved burrito. It arrived five minutes later along with Eddy Baskerville. I ripped the burrito in half before he could claim it, and watched steam escape as Eddy flopped down in front of me and said, "You won't believe where I've been."

"Eating."

"No such luck. You remember Janie Krantz, makeup girl over at Columbia always talking about how her fucking biological clock's ticking away? Well, the alarm never went off. She got pregnant last year and married Howie Smithson, that union muckety-muck over at AFTRA, all the time complaining about runaway production. I always figured they must sit around all night bitching, but I guess they found something else to do seeing as she got pregnant. Anyway, they saw me out on the street when I was going to eat, and they made me come up to their apartment over there on Las Palmas and watch videos of their kid being born—*birthed*, they called it! Videos! Howie stood there with a camera and taped it! Christ, I wanted to puke, all the blood and guts and I don't really want to *know* Janie that well, if you get my drift. What are they going to do with the fucking tape, for Christ's sake? Show it to the kid when he's fifteen? Here's you being birthed, sonny, that's your momma's snatch staring you in the face. Jesus! People got no class no more. Those motorcycle fuckers still here? Let's start throwing peanuts at 'em, see if they can catch them in their mouths. Maybe we can teach them to walk on their hind legs. Darcy! Bring a pail of grub over here, it's feeding time."

Ellie and Elsa were dancing back-to-back on stage, staying farther from the edge than the other dancers and causing a couple of the Satans to start pounding empty beer bottles on the little table in front of them. Eddy looked over at the topless girls and sighed. "Like cupcakes with cherries."

I took a bite of my burrito and sensed the chemical preservatives washing around my mouth, interacting with each of my fillings in turn before sinking with the beans and beef into my stomach like blobs of liquid mercury.

Eddy leaned suddenly over the table as if he had just remembered something. "Why the hell don't you ever call your office? I was trying to reach you this afternoon. I even called your apartment, but Tracy said you'd been out all day and she didn't know where you were."

"I was at Laurie's school. Turned up diddly."

Eddy's gaze drifted to the empty pitcher and he picked it up. "Jesus, you drink all this by yourself? I heard you got a pretty big keg inside you but you're not even tipsy, are you?" He squinted suspiciously into my eyes.

"The kiwis drank it. They're like Australians: beer is their birthright."

Eddy looked longingly over to the stage again. "Not an ounce of fat on 'em, is there? Unless you count the obvious." Elsa—I think—winked at us as Prince came to an end and Motley Crüe replaced it.

Eddy sat back in the booth and spread his large hands out on the table. "It wasn't important, anyway. I've got shit on the girl. But maybe that's the point. If she's out there I shoulda turned up something. Right? I mean, someone must have seen her, cute kid like that wandering the streets."

"What were you planning for tonight?"

"Go farther west, maybe up by the dance clubs on Sunset. Figured I'd start around eleven when the crazies come out, keep at it until three or so."

I swallowed the remainder of the burrito and wiped my hands on a napkin. "I'm going with you. But let's do it now. I don't want to wait. I want something to happen."

I dropped a five-dollar bill on the table and climbed out of the booth. Eddy clambering up behind me, saying, "You bring a coat? It's going to be colder than a witch's tit out there tonight."

"There's a jacket in the car," I said. "Come on, I'll drive."

We weaved through the noisy crowd, Ellie and Elsa frowning but wriggling dainty little fingers as they saw us heading toward the exit. The bikers spun around and scowled when they saw Eddy, and looked as if they wanted to follow us but turned back to the stage instead and growled at the girls.

I shivered as soon as we hit the icy outside air. The wind had picked up, and it felt as if it was going to begin raining any minute. Crummy goddamn weather to be walking around in. Crummy goddamn weather to be lost in.

Five minutes later we got to the Strip. Pulling off onto a residential street where the Buick was less likely to be broken into, we parked and walked back to the boulevard and its odd mixture of surreal juxtapositions: exclusive private clubs for the industry elite, obscenely expensive restaurants, luxury-car dealers. Along with sleazy fast-food joints, twenty-four-hour record stores, and the wandering homeless. Tucked here and there in between were clubs like the Whisky and Roxy for the hopefully hip and eternally young of all economic classes.

"We'll work together," I said and handed Eddy a handful of pictures and a stapler.

Despite the wind and the almost certain rain, the street was clogged with cars: teenagers cruising, honking at friends, sticking their heads out of windows and yelling at each other; men looking for hookers and hookers looking for men; cops in cars, cops walking; tourists wondering what the hell they'd gotten themselves into.

At a bus stop in front of an upscale restaurant, eight or ten kids dressed in black, with half-shaved heads and loaded down with silver jewelry, were wandering aimlessly, listening to an enormous ghetto-blaster, jumping on the bench and shouting to each other at the top of their voices. Posing, acting cool. None of them over fifteen. Laurie's age. We walked over, and Eddy smiled and flashed the picture. "Any of you kids seen her?"

"Fuck you, man," sneered an emaciated boy in a motorcycle jacket with a dozen zippered pockets.

"Look at it," I said.

The boy glared at me and then at Eddy, finally snatching the picture from Eddy's huge hand.

"I ain't seen her," he said at last, but his bravado was dying like an ember in the rain. He shoved the picture at a girl with a painted white face and red lips who looked at it and passed it around.

"She needs help," I said.

They looked at the ground and kicked their feet and mumbled. But no one had seen her.

"Keep the picture," I said and we set off again down the street toward the Whisky, past a toothless black man in an old army overcoat pushing a shopping cart with all his possessions; past a forty-year-old white man dressed as Jesus, holding a gigantic wooden cross; past hookers in leather skirts drifting by in groups of two or three; past gang members in bandanas; and young men openly selling drugs.

We talked to everyone, stapled the picture to telephone poles, and walked some more. "Look at the sidewalks," Eddy said, and I did, seeing weeds pushing up between the cracks, sometimes growing in large brownish clumps in the gutters. "It's nature moving back," Eddy went on. "Reclaiming the city. A hundred years ago this was uninhabited countryside; in another hundred it will be again. Civilization lost."

Shortly after midnight we came across a middle-aged man putting up pictures of his missing seventeen-year-old daughter. We looked at each other, exchanged pictures, and continued on our way.

"Most of the over-eighteen crowd is still in the clubs," Eddy said, as a fire truck screamed in the distance. "It'll be two o'clock before they're on the streets—those that don't head for the after-hours places."

I sat down on a brick planter in front of a shuttered restaurant and felt the dew and the cold rubbing my face. "It's depressing."

Eddy sat down next to me and said, "You got that right."

There was a rootlessness about all the young people around us that disturbed me. They seemed always to be moving, drifting, shouting; too much energy: It radiated from their bodies like heat from a lamp, but without focus. A street light above me suddenly flickered, went out, then snapped on again. I blew on my hands and stared across Sunset to the record store that wouldn't let us put a flier on the door or talk to any of their customers, and had an urge to drive my car through the plate-glass window.

Why can't we find you, Laurie?

And why did everyone seem to treat her as a *thing*? Gordon, Chauk, Kerry and Brandon, her teachers—they all spoke of how special she was, how sweet; spiritual, Anna Ravich had said.

But not one word of *love*. How hard it must be for her! A burden to everyone, even her parents. It made me angry just thinking about it.

After a moment I got to my feet and we tried again, wading into a group of kids dressed up for *The Rocky Horror Picture Show*. Nothing. Two blocks up the street Eddy ducked into a doughnut store for coffee, while I waited in the parking lot. I shivered in the wind and shoved my hands in my jacket pockets until a muffled sound somewhere behind me drew my attention, and I turned around. A group of kids lounging in the dark by their cars had slowly come to life, as if sprinkled with magic dust, and were moving silently in my direction. I could barely make them out as they emerged from the night like coyotes padding toward a bird floundering on the ground. Before I knew what was happening I was surrounded.

"The fuck you doing here, man?" a voice behind me said. They weren't kids, I could see now—mostly in their late twenties, wearing black leather caps and jackets with swastikas and death's-heads.

"Lookin' for pussy?"

"Trying to score some dope?"

"Exercising," I said. "Taking a walk. Minding my own business."

"You a fag?" a guy who appeared to be their leader asked with a laugh. "Comin' down here lookin' for a little action?"

"S and M," another voice behind me said. "Come down here to get beat up."

They started moving in on me, a circle getting smaller.

"How much money you got, dude? How much you gonna pay us to beat the shit out of you?"

I stood still as the circle collapsed on me.

"Crazy fucker. Wants to die."

"Crazy . . ."

Hands reached out and propelled me suddenly backwards, other hands jerking me to the front again. I felt myself start to lose my balance. A knife flashed open in front of me.

"There a problem here, Vic?"

Eddy was standing with a steaming coffee cup in each hand, staring without emotion, his hair wet with moisture from the night air.

The punks looked at him and seemed to shrink inside their jackets.

"Anthropology," I told him. "Learning a new culture. Hands on."

Eddy looked at each of the young men in turn, as if memorizing their faces. Then he handed me the coffee. Reaching inside his pocket, he produced the picture of Laurie. "Maybe you fellas can help us. . . ."

But none of them had seen her. When we left they straggled back to their cars.

"Can't be leaving you alone like that," Eddy said. "You a baby."

"I was thinking about Laurie—what would happen if they got their hands on her. . . ."

"Don't," Eddy said. "Don't think about it."

Twenty minutes later we were in front of a gas station watching an inebriated woman in a red dress and high heels trying without success to insert the gas nozzle into her Alpha. "I think I'll call my machine," I said with a sigh. Eddy said he wanted to use the restroom, so I walked over to the open-air phone booth and dropped in a quarter. Thirty feet away the woman was splashing gas on the side of her car and swearing to herself.

When Eddy came out a few minutes later, I was waiting with my hands in my pockets, shivering. He looked at my face and said, "Problems?"

"It's over," I told him. My stomach had started knotting, and my throat went dry. I took a breath. "The cops found her a half-hour ago at the Hollywood Bowl. She's dead."


The mist had turned to a heavy rain that pelted down and slapped against the windshield, as Eddy and I took the Buick over to Highland and then up into the Bowl parking lot. I felt numb; I couldn't believe that Laurie had come to such a brutal end after all, that this was all life had held for her. Fourteen years old! Goddamn it, why couldn't you have just been a runaway? There's no reason for someone so young to die! I tried to recall what she looked like. But there was nothing: My mind just wouldn't focus, wouldn't let me think about it, concentrating instead on the trivial and inane, noticing the wind as it whipped grass-like skirts from the tops of palm trees, and the sparse traffic on the roads, and the palpable loneliness of the night, and finally, as we drew into the lot, thinking absurdly that the Bowl had never looked so deserted. It was as desolate as an abandoned factory building. The huge main parking lot with its acres of black asphalt stretched vacantly toward a row of turnstiles, where three police cars waited in the dark, their noses almost touching and their lights splashing red-and-yellow glares on the wet ground. We drove up slowly, parked next to them, and stepped out into the rain.

The message on my phone machine had come from one of the detectives assigned to Mackenzie Gordon's death. He wanted to know if I knew anyone who could identify the girl's body, since the father was dead and the mother couldn't be found. I had called Hollywood Division and said I could only think of Gregory Chauk or maybe someone from the Holstead School, either Anna Ravich or

Emily Stevens. I looked around for evidence that any of the three had arrived, but it didn't appear so, unless they had been picked up in a black-and-white. Even the press hadn't shown up yet, which meant the department was probably keeping news of the killing off the car radio until the body had been removed; that usually meant mutilation.

Two uniformed cops, looking as if they were just out of the Academy, were sitting in one of the cars, smoking cigarettes and rubbing their hands to keep warm. They waited silently for us to cross over to them, the cynical look they all developed with time already in place; then the driver's side door popped open.

I flashed my ID and dropped Captain Reddig's name and said I wanted inside; they called me "Sir" and told me to wait, please. After a short walkie-talkie conversation they waved us through.

"Is Rivera in charge?" I asked.

The cop with the radio shoved it onto the dashboard and shook his head. "He's off duty tonight. It's Shenker."

I nodded, and Eddy and I went through and began climbing up toward the aisleway entrance, as rivulets of water washed down toward us. Bobby Shenker was someone I'd known for years; in fact, he had been my first boss for a few months in Hollywood, and I still saw him in Lee Wong's from time to time. Eddy was huffing along laboriously beside me, the short climb difficult because of his weight. "Why the hell the Bowl?" he panted. "There's seventeen thousand seats here. You think it's some kind of ritual or something? Or the guy gets off doing it in a public place?"

"Look around," I said and stared into the rain and gloom. "This isn't a very public place now, is it? You could stand on the stage and shoot off an AK-47, and nobody would hear you."

Eddy peered into the darkness on either side of us, and the mountains that made this a natural amphitheater that held in the sound like a fist holding a ball. It seemed as if we were a thousand miles from anywhere, an illusion that quickly slipped away when we entered the bowl itself just behind the box seats. The stage lights, a hundred feet below, had been turned on, throwing up an eerie pale glow that crept back to us on the rain and veiled the famous white orchestra shell in a thick, gauzy fog. The action wasn't on the bare stage, however, but to the side and behind, where we could make out the coroner's wagon and a half-dozen people moving in and out of the light like actors in a black-and-white film.

I felt an emptiness in my stomach as I watched and said, "I'm not going to like this."

Eddy sighed and stopped to catch his breath. "You and me both, buddy."

We started down the steps; when we reached stage level I turned and looked back: tier upon tier of empty seats fading into the rain and darkness, the final third or so lost to view.

"Gives you the creeps, don't it?" Eddy said.

"I had the creeps already."

Skirting the stage, we walked around to where three plainclothes cops and a civilian stood next to the body obscured under a black plastic sheet; the rain made sharp pat-a-pat-pat sounds as it drilled onto its glossy surface. As we approached, a middle-aged woman detective in a raincoat spun around and snapped at us. "You supposed to be here?"

"It's all right," Bobby Shenker said. He dislodged himself from the small group near the coroner's van and came over and shook hands. "Shitty business we're in," he said with a shake of his head and then turned to Eddy. "Do I know you?"

I introduced them. Shenker ran a hand over his thinning wet hair, patting it against his scalp, and said, "Yeah, maybe I heard of you." With labored movements he drew a Marlboro from his jacket pocket, stuck it in his mouth, and ducked his head to light it. "Three more years to retirement," he said when he finally got it going. "Then I'm outta here, go out to the desert. I got me twenty acres in Victorville, all paid for. I'm going to put a house trailer on it and watch game shows on TV all day while the air conditioner hums, then listen to coyotes yelp at each other at night. Nothing more important to worry about than double-jeopardy and buying vowels. No more dead kids to look at." He stared over at the blanketed corpse. "I used to like this job. I figured we was doing good, you know—putting away the bad guys, 'making the streets safe.' All that shit they told us when we were baby cops. The war's over, man. We lost. It don't do any good to put 'em in jail—two more just take their place." A long sigh escaped his lips and got lost in the wind. "Christ, let's go ID her."

I said, "You're going to have to get hold of someone who knew her, Bobby. I never met her, you know."

"The station house called a woman named Rivich, Ravich, something like that. The kid's principal, I guess. She ought to be here soon. You know what the kid looks like, though, don't you?"

"I have her picture," I said. "I could give you a preliminary, I guess."

We walked over to the body. The medical examiner was standing in the hazy wet light of a patrol car, talking in a subdued voice to another detective. "Is this where she was killed?" I asked.

Shenker shook his head and nodded off to our right. "Over in the storage area back there. The gate must have been unlocked. He took her in there—or she went on her own, who knows?—and probably raped her on the ground. Then he stabbed her—three or four dozen times from the look of it. I didn't count."

We left the still-covered body and walked over to the fenced yard where supplies were kept. Shenker held up a hand, stopping us from going inside. "The evidence team's not going over it until tomorrow, Vic. They ain't going to find nothing but blood, though. This was a psycho job, someone who wanted her to suffer; blood's everywhere. Blood and mud."

"Any indication it might have been more than one person?"

"What? A gang-bang? A cult? You got something I should know?" His eyes squinted at me in the darkness.

I shook my head. "Just thinking out loud." Rain was running down my neck to my back, and I shivered and shoved my hands in my pockets. "Might as well look at her," I said. "I'm ready to go home."

We went back to the body and Shenker said, "Dr. Ho—" and the ME stared in our direction. "You wanna—you know—we got a guy to look at the body." Shenker didn't want to be there. When Ho walked over, Shenker threw away his cigarette, took out another, and turned his back to light it.

Dr. Ho, a fiftyish and mildly overweight man with a short gray ponytail held by a rubber band, nodded in my direction as if he might know me. "Not pretty," he said in a thin voice and bent to yank back the black sheet.

I took a breath and said, "It's not her."

Shenker spun around and said, "*What?*"

"It's not her. What do you think, Eddy?"

Eddy pulled a flier with Laurie's picture out of his shirt pocket and squinted at it as the rain drummed down on us. "I dunno, Vic. She's too young, maybe. And not as cute."

I agreed. This girl looked to be maybe twelve. Same general appearance though: white, brown hair, blue eyes. Rain was pelting her face, washing mud from her hair. I tried to keep my gaze from the blood-covered torso with its multiple stab wounds. "I don't know, Bobby. I don't think so."

"Jesus," Shenker said.

"Wait until Mrs. Ravich gets here," I said. "She can make a positive ID. But I don't think so."

"Jesus," Shenker muttered again and stomped at the wet ground with a foot. "So we wait. If you two want to hang around you can sit in the unit. No reason for everyone to get soaked."

Eddy and I sat in the front seat of Shenker's unmarked Ford, watching the rain, listening to it drilling incessantly onto the car's metal surface as the police radio offered a running commentary on the night's crimes. It was twenty minutes before Anna Ravich showed up in a cruiser. I got out and walked over to the car as it splashed through a puddle and slid to a stop near the stage. The uniformed driver opened the rear door for her. She looked at my face as she stepped out, and her jaw tightened as if she neither expected nor wanted to see me. The patrolman offered her a small umbrella and she held it over her head, then turned suddenly toward me. "Is it Laurie? Is she dead?" She was wearing a scarf, and a half-dozen strands of stray black hair whipped around the side of her face toward her eyes.

"I don't think it's her," I said, but she stared at me as if I were lying.

Bobby Shenker, thirty feet away by the covered body, said, "Ma'am," and Anna Ravich stared intently into my eyes a moment before turning swiftly and walking over to him. I stayed where I was and watched as the medical examiner came up, and the three of them exchanged a few words. Then the ME pulled back the sheet.

Anna Ravich's body tensed, and I heard her moan and say something to Shenker. A moment later she came past me, supported by the patrolman, toward the car. Stopping abruptly, she turned in my direction without moving from where she was. "I need to talk to you." Her voice was low and ragged, torn by an emotion I couldn't identify: rage, almost. Or fear. Or hatred. "Call me tomorrow. *It is vital I talk to you.*" Then she climbed back in the police car and stared straight ahead.

Shenker waited until the car disappeared into the darkness before coming over to me. "She never saw the girl before." He patted his hair against his scalp again. "You know what that means?" he asked disconsolately. "It means maybe we got a serial killer. This girl, your girl. Or we got two different kid killers. Either way—"

"Or maybe Laurie's just a runaway," I said.

"Never bet on a happy ending, Vic, my boy. Not in Hollywood. Not anymore."

# 10

THE NEXT MORNING, THE STORY OF A YOUNG GIRL'S BODY BEING discovered at the Bowl led the local television newscast. It wasn't Laurie, was it? Tracy asked worriedly at breakfast. No, not Laurie, I said. But the body was still unidentified. Could it be related to Laurie's disappearance? she wondered. Could there be someone out there killing young girls? No, I didn't think so: two different crimes. Besides, Laurie was just a runaway; let's not make it into something it's not. But why didn't I drive her to school today instead of her taking the bus? I had to be out anyway.

Half an hour later, on the way back to the apartment, I began to wonder again about Mackenzie Gordon and Howie Wiltz. It still didn't make sense to me; what did the well-known film producer with a reputation to protect want with the publisher of a notoriously sleazy, many-times-sued porno magazine. Time to find out, I decided; Kerry Daniels claimed not to know anything about it. Not that Kerry's reputation for honesty meant a great deal to me at the moment; Kerry had her own agenda, which I hadn't figured out yet.

I waited until after nine, when the rush-hour traffic thinned, then drove over to Santa Monica Boulevard where Wiltz's offices were located amid the sexual seediness of Tinseltown porno joints, topless bars, and boy hookers. *Hollywood X-T-C* was housed in part of a two-story brick building that had been reinforced at least twice over the years because of earthquake damage, but still looked unlikely to make it through the next one, even if it wasn't The Big One. As I stood outside and stared at the building, I wondered if they had conscientiously stored up bottled water, and what sort of provisions would be deemed crucial to the survival of a porn king. Inflatable dolls and dildos and lots and lots of pictures, probably. The ground floor featured a dreary-looking Truman-era beauty shop that had gone unisex, failed, and was now boarded up; a shoe repair place with a sign that said H ELS REP IRED; and a bookstore of the sort that drove Moses Handleman to mighty paroxysms of rage and despair. "Bookstore? Hardly, Victor. More a hardware store of the perverted: chains and whips and the paraphernalia of pain."

The magazine's offices were in a series of rooms up an outside stairway, presided over by a matronly, heavyset black woman who glared at me with the same practiced disdain as Mackenzie Gordon's secretary, a skill for which Hollywood office workers were evidently closely tested before employment. When I told her I wanted to see Howie Wiltz, she pushed her "I'm sorry, he's not in" button and frowned meaningfully.

The door behind her was cracked open an inch or so. I raised my voice slightly. "It's about Mackenzie Gordon."

"It's all right, Mavis," a disembodied voice announced. "Send him back."

She nodded me toward the rear with an exasperated look and then began to shuffle through a stack of color prints of nude men and women in athletic if somewhat fanciful combinations. I pushed through the door on which had been hand-lettered "The Den of Inequity" and found myself within the midst of quiet chaos. Papers, magazines, computer printouts, coffee cups, empty pizza containers, mailing labels, beer cans, napkins, and wadded-up trash of various sorts flowed and tumbled over almost every available inch of floor and desk space. A stack of what looked like article manuscripts teetered precariously in a corner, a TV tuned to a soap opera with the sound off was in another, and a radio buried somewhere in the confusion was blaring a rock station.

The voice, now embodied in Howie Wiltz's well-known pear-shaped frame, came from a table where the publisher was standing amid more clutter, evidently working on a page layout. He was wearing rimless glasses on his round and pinkish face and had a neat little mustache like a 1930s screen hero, a tubby William Powell perhaps. He held up a small color photo in each hand and squinted thoughtfully at them. "Whatdaya think? Hard to choose, huh? But I can only use one."

They were pictures primarily of body parts disappearing into other body parts. I pointed to the one in his left hand. "The gypsy bareback riders."

He nodded earnestly, evidently pleased with my good taste. "Yeah, me too. The computer repair technicians are a little too cerebral for my readers. Hold on a sec and I'll be with you." He bent over the page spread again. "Find yourself a seat. . . ."

Easier said than done, I thought as I glanced around at the paper storm. He looked up a moment later and grasped the problem. "Sweep all that shit out of that chair. It's screenplays, believe it or not. I can't imagine why people send them to me. I take them home and build fires on long winter evenings."

I watched as Wiltz fussed energetically over his work. He was dressed in slacks and a beige shirt with the sleeves rolled up, and bright red suspenders, *de rigueur* in porndom as well as yuppiedom evidently. After a moment he sighed happily, pleased with his layout, and dropped down in a wooden swivel chair behind his desk, smiling cheerily as he cranked his feet up onto the desktop. "Do you read my magazine?"

I said no.

"Hey, don't feel bad," he said with a wave of his hand. "Two hundred and whatever million Americans don't. I don't give a shit, because one-point-three million do. Maybe they're not rocket scientists, but at least they're reading, right?"

"The New Realism in California education," I said.

"Yeah, whatever. I heard you mention Mackenzie Gordon, America's asshole. You a cop?"

"Private. I'm looking for his daughter."

"Gordon had a daughter? What'd he do, construct her out of cadavers he dug up at midnight? Come on, the single redeeming feature of creatures like Gordon is that they don't reproduce in captivity."

"This one did. Evidently."

But Howie Wiltz was having none of it. "Gordon was a self-indulgent toad sucking up the talent of everyone he worked with.

He wouldn't have the fucking time or inclination to actually *father* anyone; it might make people feel he's human, ruin the God Almighty reputation."

"You weren't a fan," I guessed.

"Not until I heard what happened to him. Spread himself a little thin, didn't he—over an entire parking structure." He reached for a half-smoked cigar in an ash tray and put a match to it. Gordon's death was evidently not causing undue grief or leading him to muse despondently on the ephemerality of life. He puffed the cigar alive as if he were giving it mouth-to-mouth resuscitation, letting loose a cloud of toxic waste that rose slowly and settled over our heads.

"What did Gordon do to earn such joy at his demise?" I asked, when he seemed able to go on.

Short fat arms flailed out wildly from the elliptically shaped-body. Like Humpty Dumpty gone mad, I thought, or a dwarf attacked by wasps.

"What'd he *do?* What he'd do to everyone he dealt with? He screwed me, that's what. Out of money and lots of it, the little prick. Remember *At the Hop?* Ten years ago he was going around town selling twenty limited partnerships in the film for four hundred G's each, profits to be split evenly. So I bought a piece. I figure the guy must know what he's doing, all the movies he made. After the film came out I learned how limited the partnership was. According to the accountants—his *and* mine—there *were* no profits. So I got a tax write-off and he got the gravy. Gordon was an A-1 asshole, Canada's revenge for acid rain from America. When he died I became a Catholic again. Hail Mary, full of grace, something exploded in Mackenzie's face. Do the cops know who did it yet? I'll pay for his lawyer."

I shook my head. "Do you have any ideas?"

"Yeah." He rocked forward in his swivel chair and began to rummage wildly around the clutter on his desk, papers flying this way and that, all the while puffing madly on his cigar, until he found what he was looking for and then threw it to me. "Here's a partial list of suspects." It was the Beverly Hills phone book. I added it to the collection of litter on the floor, where it seemed to sink from sight like a rock in a pond.

"Your name's in Gordon's appointment book," I told him. "Once the cops turn it up they'll want to know why. Were you still doing business with him?"

"Cops? No shit!" His head froze for a moment, the idea seeming to electrify him. He took the cigar out his mouth and stared at me. "They coming to my office? You know when they'll be here? Maybe I should get some reporters out here. I could tell Mavis not to let the cops inside, talk up the First Amendment for the cameras. We could probably drag this out for two or three days. Get some of that 'film at eleven' shit, show me guarding the citadels of culture against the storm troopers."

His face had taken on an intense, calculating mien; he'd lost track of my question and was beginning to mentally wander away in a reverie of hoped-for publicity. "Howie Wiltz Stands Up for the Constitution," front page of the *New York Times*.

I tried again. "Why would Gordon have your name in his appointment book?"

"*My* name?" He came reluctantly back to earth, staring at me through thick glasses and wiping absently at his nifty little mustache with the short, fat fingers of his left hand. "Oh. Hell, no, we weren't doing business. Not yet. Maybe we never would have. We were at what they like to call the negotiation stage."

His eyes narrowed suddenly as he looked at me; he seemed almost to see me now for the first time, an intruder in his garden paradise, a serpent pointing to the apple that could destroy everything. "Why am I talking to you about this? You're telling me the cops are going to show up; maybe I'm a murder suspect since my lack of love toward the bastard is no secret. I'm thinking I should call my lawyer."

"Whatever you tell me won't go any further," I said matter-of-factly. Once he was talking, I didn't want him to stop or even think about it. This was going to be my one chance with Howie Wiltz alone, unprotected by bright young guys from Harvard Law in matching Brooks Brothers suits. Keep it moving, I told myself and smiled my harmless, just-another-guy smile and relaxed back in my chair. "I'm not a cop and I don't much care *who* killed Gordon. I'm trying to find a retarded fourteen-year-old girl who's evidently living on the streets somewhere. She probably doesn't even know her dad's dead."

"Yeah?" he said without interest and shoved the cigar back in his mouth. "I heard something about a missing kid—never made the connection to the asshole, though. Been too fuckin' busy trying to get the magazine out. We're behind schedule again. Retarded huh? Yeah, well . . . OK. This is all between you and me, though. You got no proof of any of it. You go to the cops and I deny everything. Then I'll sue you for libel. I know how to do that, brother. Believe me, it's a well-traveled road."

I agreed and Wiltz went on. But carefully now, thinking about his words, still wondering a little about me. "I bought some *feelthy peek-shurs*. . . ." He pondered a moment, then reached into his trousers pocket with a jerky movement and pulled out a small gold key which he used to unlock the top drawer of his desk. He yanked the drawer back and drew out a video cassette and grinned at me. "Mackenzie Gordon in a starring role." Pushing abruptly out of his chair, he took the tape over to a VCR on top of the TV, popped it in, and jabbed the play button. A moment later Gordon was on the screen, naked in middle-aged splendor on a disheveled water-bed while a heavy-breasted blonde about eighteen was holding his erection like an ice cream cone. After a moment Wiltz flicked it off and brought the tape back to the desk.

"You get the idea. Not real exciting stuff. I mean, that wasn't Charles Atlas there. His name's the only thing about him that's big. But it is a *very* big name in this industry. A few of those pictures in my magazine would be a nice little boost to sales, a sort of Lifestyles of the Rich and Creepy. Some of the later stuff is pretty good— actresses you'd recognize, TV shows and the like. Gordon never met an actress he didn't want to hump."

He shoved the tape back in the drawer and locked it.

"And you were going to publish some of this?"

He tilted back in his chair and thought about it a moment, the cigar clamped between his teeth and waves of smoke circling his head like incense around a Buddha. "I don't know what I was going to do. Maybe publish. Maybe work out something else."

"Stupid question," I said. "But where'd you get the film?"

"Stupid question is right. But I'll tell you this—I paid sixty thousand for it. In cash. And I intended to get a hell of a lot more back than that on it."

"But you weren't sure if you were going to publish?"

He smiled at me, a little boy with a big secret. "Like they say on TV when someone gets fired: I was exploring my options."

"Which were?"

"Number one, sell it to Gordon."

"Had you talked to him about it?"

"Not about the pictures. I just told him we should meet about a business deal. The bastard started salivating as soon as I said 'business.' He probably thought I was ready to drop another four hundred grand for the privilege of associating with Hollywood dipshits. We were going to meet here tomorrow night. I was planning to make a little popcorn in the microwave, pop in the video and see if *he* wanted to invest this time. I figured it was worth about what I dropped with him."

"Did you really think he'd pay you four hundred thousand for that tape?"

"I didn't know what to think. Like I said, I was exploring my options. But in the back of my mind maybe I was thinking he might give me a piece of a film. A real piece, this time. Christ, he could afford it. Everybody else in this town is raking off somewhere; why not me?"

The phone buzzed, and Wiltz picked it up and started talking about paper stock and other workaday printing matters. I pushed out of my chair and tip-toed around the office clutter like an explorer trying not to step in quicksand or concealed tiger-pits. There was a sort of happy sophomoric confusion about it all, like a dorm room in a college for manic-depressives. Desks and tables had been shoved up against the wall and overflowed with ash trays and dirty coffee cups and chewed-up pencils. Magazines and pictures lay strewn everywhere: on desks and tables, on the floor, on bookcases and chairs. Despite what Howie Wiltz said, his readers weren't readers at all: they were gawkers; words probably confused them; they needed the visual stimulation of pictures the way addicts needed drugs. A small desk in the rear held a neatly framed photo of Jimmy Swaggart preaching hellfire and damnation; on another there was a telephone shaped like a penis. Which end do you talk into? I wondered. And where the hell *was* everybody? It was like Pompeii, like a city destroyed by a volcano, the populace suddenly rushing out in the middle of the day and leaving everything exactly as it was when the lava and ash descended. And now thousands of years later archaeologists were poking around, trying to make sense of it all. When Wiltz finally got off the phone I picked my way back to the chair. "Do you put out *Hollywood X-T-C* by yourself?"

He laughed cheerfully and waved the cigar at me. "God no! There's a dozen of us in editorial and more down at production in San Pedro. The editorial staff's at the funeral for Stacy Lovett, the porno star who OD'd on coke. Lovely girl. Did you know the cops discovered she was only seventeen?" He made little tsk-tsk motions in the air with his finger. "Some local filmmakers are going to be in deep doo-doo about using a minor. We're going to do a story about it. How do you like 'Going Up the River for Going Down on Stacy' as a title? Not too cerebral, is it? Too many words?"

His mind began to work it out; maybe the allusion was a bit too recondite after all. I tried to refocus him on the more immediate problem of Mackenzie Gordon and the incriminating tape that suddenly didn't seem so valuable.

"Now that Gordon's dead are you going to go ahead and run the pictures?"

He stood his pear-shaped form up from behind the desk and shook his head thoughtfully. "I don't know. It's a problem, isn't it? I'm not too keen on the cops finding out about the film as long as that prick's killer's running loose. I can see them weaving a nice little fantasy about Gordon and me arguing about it, and me killing him; that would clear everything up for them, wouldn't it? Make them look good while I take a dive. No, I don't know if I'll run the pictures or not. I'll have to give it some thought."

"It looks like you could be out sixty thousand, then."

"No, I don't think so. There is another option, remember? I only told you option number one. I'll have to give it some serious thought, though."

After leaving Wiltz, I stopped at the bar next door, a smallish dark room smelling of beer, with a dozen tiny tables and an aging pool table half-visible under a phony Tiffany lamp in the rear. Everything seemed covered with a layer of grime, as if nothing had been washed since Phillip Marlowe had stopped in for a shot of bourbon a half-century ago. I stood at the end of the bar under a TV blaring a soap opera, ordered a Bud, and asked for a dollar's worth of change.

The bartender gave me a bottle without a glass, and four quarters. Holding the bottle in one hand and the change in the other, I walked back to the pay phone in a tiny alcove that led to the single restroom, and dialed Brandon Stiles's number. The phone rang for two minutes without an answer, so I hung up and called Kerry Daniels. Same result. Maybe they went out together to celebrate their sudden unemployment.

Now what?

Two bright-eyed young men with luxuriant, surfer-style blond hair flowing over their ears strolled out of the restroom and smiled at me. "Going to be here long?" one of them asked.

"Just making a call," I said as I dropped a quarter in the slot.

They shrugged and went out to the bar.

I dialed Rudy Cruz.

"No news, amigo. Don't-Call-Me-Geraldo's got Gordon's girlfriend in the interrogation room. Reddig's in there too, but they don't expect anything. What's with you?"

"Dead end, I guess. You folks don't have Brandon Stiles down there too, do you?"

"Not as far as I know. Unless he's in the dungeon with the whips and fingernail pullers. What we do have is an army of reporters hanging on; they're oozing in from all over the country now. I guess they smelled blood: Celebrity Explodes in Hollywood, and all that."

"Anything on Gordon's daughter?"

"Missing Persons put it at the top of the list. They're moving on it now, Vic: Hollywood, Bel Air, even the beaches. The Beverly Hills police even brought in some Boy Scouts to help. Someone'll find her if she's out there to be found. Suddenly she's big news."

"And the mom?"

"Haven't heard, but Rivera's not talking to me anyway; let me check around."

Someone in the bar put a country-western song on the jukebox; somehow it wasn't what I expected in here. Why did everyone in LA want to be a cowboy? "This might be a stupid question," I said to Rudy, "but is there actually proof Laurie Gordon exists? She's not a figment of Mackenzie's cinematic imagination?"

Rudy's humorless chuckle came rumbling down the line. "She exists, Vic. Or she did a week ago."

I was about to ring off when I remembered something. "What did the bomb squad come up with at LAX?"

"A homemade explosive device, very simply constructed, with easy-to-procure materials. But rigged to explode remotely. They're not sure how yet but probably something simple like those remote activators for car alarms. Or an FM transmitter like the special effects guys at the studios use. This interesting to you?"

On the way out of the bar one of the surfers offered to buy me a drink. On the sidewalk out front a girl in stiletto heels offered to show me a good time. On the corner an elderly man with a three-day beard offered to sell me a map to the stars' homes, and a Vietnamese kid offered me a Rolex for sixty dollars. What a fun town, I thought. Film at eleven.

# 11

I DROVE BACK TO THE OFFICE, LEFT THE BUICK IN THE LOT AND hurried around to the lobby door, blowing on my hands and huddling inside my jacket as the wind snatched up scraps of paper and fast-food wrappers and whistled them along in front of me. Moses Handleman was just opening up his bookshop; he stuck his great hairy head out the door and yelled "Comic books!" and waved a contemptuous hand heavenward. Instinctively I glanced up at the purple-and-gray sky, expecting to see the clouds suddenly part in a thunderous burst of Godly indignation, and lightning bolts explode out to smite the philistines of Hollywood. Instead, I saw a small red airplane trailing a sign advertising an "adult" phone service.

The tiny elevator in the lobby was crammed with the usual half-dozen young women in high heels and designer dresses heading for the modeling agency down the hall from my office. I held my breath as Giorgio swirled around me like the mists of Avalon until we were all disgorged on the third floor, the women heading in one direction and me in another; not unlike the story of my life, I thought. My office was chilly, since I'd turned off the thermostat the last time I'd been here. When was that? Two days ago? I retrieved a small pile of mail from the floor and quickly flipped through it, marveling at my good fortune at winning once again—GUARANTEED, this time—a prize from column A for viewing a time-share condo in Calexico. Let's see, column A: a new Ferrari, a two-carat diamond ring, a month in Europe, or a set of luggage. Perhaps some other time, I decided after a moment's reflection and let it fall with the rest of the mail into the waste basket. Finally I grabbed a coat from the closet, turned on the heat, and left again, locking the door behind me.

Rather than wait for the elevator, I trotted down the narrow rear stairway, exiting the building near the corner coffee shop. Waving a frozen hand at the white-garbed counter help on the other side of the foggy windows, I hurried down Bronson. At the Paramount gate the uniformed guard nodded abstractly, huddled inside his tiny enclosure, as I went through and wandered down to the squat two-story building where Mackenzie Gordon had had his office. Brandon Stiles was outside in his shirt sleeves, shoving boxes and papers from a supermarket shopping cart into the back of a trendy four-wheel-drive Range Rover equipped with the oversized tires of an army assault vehicle.

"Do you have to ford a lot of streams in your line of work? Maybe help the Marines make amphibious landings?" I ran my finger over the highly polished finish of the tank-like wagon; there wasn't a scratch or a flake of dust anywhere on its glossy, lovingly cared-for surface.

Stiles's reflection flashed across a fender as he glanced at me angrily, but he didn't respond, continuing to toss boxes from the shopping cart into the car. When he was finished, he slammed the door shut and started to push the cart back toward the building. I braked it with my foot and tried an easier question. "Moving out?" That at least seemed to explain the Rover; it would have taken a half-dozen trips in his Corvette to transport all the junk he'd thrown in the passenger compartment.

Stiles's pale blue eyes glittered hatred, and his fingers tightened on the shopping-cart handle until the knuckles turned white. "Well, I'm out of a job again, aren't I? When the great one exploded so did my career. Or what was left of it. You think it's funny, don't you? You really get off on other people's failures."

I felt a sudden urge to hit him; not many people affect me this way, but Stiles and his determined adolescent whininess grated like finger-nails on a blackboard. Instead, I removed the temptation by thrusting my hands in my jacket pockets as I tried to keep my voice calm. "Does this mean production is definitely off? The film's shut down?"

"No, that's not what it means! The goddamn bankers own it now;
it was part of the partnership agreement Gordon had with them.
They decided they didn't want their investment going down the
drain, so they hired the lovely Kerry Daniels to produce. How nice
for her: she's finally fucked her way to the top. Meanwhile I'm out
on my butt."

I took my foot off the wheel and stalked along with him as he angrily shoved the cart back into the building. "Kerry fired you when she
took over?" I asked. If so it surprised me; I had seen her as mother-
hen protective of Stiles, even if he hadn't seemed to appreciate the
fact.

He was stalking rapidly down a deeply carpeted hallway, pushing
the cart as if it were a battering ram and ignoring the curious stares
of secretaries and executives shrinking back against the walls as he
brushed past. When we got to his office, he turned abruptly in and
gave the cart a furious shove. It crashed into his desk and toppled
over. The office was half-empty, boxes and books piled haphazardly
on the floor, framed pictures and awards strewn on the desktop,
ready to be swept into the cart. Stiles's Oscar was balanced precariously across the seat of a chrome-and-leather director's chair, and he
knocked it to the floor with his fist, sitting down angrily and staring
at me.

"Did the bitch fire me? I guess it depends on who you believe.
She says no, the bankers did it, they didn't want the 'erratic' and
artistic Brandon Stiles around to fuck up their precious picture!" He
gave the Oscar a kick with a Reebok and it rolled dolefully away.
"That was *her* story. So I called the bank. I had to satisfy myself with
talking to some half-assed assistant vice president in their entertain-
ment-loan department." He assumed a mincing tone: "'Miss
Daniels is the producer, she's in charge of the cinematic project'—
he really said *cinematic project*—'and she makes all the decisions;
we're just investors.' So if I'm fired, she did it. I guess I don't give a
shit anymore."

He came suddenly out of his wobbly chair and stared at me in
disbelief. "Do you know what she's planning for this film now that
that idiot Gordon is dead? The same thing he did, exactly, down to
the tiniest depressing detail. She's a goddamn *clone!* She's going to
make the *same . . . damn . . . film.* And someone in production told

me she's going to get Jason Esserton to direct. Jason fucking Esserton!"

"Never heard of him," I said. I had taken the chair behind the modern glass-topped desk; all the drawers had been yanked open and emptied. Feeling an instinctive urge to tidy up, I shut them one by one as Brandon rambled on, then relaxed back with my feet on the desktop.

Stiles flopped down again in his director's chair. "He's a *music video* director. Can you *believe* that? She replaced me with an MTV bozo who's never done a scene longer than eight seconds!" He ran his hand through his long, stringy hair and stared at a spot on the floor through thick computer-nerd glasses.

I was going to have to pull him out of this mood if I hoped to learn anything. But it wasn't going to be easy. Brandon Stiles was the archetypical Hollywood egoist, taking to self-pity like a starlet to a hot tub; he and his problems were the only subjects worth considering, the still point about which the universe turned. I imagined him, like Hugh Hefner, hoarding dozens of scrapbooks and diaries, beginning at the age of seven or so: here I am with my dog Sparky; and here's a picture of my first lemonade stand. Here's the kid who beat me up for my lunch money. And here's where I set his house on fire. Treasure it all: someday the world will want to know.

I tried to blunt him back to reality. "I understand the police pulled you in to talk about Gordon's death."

His head jerked up and he shot me an icy look from behind the distorting glasses. "Wrong! I went in on my own. I volunteered. They seemed more interested in you, boyo. It *was* you I saw coming in, wasn't it? How did you explain that away?"

"I haven't yet. Did they buy your story about going there to meet Catherine Wilbourne?"

"Why shouldn't they? It's true. It'd be easy enough to check. But when I saw she wasn't there I turned around and left."

"What made you think she would be there?"

He scrunched down in the chair as if he were trying to disappear, and his voice went soft. "She called me from New York two nights ago and said she was coming home because of Laurie. She sounded frantic. But she didn't tell Mackenzie; she was fed up with him and blamed him for Laurie's disappearance. She was going to get in to

LAX about three in the morning and wanted me to come by the house at four-thirty. Later on we were going to go to the police station to see if there was anything we could do to help. Mackenzie was supposed to be in Malibu. . . ." He left the sentence dangling, as if he didn't want to go on.

I said, "Her plane got in at three?"

He nodded silently, staring again at the floor.

"So about the time she was picking up her Louis Vuittons from the luggage carousel, her husband was being killed across the street in one of the parking lots."

Stiles's eyes blinked open and looked at me. "Yeah, I guess so. . . . Hadn't thought about it like that before. Sort of gruesome . . . " Then he gave a little start and sat up straight as he realized that he had just placed his lover near the scene of the crime. "Except that she left the airport the minute she got in."

"How do you know that?"

"She called me this morning. She said the minute she got in she took a cab to Beverly Hills."

"She called you? She's here in town?"

"Of course she's here. I said—"

"Then why didn't anyone know? Why'd she disappear?"

He looked at me irritably. "She didn't disappear. She didn't tell anyone in London because she didn't want Mackenzie to know. She was furious with him, blamed him for Laurie's running away. When she got in she came by the house, like I did, and saw Kerry's car, so she went out to Malibu instead. I guess she called her attorney and he said to sit tight for a while so he could look into things. I really don't know. I only talked to her for a minute. She was on her way to the police department—the Beverly Hills police. I guess she was down at the LAPD last night. Her attorneys wanted to go there instead of to Hollywood Station. You'll have to ask her why."

You're damn right I'll ask her, I thought. Catherine's daughter disappears, her husband's murdered, then no one can find her for a day. Why the hell would her attorneys try to keep her bottled up? I said to Brandon, "Why did she want to meet you as soon as she got home?"

He glanced over at me without emotion, looking for once almost like an adult. "Look, it's no secret, I've been through all this with the police. Catherine and I were close—we were seeing each other."

"Having an affair—"

"Don't be so goddamn moral! We were fucking each other. Is that what you want to hear? People do those things, you know." His voice faltered and he seemed to sink within himself. "We're not 'having an affair.' We love each other, we're going to be married."

"Oh?" After all these years, Hollywood pairings, divorces, and re-pairings shouldn't surprise me. But this one did. And not only because Catherine Wilbourne was probably old enough to be the boy-genius's mother. It was bad form to show my surprise like this, I thought, but the word had blurted out and now hung between us like a dagger that couldn't be ignored.

Stiles looked at me defensively, starting to revert again to adolescence, and looking for an argument where there wasn't one. "Something wrong with that?"

"Not at all," I said. "Did Mackenzie know?"

"Hmppf!" The noise burst from him like air from a balloon. "Do you think I would have been on that goddamn film if he had known? Besides, he was too busy sticking it to Kerry to know what anyone else was up to. Mackenzie always had old Number One so much in front of his eyes that he couldn't *see* other people, including his own family. Catherine had had it with him years ago. The only reason she stayed around this long was Laurie. She didn't want to upset her; Laurie kind of flies off the handle sometimes. But Catherine was hoping she was old enough to accept it now."

"When were you planning to get married?"

"She was going to file for divorce as soon as her film was through shooting in London. She was going to tell Mackenzie to move out to the Malibu house; he spent most of his time there anyway. But after I started this film we thought we ought to wait until it was through or at least in post-production. This was supposed to be my *entrée* back into the business. I didn't want to screw it up."

Something about Brandon's assurances didn't sound right to me. "How long have you and Catherine been seeing each other?" I asked.

He thought a minute and shrugged his narrow shoulders. "Six months, maybe seven."

"Then what makes you think Mackenzie didn't know? These things are hard to hide."

He looked at me irritably. "Who would tell him? Besides, you just know these things. You're dickin' some guy's wife and he knows about it, he'll let you *know* he knows."

I decided not to ask the barely post-pubescent director how many other wives he had been "dickin'" to gain this invaluable insight into human behavior and instead said, "Did Kerry Daniels know?"

"Hell, I suppose so. But believe it or not, we didn't sit around discussing balling various members of the Gordon clan." He came suddenly out of his chair as if he remembered what he was supposed to be doing and began to shove unbound books and manuscripts into the shopping cart. More screenplays, I thought ruefully and envisioned the rain forests being depleted for another mutant-killer-on-the-loose or college-kids-on-vacation film; somehow the trade-off didn't balance.

As Stiles dropped a portable radio into the cart, I asked, "Why wouldn't Kerry tell her boyfriend if she knew what was going on with his wife?"

"Because she's a friend of . . . " he started and then stopped when he realized the inanity of what he was saying. "Oh hell, I don't know. But Gordon didn't know about us. I'm sure of that. Catherine is sure of it. What difference does it make, anyway? The man's dead."

"It makes a difference *because* he's dead," I said. "The police are looking for a motive."

"A motive?" He stopped what he was doing and stared at me. "A motive? Do they think *I* killed the asshole?"

I said I didn't imagine the police had gotten to the point of thinking anything yet; they were just digging around. But he didn't seem to be listening.

"Why the hell would I kill the guy that was finally giving me some work?"

"Maybe he changed his mind."

Stiles looked at me furiously. "I was *on* the film until he died and the bitch took over—"

The sleekly modern telephone on his desk gave an irritating electronic ring, and Stiles reached automatically for it, then changed his mind and yanked it from its plug and threw it like a baseball against the wall, where it shattered into a dozen pieces. I was still seated behind his desk, tilted back in the chair and staring up at him; his face was twisted in rage and his fists clenched and unclenched at his sides. Then he started throwing papers in the shopping cart again, muttering obscenities to himself. I said, "The night before Gordon was killed, you left a message on my phone machine. What was all that about?"

He looked at me angrily, tiny beads of perspiration forming along his upper lip. "Something funny was going on with Mackenzie. He wasn't acting like a distressed father, if you know what I mean; he was pissed, batso, storming around the fucking office, screaming at people. . . ." He trailed off. "What the hell difference does it make now?"

I was thinking about Gordon's temper, his vindictiveness, and his odd relationship with his wife's lover. I asked, "Do you think Gordon might have hired you *because* he knew about your affair with his wife?"

Stiles stopped abruptly and stared at me. "Why the hell would he do that?"

"To play with you a little, maybe carry you a while on the film and then drop you. He could make some noises to the press about how your final chance just didn't pan out, how *difficult* you were to work with, how no one got along with you no matter how hard they tried. What would that have done to your career?"

Before he could answer, a soft, timid voice came wafting to us on gentle puffs of perfumed air. "Terribly sorry, Brandon—" We both turned to see Kostas Sikelianos, an executive VP of indeterminate but highly remunerative duties, standing at the door with his long, diamond-studded fingers clasped humbly in front of him like a penitent seeking absolution. He was fiftyish, plump and silver-haired, dressed in a mist-gray Savile Row suit, Gucci shoes, and impeccable tie. He was said to be someone's brother. He smiled brilliantly, dewy brown eyes shifting easily from Brandon to me. "Do you boys think you could quiet down just a tad? The secretaries are getting a bit nervous and—"

"Fuck the secretaries!" Stiles shouted in a rage.

"Yes, no doubt. But you can be heard all over the building, don't you see, and—"

But Stiles lunged for a heavy three-hole paper punch on the desk and threw it violently at the quickly retreating head. It slammed off the wall, leaving a dent, and clattered to the floor along with a dozen tiny chunks of plaster. For a moment Stiles stood with his arms hanging loosely at his sides, a strange smile beginning to emerge on his thin lips. Then suddenly he began laughing, and in a minute he was roaring so hard he had to sit down. "Christ!" he shouted with an almost euphoric rage and gestured angrily toward the door with his victoriously clenched fist. "I've wanted to do that for a long goddamn time. Christ!"

It was as if a dam had suddenly given way, and he howled with uncontrolled laughter, tears streaming from his eyes and rolling along his cheeks as though he were sobbing. But as the reality of his situation slowly set back in, his voice weakened and he began to choke to a stop. For a long moment he sat sullenly, odd-sounding moans coming faintly from his throat as he wiped at his face with the sides of his fingers. When at last he seemed ready to go on I tried again.

"Do you think Gordon could have been playing with you like that? Just stringing you along?"

Stiles shifted uncomfortably in his chair; his gaze moved away as he thought about it. For a long moment he didn't respond and when he finally did his voice was so faint I had to lean forward to catch the words. "Maybe he *did* know. Christ, it'd be like him to pull something like that, wouldn't it? What a blow to the great Gordon ego to discover his wife was no longer interested in him!" He paused a moment and his eyes seemed to water. "If he found out, he'd strike back. He'd have to. He'd have to show us he couldn't be fucked with. Power! That was always the name of the game to Mackenzie. Power . . . crush people, make them crawl. Maybe that was what he was planning all along." He leaned forward, his elbows on his knees, and rested his forehead on his hands. "God, how I hate him."

I waited without saying anything.

Still staring at the desktop he said softly, "Catherine was nothing to Gordon. Nobody was. Even Laurie meant nothing—just another problem that had to be dealt with." He sat back and looked at me, his voice rising with anger. "Anyway, he was too busy to care about other people, the way he was always looking after his own hormones."

Kerry Daniels, I thought but then, remembering the name from Gordon's appointment book, said "Sharon Haynes?"

Stiles smiled at me through his rimless glasses and ran a limp hand through his hair. "You found out about that, huh? Well it didn't take much detecting, did it? There's more, believe me. Mackenzie wouldn't have noticed his wife if she were in the same damn room with him, but he always had time for this week's bimbo." His small fists clenched and he said bitterly, "The bastard . . . "

I wondered if Gordon *had* found out about his wife and Stiles. He wasn't an idiot, and he would have had the typical philandering husband's jealous distrust of his own wife. If he had found out, it gave both Stiles and Catherine Wilbourne reason enough to want him dead: an angry spouse could definitely muck up the divorce proceedings, especially the all-important division of assets. Much neater and cleaner and more rewarding all around if the husband were simply removed entirely from the scene.

More curious to me at the moment, though, was the surprising and unlikely coupling of wiry young Brandon and the ageless but erotic Catherine; it was something I wanted to pursue but without, if possible, upsetting him, always a danger with Brandon. Keeping my tone neutral, I asked, "When did Catherine make up her mind to leave her husband?"

"Just before going to London. For Laurie's sake she had to put up with more from that asshole than anyone will ever know. But it just got to be too much."

"What finally caused her to make the break?"

He sat up suddenly in his chair and looked at me with surprising earnestness, as if glad that I had asked, and at once I realized why. I was giving Brandon the opportunity he craved to defend Catherine to a stranger, to publicly proclaim his love, and he seized it eagerly. Oddly, I found myself warming to him, even sympathizing with his perhaps too-exuberant enthusiasm. Maybe throwing telephones and yelling at studio executives gave Brandon something he had lacked before: a personality of his own, something beyond the cardboard boy-wonder image created by the press. His voice was eager and clear as he recounted their plans. "Catherine made up her mind

when we started getting . . . close." He made a funny little gesture
with his hand. "We'd been seeing each other for a while, we enjoyed
each other, enjoyed talking to each other. It was only natural we'd
start thinking about marriage. And she thought—she hoped—Laurie would be able to handle it now."

"Do you think Laurie could have run away because she found out
her parents were getting a divorce?"

"It's the first thing I did think! But when I talked to Catherine in
London she said Laurie couldn't possibly know."

He spread his hands in a decisive gesture; it just wasn't possible.
Brandon, it was clear, lived in a world of absolutes: Gordon was a
fool, Catherine a goddess, Kerry a bitch. How much simpler life
must be for him without shades of gray to obscure and muddy his
perceptions. I said, "Then Catherine's known all along that her
daughter is missing?"

"Of course, or at least since Monday when I found out—"

Before he could finish we were interrupted by a discreet scraping
sound at the door and we turned to see two studio security guards in
full paramilitary livery standing with their hands on their holstered
batons. No longer the aging retirees of simpler years, these were
both ex-cops, one from Culver City homicide, the other from Bur-
bank. The older and bigger of the two was Leo Perlea; I'd worked
with him several months earlier on a bribery case involving a studio
purchasing agent, and we'd shared a few drinks since then. He
looked at me apologetically. "Oh, it's you, Vic. We got a report from
upstairs about a disturbance." He glanced down the hall and his
voice dropped to a whisper. "You know, from Mr. S. He wanted us to
kinda help Mr. Stiles outta here. Quietly."

"It's all right, Leo. I'll take care of it."

Both of them looked as if they didn't want to step into the room
but didn't want to stay in the hallway either. It reminded me of my
own edginess when I had worked patrol and was called to quell a
domestic disturbance: husband and wife can be at each other's
throats until you show up and become the instant enemy of both.
Mostly you just want to get the hell out of there before it explodes.

"You sure there's no trouble?" Leo asked dubiously. His eyes went
from me to Brandon who was looking uneasy; authority figures
seemed to bring out the worst in him.

"Performance art, Leo," I said with a smile. "We'll be out of here in ten minutes."

They both looked at us uncertainly, shifting their weight from foot to foot and glancing down the hall. "Yeah, OK, but keep it down, all right? Do your performance stuff outside the lot."

After they left Brandon seemed to go limp. "Thanks." He ran his hand through his hair again, a nervous gesture he seemed to be unaware of. "Can you imagine what the trades would've said if I was kicked off the lot? Christ, they would've made me look like an idiot."

I walked over to the door and closed it, then came back to the desk and sat down again. I didn't particularly relish doing it, but I needed to start easing into what I really wanted to find out: what Gordon's demise meant financially to his widow. Who benefits, again. I expected Brandon to react angrily, but emotion is often the quickest way to the truth. I said, "Mackenzie's death will make things pretty tough for Catherine now, won't it? I guess he'd been their main source of income, what with his production company."

Brandon shot me a contemptuous rather than angry look. "Are you kidding? Catherine could buy Gordon a hundred times over. Don't forget, she's been in pictures for thirty-five years and that wasn't in the Jackie Coogan era either. Her money was invested in real estate, stocks, you name it. She owns half of Gordon's production company in her own name. She could kiss it off tomorrow and not give it another thought. In fact, she was going to let the asshole have it in return for not tying up the divorce in legal bullshit. She didn't want it anyway; she wanted to *act* in movies, not make them."

Meaning there was no financial reason for Catherine Wilbourne to want her husband dead. Or, as far as I could tell, no reason Brandon Stiles would want him dead. So far only Kerry Daniels appeared to benefit financially. On the other hand, I reminded myself, only a minuscule percentage of murders occur for a financial reason. Passion, of one sort or another, is a far more potent motive and there was passion galore hereabouts.

Stiles had struggled to his feet again and was shoving the material from the desktop into the shopping cart. But he was going about it slowly now, with a lack of interest, as if all the fight had drained out of him. He didn't look like someone who had seen the only obstacle to his marriage unexpectedly removed. But then love manifests itself in many and varied ways, I thought. Even in real life. Even in Hollywood.

Suddenly he turned around. "Laurie should have turned up by now, shouldn't she?" he said unexpectedly. He looked at me with an odd, almost pained expression. "She should have been found. A kid shouldn't be lost this long."

"It doesn't look good," I said.

Brandon's gaze turned inward and his voice sounded sad and dreamy. "She's a good kid. And she likes me. I'd be a good dad for her—better than Gordon ever was. She's got a streak of real creativity in her, you know. She draws, paints, builds things. Catherine says retarded kids are sometimes like that. It's too bad this had to happen. I hope she doesn't end up like that girl at the Bowl last night. All the crazies around here. . . ." He paused, then added, "That's why Catherine came home. For Laurie." He let out a sigh, his gaze shifting to the carpet.

I remembered the picture of the young man in my pocket and held it out for Brandon to look at. "Do you know him?"

He took it out of my hand and shrugged.

"Turn it over," I said.

"Richard!" He smiled slightly. "Laurie's 'boyfriend.' I never met him. But she told me about him when I was out at the house once. I think it was kind of a secret." He gazed quizzically at the picture a moment before handing it back.

A boyfriend! So I had been right. Then maybe we've been looking for her in the wrong places. Maybe she fled to her boyfriend's house. Maybe she wasn't running from but *to*, to someone who loved her. I felt suddenly happy for Laurie. *Love*. And now also I had a place to look, my first real lead. My pulse quickening, I said, "Do you know his last name? Or where he lives?"

"Sure. Richard Ravich. His mother's the owner of that school she goes to. He's a student in Laurie's class."

I stared at him dumbly, a lump of anger swelling in the pit of my stomach. Ravich! That was probably what Emily Stevens had started to tell me before changing her mind: Laurie and Anna Ravich's son. But why? Why was it so important that I not know about Laurie's boyfriend. Especially since it may have helped me find her. The more I wondered about it the more my anger grew. "Did Kerry know about Richard, too?"

"Kerry?" He shrugged, uninterested. "I don't think so. I think it was Laurie's secret. Laurie's and mine."

I slipped the picture back in my pocket. Brandon was again silently dropping papers into the shopping cart. It was time to leave him alone. "What do you do now?" I asked as I came to my feet.

He tilted his head and gave me a tight little smile as he worked. "Announce my 'availability for employment.' Call the trades, harass my agent, collect unemployment. I've been through this before, you know."

"Have you set a wedding date?"

He dropped the last of his framed pictures in the cart; he reached down and picked up his Oscar. "I haven't talked to Catherine about it since before Mackenzie . . . "

He fell silent and sank back down in the director's chair. There was nothing left in the office but the paper punch and the telephone, lying in pieces on the floor. His gaze wandered around the barren room for at least a minute. Then he got to his feet and walked out, leaving me and the shopping cart behind.

# 12

I STOPPED AT ONE OF THE TWO PAY PHONES OUTSIDE OF BRANDON'S building and called Eddy Baskerville. "Didn't sleep none too well," he said morosely. "Kept dreaming of stabbed and raped kids."

I told him I knew what he meant.

"Guess I'll go out again after lunch," he continued. "Don't know if one or two guys are going to make any difference now, though. Seems like half the cops in southern California are looking for her. See her picture every time I look at the TV. Even had it on the 'Today' show. But I figured, what the hell, maybe it wouldn't hurt to check out the area around Plummer Park. Then maybe I'll poke around Hollywood High. No point in you coming along; I don't figure to turn up nothin' during the day. Mostly just keeping busy. Better if you go at it from your end."

I said that probably made sense. Especially since I finally had a lead of sorts. I told him about Laurie's boyfriend. "Last night his mother said she wanted to talk to me. Maybe that's what's on her mind. It's sure as hell on mine. There's also something going on with Catherine Wilbourne. Brandon Stiles says she's back in town. I'm going to see what I can find out about that."

"The missing momma, huh? No shit! Well, let me know. If you don't come up with anything maybe we'll try West Hollywood again tonight."

After Eddy hung up, I took out another quarter and called Parker

Center, trying to run down Catherine Wilbourne. Where would she be—Homicide or Missing Persons? I didn't know anyone in Missing Persons, so I tried Homicide and got put through to a detective sergeant Leavitt, who knew me vaguely. "Yeah, she's here, or so I heard. Haven't actually seen her. Everyone's talking about it, though. She's up in an assistant chief's office, getting the star treatment. You wanna know when she leaves?"

I said yes and asked him to leave a message on my phone machine as soon as he heard anything. Then I called the Holstead School. A man answered, said the receptionist was gone for an hour or so, and Mrs. Ravich was out. No, he didn't know when she'd be back. Would I care to leave a message? I said no, I'd call back later. I used my last twenty cents to dial my office to see if Anna Ravich had left a message. Nothing. So what was all this about *having* to see me? *It's vital I talk to you.* Maybe last night's emotion had fizzled out with the light of day. No matter: I was going to talk to her whether she liked it or not.

So now what? Until I could get hold of Anna Ravich I was lost. Like Eddy said, not much point in hitting the streets with everybody in LA aware that Laurie was missing and knowing what she looked like. Catherine Wilbourne's daughter! If she's out there, someone's going to see her.

So . . .

Hell, take a walk. Relax, think it out, maybe something will come to you. Maybe.

Feeling useless, I turned from the phones to see Kerry Daniels striding toward me from a soundstage fifty yards away. "My partner in crime," she said with a conspiratorial smile as she approached.

She was dressed in dark, wintry-looking slacks and a blouse, and had on a floor-length leather overcoat of the type seen outside of Spain only in Hollywood or the back pages of *The New Yorker.* Evidently Rivera hadn't kept her for questioning very long. I said, "How'd things go with the police?"

She looked at me with an infectious, good-natured smile, and I found my mood improving a little, drawing strength from her own uplifted spirits. Her voice was buoyant as she stared at me from her pretty, brown eyes. "Actually, they were quite nice until they found out I knew you. Then it was electric cattle prods and bamboo shoots under the fingernails. You are not universally loved, I was shocked to discover. Let's go to the commissary; I'll buy you lunch and tell you all the gory details."

I shook my head as a '52 Studebaker and a '40 Ford crept past us on the way to where a television miniseries on Eisenhower was shooting. "I was just about to take a walk. It's my therapy—it helps me think things out. You can come along if you want."

She looked at me in disbelief, as if I had just asked her to have sex in the back of the Studebaker. "Walk? In LA?"

I stuck my hands in my jacket pockets. "Sounds bizarre," I agreed. "Sort of primitive, like life before the networks." I smiled encouragingly. "Why not be bold and give it a try, though? I'll take you to my office building afterwards and buy you a lunch of alfalfa sprouts and just-picked Tibetan spinach."

Her eyes narrowed as if she was learning something unsavory about me. "If you want exercise, why don't you join a club or run like everyone else?"

"I used to run to keep in shape. Still do once or twice a week. But this is more for emotional than physical health. I try to go out every day; it's relaxing."

She looked at me dubiously, not quite willing to venture something so uncivilized. "God, what if someone saw me? They'd think I was out of work!"

"We'll go south," I said. "No one in the industry has been south of Melrose in a generation." I had already started toward the gate, so she had to hurry to catch up, almost colliding with a 1950 Ford convertible driven by a woman in a one-piece swimsuit and bathing cap.

"Well hold my hand, then," she said peevishly. "I don't feel safe out there with all the muggers and gang-fighters. If someone starts shooting, place your body firmly in front of mine."

Which was, I thought, a pretty good plan even if no one was shooting. Taking her hand, I steered us out onto Windsor, past rows of cute little Mediterranean-style homes from the thirties with neatly trimmed yards and straight-as-a-ruler gardens, huddled next to new apartment buildings that looked as if they had been inspired by a train wreck. Los Angeles is a city without zoning or common sense when it comes to building placement, and all the livable and affordable areas of the city are gradually being transformed into these

Brave New World fortresses, where flowers are as alien as smiles between neighbors. We walked in silence for several minutes, Kerry huffing and puffing with the unexpected exertion of non-automotive transport. Her mind seemed still off-balance with the novelty of our exploits. "How did you know I was on the lot?" I asked as I jacked up the pace a little.

"*Everyone* knows," she panted. "You and Brandon were our mid-morning entertainment. Half the staff was crouched behind locked doors, listening. I was afraid Brandon might commit ritual suicide in the hallway in front of my office."

"Is it true you fired him?"

"Damn right! I don't need a personality problem on my first film. Brandon's out. Maybe I'll use him in the future when I have my own projects, but not now. This film is too important to me."

"Yesterday out of a job and today a big-time Tinseltown producer. Another Hollywood success story. Next it'll be Monday nights at Mortons."

"You sound like Brandon. He's ready to kill me, but I'm not going to screw up this opportunity. I was as surprised as he was that the bankers wanted to go ahead, but they said they'd sunk several million dollars into the film already, so they may as well try to get what they can out of it. Brandon will do OK once he learns to control his temper. He really can be quite violent."

We had walked all the way down to Beverly Boulevard and turned west, houses and apartments gradually giving way to banks and insurance companies. "I guess everything's worked out OK for you then," I said, raising my voice above the sudden hiss and growl of traffic.

She yanked her hand from mine and stopped cold, as traffic whizzed by us in a blur. "What the hell does that mean?"

I kept walking, and she scurried along to keep up. "Did you know that the bank was going to end up owning the film if Gordon died?"

Her voice rose with anger and wounded pride. She wasn't sure what I was getting at, but she didn't like it. "I did Mackenzie's paperwork. Of course I knew."

"So you can't have been too surprised that they would want to go ahead with the film."

"I *was* surprised! And more surprised when they picked me to replace him. I didn't expect that for a minute. In fact, I was ready to file for unemployment."

"I guess with all the trouble the project's had, the storyboards being 'lost' and all, you were the logical choice. The bank wouldn't want someone else to have to spend weeks learning the film. They want their money working for them."

She grabbed me by the arm, her fingernails digging through my overcoat. "I don't think I like the sound of this. It almost sounds like you're saying I benefit from Mackenzie's death."

A giant RTD bus wheezed by us, its massive tires crunching the curbs, and clouds of exhaust coughing from the rear and swirling in the clear icy wind whipping down from northern California. "You do benefit," I shouted above the diesel blare. "You get a chance at producing that it might have taken years to get otherwise. And you've already said Gordon meant nothing to you personally; this get-up you're wearing isn't mourning, is it?"

Kerry hunched her narrow shoulders together, shivering. "Yeah, well . . . " She was silent for a moment beside me, her hands thrust deeply into the pockets of her coat, as we trudged along with the noisy traffic shooting by us as if we were in parallel universes. After a moment she said, "The bank picked me because they'd heard good things about me—wait a minute! You're working for them, aren't you?"

"I was. I turned in the storyboards yesterday." And the check was still warm in my pocket, I suddenly remembered; I had forgotten to deposit it. I made a mental note to stop by the ATM before dinner. On second thought, I'd better do it in person tomorrow. I don't want any machine crunching up *that* deposit.

"And they asked you about me—"

"I told them I don't know anything about making movies," I said, as two more RTD buses coughed and sputtered down the street like angry TB patients. "But I said you knew more about that film than anyone else. I guess they thought you were a logical choice."

Kerry halted suddenly and seized my hand as if she were pressing alms on me. Her eyes gaped at me in disbelief. "Hey! You did that for *me*, didn't you? *You* convinced them! Damn! *Damn!*"

She dropped my hand and started striding rapidly down the street, and I had the terrifying impression that she might start skipping at any moment. Or worse, break into a Ginger Rogers routine, with the expectation I'd turn out to be a closet Fred Astaire, tapping my way to happiness. Just then, a group of low riders cruised by in a metallic maroon '65 Chevy and started yelling and whistling at her. She pirouetted, matador-style, her coat billowing out at the bottom, and smiled and waved, and the driver yelled something happily obscene in Spanish and floored the Chevy, tearing off down Beverly in a screech of burning rubber.

"*Damn!*" she said, coming back to me and kissing me on the cheek before grabbing my hand again. "I wondered why they picked me so fast."

We had worked our way down to Rossmore, where we turned north again into an area of stylish apartments across from the Wilshire Country Club and golf course.

She stopped suddenly. "My God, look at these beautiful old buildings." Staring up in surprise at the ten- and twelve-story apartment houses on our side of the street, she said, "I thought everything in south Hollywood was covered with graffiti and propped up with two-by-fours."

"This street becomes Vine further up. Then it does look like that. But for a mile or so it's 1920s elegance. Speaking of aging elegance, did you know about your pal Brandon and Catherine Wilbourne?"

She laughed happily and squeezed my hand. "Boy Wonder and the Earth Mother. Yes, I knew. Who didn't? I've tried to picture their couplings but couldn't—pale anorexic Brandon lost within the folds of Catherine Wilbourne's middle-aged baby fat. She reminds me of Elizabeth Taylor in one of her more unflatteringly chubby phases."

"They're planning to get married."

She stopped and gaped at me. "No! Tell me you're kidding. She's old enough to be his mother."

"Love has no bounds."

Kerry was half-laughing, half-bewildered. "I don't believe it!"

I said, "Did Mackenzie Gordon know about their affair?"

"Of course he knew. There aren't any secrets in a gossip-driven town like this. Catherine has always slept around. Mackenzie just accepted it, I suppose. He was obviously in no position to complain."

"And yet he hired Brandon for his new film."

"I don't think Mackenzie knew about them at the time. I guess when he found out, he didn't want to upset Catherine by firing him. But Mackenzie definitely didn't like having him around. You saw how he treated Brandon."

"Why wouldn't he want to fire him?"

Kerry stopped and looked at me like a waif in an illustrated Charles Dickens book, tiny beads of perspiration lining her forehead and her hair in mild disarray. "Can we sit on this bus bench for a minute? My calves are killing me. God, I hope this doesn't mean I'm going to build up my leg muscles. I hate women with leg muscles." She slumped down on the bench and thrust her un-muscled legs in front of her, as if she were determined to stop any other unwary pedestrians with her feet, then put her head back and closed her eyes to the sun. "Mackenzie couldn't afford to upset Catherine. She actually controlled his production company, you know. Mackenzie said she owned fifty-one percent in her own name, since she put up the initial investment. He ran the whole show, of course, while Catherine was off making movies or allowing Brandon to lose himself within her layered rows of body fat."

With some effort, I restrained myself from pointing out that Catherine Wilbourne, besides being one of the few real stars left in Hollywood, was a remarkably attractive woman, and several million men would have gladly traded places with lucky young Brandon. Instead, I said nothing and plopped down on the hard wooden bench next to her. After a moment of watching the sparse traffic on Rossmore, I asked, "How do you like being an executive so far?"

She rolled her eyes and smiled bewilderedly, as if it hadn't quite hit her yet. "I heard about it this morning when I came in to clean out my office. So instead, I carried my few worldly possessions over to Mackenzie's office. Before I could even put anything in the book-cases, the temp in the front office rushed in and dumped a script on my desk. Something about a nuclear power plant. I said, wait a minute, I'm already *making* a movie, and she says 'OK, how about a family of illegal aliens getting caught in a drug raid.' Then she starts hyperventilating: 'How about a high school boy who builds a girl out of Tinkertoys. Or two women with incurable diseases who live together but can't stand each other.' She's pitching a mile a minute and finally I say, Jesus, go out front and *type* something and she says she can't type. She can't file. Even the phone gives her trouble. . . . How far is it to the lot? I want to call a cab."

"It's about ten minutes," I lied. "You can do it. Think of the pioneer women."

She struggled to her feet and looked around wistfully as if a studio limo would magically appear. But that was only in MGM films, I reminded her, and started walking again, but more slowly.

Thinking about what Stiles had said about Richard Ravich, I asked, "Does Brandon know Laurie very well?"

"Oh, pretty well, I suppose. I'd see them at Mackenzie's house for a meeting or story conference or whatever and Brandon and Laurie got on quite well. Sometimes too well, I used to think—the way he'd be kidding and playing with her and hugging her. She was getting too grown-up, if you know what I mean. It seemed a little odd at the time, but I suppose not if he was planning on becoming her step-dad. You still don't have anything on Laurie, do you? God, I feel so bad celebrating my luck while she's missing."

"Both the LAPD and the Beverly Hills police are looking for her now. And everyone in LA's seen her picture on TV. She'll turn up." That, at least, was what I had to keep telling myself. After a moment I asked, "Did you know about Laurie's boyfriend?"

She glanced at me quickly. "Boyfriend? Laurie?"

"His name is Richard Ravich. His mother is the principal of Laurie's school."

"It's news to me. Of course, I didn't see Laurie all that often. But Mackenzie never mentioned it either. I guess I'm learning there's a lot of things he didn't discuss with me. What ever happened to that porno publisher? Did you ever talk to him about Mackenzie?"

"Howie Wiltz is a problem," I said. "I'm not quite sure what it all means. He's got a video of your Mackenzie and some of his girl friends dallying in bed. Mackenzie's home movies, I guess. He was planning to sell it to Gordon when he was killed. Now he's not sure what he'll do with it. Maybe publish some of it in his magazine."

Kerry had stopped suddenly and was a step behind me. "Oh, Christ, no!" Her face had paled and she grasped my arm tightly and stared at me. "*Wiltz has the video?*" The wind was eddying around us and I felt a chill go through me as Kerry's fingernails dug through my overcoat into the flesh. Then it suddenly hit me.

"That's what Mackenzie was looking for all this time, wasn't it? That's why the two of you were so upset about this missing script material. There never *was* any script material. Or a cartoon video. Laurie left with a tape of Mackenzie and his playmates."

Kerry was beside herself, her eyes wild with fear, not listening to me.

"Vic, you've got to get that tape back. You've got to. I could lose everything now if that got out. God, I've finally got my first real chance. I can't . . . You've, *we've*, got to get that film. We've *got to!*"

I was looking at her as she half-pleaded, half-screamed at me, and the sense of what she was saying finally sank in. "You're in the film."

I hadn't even considered that before but, of course. Wiltz had said Mackenzie and some others. Why not Kerry?

"Oh, Jesus!" She was hanging on to me; her body had gone limp. "I didn't know it at first, but Mackenzie had a video camera set up in his Malibu house. That's one of the reasons he spent so much time there. There are two cameras in a back bedroom shooting through mirrors, one directly over the bed. He'd bring a girl over, usually an actress, someone who needed him, needed to keep him happy. He'd do a little coke and then a lot of sex. All the time the cameras were running. Later he'd cut and splice to make a fifteen- or twenty-minute film. Then the next time he'd show it to her. Or show a film of him and someone famous. Some of them got mad, some of them thought it was funny and wanted to do it again. He's got a dozen different cassettes now, probably a hundred different actresses. None of them were well-known at the time, but a couple have become big since then. Look, Vic, I'm in that film. I've got to get it back before someone at the bank finds out."

"Did Gordon's wife know about the film?"

"No. That's the one thing Catherine never found out about. In fact, she almost never went out to Malibu. She knew he was out there with his girls, of course."

"Then that's why Gordon was so anxious to get it back. Why upset your multimillionaire wife, especially if she's the majority owner of your film production company? Did Laurie really run away or was that another of Gordon's inventions?"

"Laurie's gone, Vic! Just like Mackenzie told you. She got mad at

Mackenzie when he wouldn't let her watch a cartoon video that night. When she ran away, she grabbed a cassette from the den, probably thinking it was the cartoon. Mackenzie was frantic; he needed it back before the cops or anyone else found it and it became public knowledge. That's why he made up the story about the storyboards and script material. It never was missing, but we couldn't tell Brandon or anyone else; we went ahead and recreated everything. When you found the storyboards at Mackenzie's I wasn't surprised, but I couldn't let you know that either."

"That's why you called Chauk even after I'd found them."

"I knew what we were really looking for was still missing, unless it was somehow in Mackenzie's car when it blew up. I guess that's what I was really hoping for. When the police didn't turn up any evidence of the tape, I thought it might be gone for good. But I couldn't be sure, and I couldn't tell you or anyone else. I had to find Laurie—"

"Do you think Laurie could have known what was on that video? Do you think she could have taken it on purpose?"

Kerry shook her head and her hand slipped from my arm. She was still distraught but seemed relieved to be finally telling her story. Too much had happened to her recently, too much she had had to face alone. Just talking about it was like setting a burden down—if only temporarily—that she had been carrying for too long. Her voice softened as she answered. "I don't think Laurie had any idea what she took. She's very retarded, Vic. I don't think the film would make any more sense to her than it would to a four-year-old. And Mackenzie was really upset by her running away—and not just because of the video. He really did love her."

We had started walking again and were coming up to The Keep, a quirky 1920s apartment building with brooding medieval turrets, arches, and dark corner staircases, and where I've lived for five years. I had brought her this way purposely to show her its haunting Transylvanian moodiness, oddly fitting right into its location on Rossmore, just blocks from Hollywood and Vine. But I said nothing about it now and kept on walking; Kerry was staring with a hazy intensity at the sidewalk. After a moment, I said, "Did you or Mackenzie ever get a line on Laurie? Did you have any idea where she might be?"

She shook her head and then dabbed irritably at her eyes as if she didn't want me to see that she had been crying. "Nothing. But even after he hired you, Mackenzie kept looking. *He* wanted to find Laurie, if he could, so no one would get their hands on that videotape."

She stopped again and looked steadily at me as the wind lifted her hair and whipped it around her face. "Look, Vic, you've got to get that tape back. I'll hire you. I don't care how much it costs. I've got to have it."

I put my hands in my pockets. "Wiltz is talking about four hundred thousand."

Her arms fell to her sides, and she seemed to shrink inside her leather coat. "Oh, God." Her voice weakened. "Then you've got to steal it."

"Sorry," I said. "Not my sort of role. Try one of the gunsels from Central Casting."

Kerry fell silent as we turned east on Clinton and walked on. There was little traffic except for an occasional mother bringing her kids home from preschool, and gardeners rumbling by in rickety pickup trucks with lawn mowers bouncing in the back. Kerry strode beside me, hands in pockets and lost in thought. After a moment I said, "That's what was bothering me after I talked to you at Gordon's the morning he was killed. Do you remember what you said when I told you I thought Gordon might be planning a porno film with Wiltz?"

She shook her head, eyes still on the sidewalk.

"You said, As a producer or an actor? I thought that was an odd thing to say. And when I asked if you had just stopped in early that morning you said no, you'd spent the night, and then asked if I wanted to watch your videos."

She looked up at me with a wry half-smile. "Kind of a bitch, wasn't I?" After a minute she added, "Sorry." And smiled again, a sad, cheerless smile that just flickered across her face and then disappeared. But bit-by-bit she was beginning to regain some of her normal equanimity, the determined open-faced pluck I had seen earlier in her dealings with Brandon Stiles and myself. Still, failure loomed closely, and the easy-going Kerry of earlier in the week lay buried beneath the weight of the past few days, as fate had jerked her first this way and then that: Laurie disappearing, Mackenzie murdered, her job vanishing, then her dreams suddenly realized, as she was named producer of a film ready to shoot. But now that could be yanked away, too, and her career again sent reeling if the video turned up in the wrong hands.

We turned on Bronson and walked a while in silence, Kerry lost in thought, until we found ourselves in front of the McKay Building, just half a block from where we started at Paramount. I nodded at it and said, "Let's go in here."

She stopped and stared at the aging four-story building with startled disbelief. At first she didn't seem to think I was serious. "Why would I want to go in there?" Her gaze passed briefly over the smooth granite façade and mock Greek pillars in front. "God, look at that: a revolving door." More disbelief in her voice.

"You have the Californian's instinctive distrust of anything over ten years old," I said. "Come on."

I took her by the hand and stutter-stepped through the brass and glass door and into the large high-ceilinged lobby, alive with clumps of chattering workers streaming through to and from lunch. She stood still and stared at the polished marble walls, gilt-and-cut-glass elevator, and the large old-fashioned clock hanging on the wall. "What is this place? It looks like something out of a 1940s musical. It's a film-set, right? Or a model for a train station?"

I pointed her in the direction of the elevators and began walking. "It's where we're going to solve a murder, launch your career, and have a glass of wine."

# 13

KERRY DANIELS LOOKED AT THE SMOKED-GLASS WINDOW IN THE DOOR as I put a key in the lock. "I'm surprised it doesn't say Spade and Archer."

I curled my lips and tightened my jaw until it hurt. "Archer's dead, sweetheart. The dame shot him in the alley and the falcon's disappeared again, and now the fat man's after me." But it sounded more like Pat Sajak than Humphrey Bogart, I thought, as I ushered her inside and shut the door behind us. Leaving the light off in the waiting room, I brought her into the inner office; she stood for a moment in the middle of the large room and looked around appreciatively.

"It's not what I expected."

"A decorator did it," I admitted. "From Columbia. It was part payment for a job I did."

"Sort of English clubby. Lots of wood and leather. I like it. Comfortable."

I walked over to the phone machine and played back my messages as she wandered over to the window and looked out. There was a call from Rudy, terse as usual: call him at the station, no indication of what it was about. And a message finally from Anna Ravich: call her at the school. She needed to talk to me. Right! I thought with a renewed spark of anger: And I need to talk to you, too. A few words regarding your son and Laurie. But not with Kerry in the office.

And also a curious message from the ever-curious Howie Wiltz.

"Hey, wise guy. Come over to the office tonight at nine. I got a few things to tell you about your new-found friends."

"Sounds like a pleasant man," Kerry said with a weak smile. She had been staring over at Paramount and stood now silhouetted by the window. She was an attractive woman, I thought, as I looked at her. Hell, she was more than attractive. It was still hard to imagine her frolicking in the hay with the rotund, balding, and fiftyish Mackenzie Gordon, joining his stable of homemade porno stars trying to advance their careers on the age-old casting couch. According to Kerry, her own motivations were different, and perhaps they were. Brandon and Catherine, Kerry and Gordon. Gordon and a cast of thousands. What a fun industry this is. And I found myself wondering if General Motors or IBM was any different. Probably not.

"Howie Wiltz is actually an interesting person," I said as I sat behind the desk and picked up the phone. "I don't know why, but I kind of like him." I punched out a number and scrunched the phone between my cheek and shoulders as I put my feet up on the desk and waited for it to be answered. Kerry walked over to the bookcase and stared at the foot-high plaster bust staring back at her. "Is this who I think it is?"

"Oliver Hardy," I replied.

"Of course," she muttered to herself. "Another fine mess . . . "

Finally I heard Moses Handleman's Pavarotti-like voice on the other end of the line. "Bronson Rare Books,"—sounding as if he was auditioning for the Met.

"How's business?" I asked.

The voice became ebullient. "I have just sold an unpublished and heretofore unknown Faulkner screenplay in typescript. It was fortuitously discovered in a box in a studio prop room with hundreds of other unproduced scripts awaiting the trashman. Business, in short, is wonderful."

"Then we will have a 1975 Lafite Rothschild. And three glasses."

"An excellent choice, monsieur."

After Moses hung up I called Ernesto's coffee shop downstairs and ordered a ham and cheese with chips for Kerry. A proletarian meal for a producer and perhaps the last of its kind she'd see. The preliminaries completed, I took her coat to the rack in the waiting room, then settled her down on one end of the leather couch as I took the other. "You do seem to have acquired a problem," I said rather needlessly at this point and added, "The question now is how do we go about dealing with it?"

"Does that mean you'll work for me?" She looked at me eagerly, brown eyes growing large and her mouth opening in an expectant half-smile that was already preparing to be disappointed.

"Not exactly," I said. "My first obligation is to find Laurie. She's still out there somewhere, probably unaware that her father is dead. If I can get you the video while I'm at it, I will. But I'm not working for you. If I dig it up you can pay me back by throwing some work my way when you're a big-time studio executive."

She smiled uncertainly. "Are you sure? You really don't want to be paid?"

Another concept alien to Hollywood, I thought to myself. First walking and now this. But I told her I was sure, and she relaxed a little. The next step was going to be more difficult. Kerry Daniels, despite her determined veneer of perky optimism, was on the edge: her whole career, just a few minutes ago seeming to stretch brightly away into the indefinite future, was suddenly in doubt because of the uncertainty over her and Gordon's idiotic little sex flick. She was keyed up, her fingers drumming the arm of the chair, as her mind's eye saw everything coming crashing down if the film became public knowledge. She wasn't going to be any good to me like this. I needed her to relax so we could talk it out: somewhere, I was sure, in Kerry's memory, from something Gordon had said or something she had seen, was the key to Laurie's disappearance. We just needed to start talking, moving things around to see what happens. But I knew I wasn't the best person to get her to do this. She needed someone disinterested, someone who didn't come to the problem with the prejudices and preconceived notions I had; someone who would listen and not judge. Trying to keep my voice matter-of-fact, I said, "A friend of mine is going to be here in a minute. I want you to talk to him as openly as you have to me. He helps me think things out sometimes."

She looked alarmed. "But I don't want—"

I gave her hand a paternalistic pat, smiled my fatherly smile, and whispered, "Trust him. He's a doctor!" Which he is, a Ph.D. in classics, the subject he taught before rejoining the real world ten years ago. And he ought to be here any minute, I remembered suddenly. I reached over and quickly flipped on the radio. An oldies station; better switch. KUSC: ah . . . Pappa Haydn, charms to soothe even the savage Handleman breast. Just then the outer office door squeaked open and shut, and seconds later Moses tramped bear-like into my office, all six-foot-four of him, bushy-haired and bearded, a bottle of wine in one hand and three wine glasses held precariously by the stems in the other. I made the introductions and Moses responded with an old-world litany of "delighteds" and "charmeds" and then flourished the wine bottle, holding it in two hands like an enthusiastic sommelier.

"A mere California Cabernet," he explained, "but quite good. I have been assured that it has been passed upon by all the proper experts and praised in the best homes in Encino. The grapes for the vineyard were brought to this country in the nineteenth century from France by Shirley MacLaine in a previous life. Note the bouquet and coloration. Don't get so close, please, Victor! Allow it to breathe!"

Just then there was a knock at the door and Ernesto himself, dressed in white shirt and white pants, bustled in with a covered platter. "Ham and-a cheese," he said, identifying Kerry immediately as a "movie person" and sounding suspiciously like Chico Marx. He put the sandwich and chips on the coffee table where he spotted the wine bottle and gave Moses a scowl. "California!" He turned back to me. "I coulda brought you a nice Chianti. Why you wanna this? Abomination!"

"It's Napa Valley Thursday," I told him. "A traditional American folk holiday. Humor us."

After Ernesto stalked off grunting Latinate monosyllables, Moses poured out three glasses of wine, and Kerry and I sipped appreciatively while he attacked his own with somewhat more gusto.

"Kerry is a producer at Gordonfilms," I told Moses, and then explained to her about his cinema and related-matters bookshop. "I thought you two should get to know each other," I added.

"And so we should," he agreed, and for some time we talked back and forth about moviemaking. Finally, the wine gone, I said, "Kerry has a bit of a problem, Moses."

"Yes?" He looked at me.

"Maybe you could hit the high spots," I said to Kerry, allowing her the opportunity to leave out anything she wanted to. But it was testimony to Moses's instant empathy that she left nothing out, including her appearance in Gordon's video. Moses finally leaned back in his chair, stared at the ceiling, and said, "A problem indeed."

"Beginning with the video," I said. "We don't want Kerry's career to go down in flames the same week it's launched."

Moses peered at me. "You say the odious Howie Wiltz is determined to make money on it?"

I agreed that money certainly seemed to be his objective, but noted that he didn't seem particularly odious to me. Certainly not outside the norm for Hollywood. Moses shook his great hairy head. "His whole life is devoted to exploitation and sadness, but we'll discuss that some other day, Victor. If he can no longer sell—blackmail is a more honest word—the video to Gordon, his only other option would seem to be to publish, and reap the whirlwind of publicity."

"He indicated to me that he had another option," I said. "But he didn't say what. Maybe that's what he wants to talk to me about tonight."

Moses turned it over in his mind a moment. "Kerry is obviously in no position to come up with the kind of money Wiltz is talking about, if he still has blackmail on his mind. Are there any other, uh . . . actresses, on that film who could?"

Kerry mentioned a couple of names, both up-and-coming stars. But not blockbusters. And not the type with an extra four hundred thousand lying around. She added, "I don't think either of them would be very upset if the film *was* made public. They're not going to be trying out for parts at Disney. Or trying to get bank loans as a producer."

"Which leaves us where?" Moses asked, looking at us both.

"Confused," I said. I added, "And of course there's still the problem of Laurie."

"Ah yes. The unfortunate little girl."

Kerry said, "I don't understand how Wiltz ended up with that film, anyway. Laurie took it with her when she left. Where did Wiltz get it?"

"He bought it," I reminded her.

Moses stretched out in his chair and stared at his shoes. "That, of course, is where the mysterious seller got the film: from the girl, somehow. But where's the girl? If we knew who sold the film to Wiltz maybe we'd know where the girl is."

"And if we knew where the girl is we'd find out who sold him the film. We're going in circles."

Moses rubbed his eyes with his large, thick-fingered hands, laborer's hands, I had always thought, and remembered him saying he'd worked summers during college on a fishing boat out of San Pedro. He opened his eyes, gazed up at the ceiling and then turned to me. "Do you think Wiltz could be thinking of selling the film to Catherine Wilbourne?"

"It's possible, I suppose. It wouldn't do her image any good if her husband's private life was made public. Maybe I'll get a chance to ask her when she finishes with the police. If I can get in touch with her. Maybe Brandon would help."

"Do you think Catherine could be who Gordon was meeting at the airport?" Moses asked but then quickly changed his mind. "Getting up at three in the morning to drive out to the airport in the rain to meet your wife for a furtive talk in a deserted parking structure? I hardly think so." He smiled ruefully to himself.

We fell silent for a moment and as I glanced at Kerry next to me on the couch, staring quietly at the floor, I marveled again at Moses's calming effect on people. A few minutes ago, on finding out that the tape of her and Gordon in bed together was in danger of being made public, she teetered on the edge of hysteria. Everything she had hoped and planned for for years was about to come tumbling down. But having told her story to the great silent hulk sitting across from her, she began to regain hope: someone understood, something was being done.

It is a gift of Moses's and why I had wanted him present—this instant sense of true caring that he is able to communicate to others, that causes complete strangers to trust him and open up in a way they never would to me. I used to think it was in his eyes, the way he would look at you as if you were the only thing in the world that mattered at that instant. But I've finally decided it's not definable, not even Moses could explain what it is. It's just there. Like freckles or a dimple in the chin.

My mind had begun to return to the almost mythic Catherine Wilbourne and her role in all of this when Kerry, evidently following the same track, looked at Moses and said, "I think she knows something. I think Catherine came back to LA because she knew Mackenzie was panicking, not because of Laurie."

Moses's heavily lidded eyes lumbered open and he rubbed at his bearded jaw. "I'm inclined to agree. But is she responsible for Laurie disappearing, also? And is she somehow involved with Howie Wiltz and the video?"

Could Catherine be involved in Laurie's disappearance? I wondered. No, it just wasn't possible. Catherine had been in London when Laurie disappeared. That much was certain. And she wouldn't do anything to endanger her own daughter anyway, would she? I wondered what I would be doing at this moment if Tracy had disappeared. I would have been frantic, I knew: I would have been at the newspapers and TV stations, I would have been on the streets day and night. And my mind drew up the image of the girl at the Bowl, not just killed but savagely killed, tortured, made to feel her death in the most barbaric manner. Again I thought: Laurie's dead, she's in a Dumpster or buried under rocks or stuck under bushes somewhere up in the hills.

Next to me, Moses and Kerry were talking about something, the words hanging on the edges of my consciousness, something about Catherine Wilbourne. The surviving parent. I hadn't gotten the answer yet to my question about who benefits if young Laurie, unable to care for herself, were to suddenly inherit her mother's fortune. If that was what lay behind this, if control of Mackenzie and Catherine's estate was the motive for all that had happened in the past few days, then maybe it was actually Catherine and not Laurie who was most at risk.

Forget it! I told myself at last. Just as I had when I left the Holstead School, I was creating problems and conspiracies out of my frustration at not being able to find Laurie. So far, this was only a missing person's case. Don't fantasize it into anything else.

I turned to Moses and tried something that had been nagging me for days but had been shoved into some out-of-the-way mental corner as I concentrated on more immediate concerns. "Do you know a Gregory Chauk?"

He shook his head. "The name is unfamiliar to me. Should I?"

"He teaches at UCLA."

"It's ten years since I've been there, Victor. And there must be a thousand people on the faculty."

It was a wild chance that they would know each other, and I wasn't surprised that it came to nothing. The entire week had been filled with dead ends. Kerry sighed and glanced at the two of us. There was a mixture of resignation and sadness in her voice, and maybe just a touch of excitement. "Quite a first day on the job for me."

"It'll get better," Moses assured her. "It's comforting to know that the bank is behind you. They'll give you room for mistakes, room to move around in. Don't get too uptight about things."

"Oh, Jesus, the bank!" she said and stood up suddenly. "I've got to get downtown. I'm not sure how long they'll be behind me when I tell them the other good news of the day. The Bank of California called me this morning. The day before Mackenzie was killed he borrowed a hundred thousand dollars on a six-day promissory note. The production company's only involved because it was one of the assets Mackenzie put up as collateral, but B of C expects its money in three days. If not, they could tie us, and his estate, up in litigation for months."

"One hundred thousand dollars?" Moses whistled appreciatively.

"He took it in cash," Kerry added.

Moses said, "Now at least we know what changed hands at the airport."

"But it didn't stop the film from ending up with Wiltz, did it?" I said.

"An interesting thought," Moses said as the pieces started to move together in his mind. "Maybe the person who killed Gordon and the person who sold the film to Wiltz are not one in the same. Maybe there are two people out there you should be looking for. Or two films. Something to think about, Victor."

# 14

KERRY SCURRIED OFF DOWNTOWN AND MOSES RETREATED TO HIS first floor bookstore. I called Rudy Cruz; he was out, so I left a message with a gravelly voiced sergeant named Tillotson and hung up. Then I looked up the number of the Holstead School and returned Anna Ravich's call. The phone was picked up on the first ring. The regular receptionist, this time. "Oh, yes, Mr. Eton," she said, and I could almost see her smiling down the line. "I remember. You're the one with the tragic personal problem, aren't you?"

"Promptness, yes," I admitted.

"I do hope you work on it," she said. "I've learned the only thing you get for being on time in Beverly Hills is lonely. Do you want to talk to Mrs. Ravich?"

I told her I did.

"I'll put you on hold—they do that all the time here at the school, to 'model' the appropriate behavior for you. It won't be long but it will be painful."

And it was, as she made me sit through most of "Moon River" with Andy Williams. Just as my tolerance was bottoming out, Anna Ravich's voice thudded down the line without any greeting. "I need to talk to you. Soon!"

There was a brittleness to her words that made it difficult to tell what emotion she was experiencing, but I remembered the look in her eyes when she confronted me at the Bowl: whatever she had been feeling then was still with her. I asked, "Now?"

"No. I can't now. This afternoon, five o'clock. But not here and not at your office. Someplace private."

"All right," I said and thought about it a moment. "How about the Gold Rush? It's a bar in the five thousand block of Wilshire."

"Fine," she replied. "I'll find it."

"Do you want to tell me what this is about?"

"No," she said and hung up.

I put the phone down and almost immediately it rang.

"You're the detective hired to search for Laurie Gordon?" a husky female voice asked.

Just for an instant I hesitated, as a chill, like a drop of icy water, trickled along my spine.

". . . Yes."

"I'm her mother. I'd like to talk to you."

"Catherine Wilbourne?" About time, I thought.

"Yes." Her voice was calm and clear, perfectly modulated, an actress's voice, full of promises and beautiful things. "Let me give you directions. I'll expect you in an hour."

She was in Malibu, she said; she told me how to get there and then hung up without the slightest doubt that I would do whatever it was she requested.

I stood for a moment next to the desk, feeling an unexpected little shudder of excitement. I had worked around Hollywood actors and actresses for years and had never been much affected by it. Most stars, I quickly learned, might be worshiped by the world, but they were turn-offs to the people who actually had to deal with them: arrogant, uncaring, egotistical misfits who had arrived at their success through an accident of fate or the time-honored Hollywood in-crowd of friends or friends-of-friends, and who now treated everyone else as if they were serfs or supplicants placed on earth expressly to do their bidding. "I'm a star!" was heard so often that it became a running gag among film crews: I'm a star and you're not.

But Catherine Wilbourne! An indelible presence in the entertainment community for thirty-five of her forty or so years, one of the few stars who truly was a star, whose name alone could still sell a picture. A beautiful little girl in curls who had grown up to be an even more beautiful woman. Damn! I was excited! Damn!

I whistled my way out to the Buick in the lot and hurried along
Santa Monica Boulevard to Pacific Coast Highway and the ocean,
then headed west, speeding past Paul Getty's tribute to the twin
deities of ancient Rome and Paul Getty, past Topanga and the
surfers, to Malibu and more surfers, most of them clad in bright Day
Glo wet suits, standing by convertibles with their boards perched
next to them like primitive phallic symbols. Off to my left stretched
seven thousand miles of blue Pacific, on my right the hills where
Catherine Wilbourne lived, alive and vibrant with a blazing
Mediterranean beauty even on an overcast day like this, red and purple bougainvillea erupting in fiery clumps beneath whitewashed
houses that perched precariously on stilts with a sort of hubris that
said I Don't Believe in Earthquakes. Beneath the bright sun of summer, it sometimes seemed too perfect, almost in bad taste: the sea
too blue, the bougainvillea too red, as if Van Gogh had tried to paint
like Monet. But today, in the muted light of autumn, it was beautiful.

On the way out, I tried to picture what Catherine Wilbourne
would be like in person. Smaller, right? They always look smaller.
And older, no doubt; makeup and camera and lighting people can
do magic on the screen, hiding all of nature's little tell-tale signs of
age. And not really fat at all, despite what Kerry had said. Catherine
was . . . well, she was all there. You couldn't see her bones poking
through the flesh like you could on most actresses today. She was
curvaceous, not angular. But yeah, she'd never be the poster girl for
an anorexia campaign.

But what would she be like? Bitchy? Imperious? Probably. She was
used to getting her way, probably always had. Moses had wondered
what it must have been like for her to have become a fantasy for
millions of males. It was an intriguing question: what was it like
knowing that every man she met was dying to get in her pants.
Knowing she had that power?

What's it like, Catherine?

Maybe I'd ask her.

The turn-off to their house was an obscure unmarked private
drive rising without warning off Pacific Coast Highway. I zoomed by
it the first time and had to swing a quick U-turn against two lanes of
oncoming traffic and go back and take it again. The road led up and

around a bend to a two-acre plateau hacked out of the side of the mountain like a finger dabbed into a cake. Sitting at the edge of the cliff was a single-story ranch-style house, maybe thirty or forty years old. The front was white stucco with blue trim, the sides virtually all glass, to take advantage of the unobstructed view of the sea spread out below like a great, soft blue tablecloth. A veranda with chairs and umbrella-tables and chaise lounges ran around the perimeter of the building like the decking on a luxury liner. The entire estate—house, pool, and garage—crouched behind a thicket of pines and oleander and hawthorn bushes on the three landlocked sides, making it invisible from anywhere except the ocean a quarter-mile away. The effect was of comfort and privacy rather than Hollywood ostentation, except perhaps for the red Mercedes convertible sparkling like a jewel on the circular brick drive in front. I left my car behind it, walked up the three steps to the porch, rang the doorbell, and wondered again about Catherine.

And suddenly there she was.

In a bathrobe.

Looking as if she had just stepped from the shower or pool.

Not smiling.

"Miss Wilbourne?" Christ! Who did I think it was, Kermit the Frog?

"Come on in. I'm just watching some movies."

She held the door and I squeezed past her. She was smaller than she appeared on screen. And maybe just a little older. But not fat. No, not at all. And . . . well . . . beautiful! Really beautiful. Like a movie star. Like Catherine Wilbourne. And right here next to me.

"Come along through here," she said, leading me down a hallway to a large living room in the rear of the house that overlooked a marvelous crescent of coastline and ocean from Long Beach to Ventura. I crossed over to the windows as if drawn and stared out at the beauty of the sea; it was partly overcast, and a storm was building in the west, but I could still see half a dozen different blues as the ocean stretched to the horizon where only the thinnest of lines separated it from the sky. Near the shore, the surf was rolling in at eleven-second intervals, a clear blue crest beginning on the right and gradually turning white as it slanted toward the beach. Surfers balanced precariously on the curl, riding up and down as they were flung shoreward; then the wave broke and they dipped suddenly from sight, their boards popping unexpectedly airward a moment later like toast from a comic-book toaster.

"Please—" Catherine Wilbourne impatiently pointed me to a soft peach-colored couch in the center of the room, and when I sat she crossed her arms and stared down at me from a face turned suddenly hard. "I want to know where my daughter is."

The words came angrily, like an accusation, jolting me back to reality but throwing me off balance with their tone. No introductions, no explanation, just a sudden demand issued like an order from a junior-high-school principal to one of her more intractable students. I wondered what she knew about her daughter's disappearance, if she knew that I had been looking for Laurie for days, if she knew about her husband's panic to get the video back. I gazed at her steadily, keeping my voice calm and trying to moderate this unexplained hostility. "Your husband hired me to find Laurie. That's what I'm . . ."

She interrupted before I could finish. "You haven't done a damn thing as far as I can tell."

"Maybe we'd better back up, Miss Wilbourne. Your husband is dead. Aren't you concerned with who killed him?"

She was still standing with unbending rigidity, staring at me from two feet away. She was barefoot and in a bathrobe that barely fell to mid-thigh, and I wondered what, if anything, she was wearing beneath it. Thrusting her hands in the robe's pockets, her voice rose scornfully as she glared at me. "The police can worry about who killed Mackenzie. I want my daughter back."

"How did you find out she was missing?" I asked, trying to diffuse her hostility by changing the direction of her inquiries.

"Brandon told me when I talked to him Monday. I came home as soon as I could."

"Yesterday morning," I said.

She nodded impatiently.

"Then why did you wait until today to contact me? Stiles must have told you I was looking for Laurie."

Her voice raced with anger. "I didn't even talk to Brandon again until today! When I got in, I went by the house and saw that Mackenzie had visitors, so I drove out here and called my lawyer. It was half past four in the morning, so he told me get some sleep; there was nothing we could do at that hour. We'd check with the police later. He called back before noon and told me about Mackenzie."

"Why didn't you go to Parker Center right away? Your husband had just been murdered—"

"I was looking for my daughter!" she shouted. "What could I tell them about Mackenzie? I went to the Beverly Hills police—that's where she disappeared from. We spent all afternoon driving around Hollywood and Beverly Hills in a police car looking for her. When it got dark, my attorney took me downtown to give a statement instead of going to Hollywood, so I wouldn't have to talk to the reporters hanging around. 'Entertainment Tonight' and 'Inside Edition' and all the tabloids are there trying to find out what happened to Mackenzie. I don't *care* what happened. I want my daughter back. Mackenzie hired you—why can't you find her?"

I was looking at her, watching her face, wondering how much she knew, and how much I should tell her. Are you aware of your husband's videotaped frolics with dozens of young actresses, Catherine? Do you know about Mackenzie and Kerry Daniels, who has just become the producer of a film you own through Gordon's production company? How much do you know?

Or do you even care?

I was beginning to feel uneasy as she stood there staring down impatiently from angry blue eyes, arms folded confrontationally across her chest; it's an old interrogation technique and I admired her ease at employing it: Sit down (yes, ma'am); tell me everything you know (yes, ma'am), all the while making you feel intimidated by forcing you to look up at your inquisitor. I didn't need it: I was already feeling intimidated enough by that damn short robe. I pushed out of the chair and strode over to the wall of glass and stared out again. Giant reddish splotches of bougainvillea and ice plant hopscotched down the steep hillside to the highway below; out at sea, half a dozen white sails were skudding along in a group in the near distance, teetering back and forth as if they would fall onto their sides at any minute, and another group of six or eight were clumped together farther out. A large brass telescope rested on a tripod next to me, pointing toward the horizon, and I was tempted to look through it, but Catherine Wilbourne was making impatient noises behind me. I turned and faced her.

"We can stand here and play word games with each other if you want," I said calmly. "You can try to intimidate me and I can lie to you. Or we can work together and try to find your daughter."

"Mackenzie hired you!" she said angrily.

"He hired me to find some script material Laurie took when she left. I found it and I've already been paid. I'm looking for Laurie because I want to. No one is paying me. So you can't fire me. And you can't threaten me."

She was standing ten feet distant, hands thrust again in pockets, staring at me, a face I'd seen in two dimensions all my life on theater screens or on television. It was stirring the strangest emotions within me, almost as if I were meeting my past, the same sort of feeling you get when walking into a school room you last visited twenty-five years ago. Her eyes stayed focused on mine as she struggled to make up her mind. Then abruptly her expression softened, and she shook her head as if she were clearing away the horror of the past few days: her daughter's disappearance and then her husband's murder. She smiled feebly, those famous cheekbones rising and her lipstick-free mouth opening slightly as she approached me with one small hand outstretched.

"Let's start over, Mr. Eton—Vic! My name's Catherine Wilbourne, I'm happy to meet you, and I thank God you're looking for Laurie. I'm sorry for being rude but you can understand, I hope. Laurie is my only child and she's . . . she can't take care of herself. I've been worried sick. Brandon said you were working for Mackenzie so naturally I called you."

We shook hands, a little foolishly at this point, I thought, but she was determined to get off to a better start. She led me over to an octagonal oak table next to the windows. "Please sit down. I'll get some coffee from the kitchen."

I said no to the coffee but she kept at it. "Tea? Orange juice? I'm afraid there's no alcohol. I don't believe in it."

I said tea would be fine, and she padded off in her bare feet to the kitchen, coming back shortly with hot water and tea bags and two dainty blue and white china cups. She sat across from me at the table, and I envisioned that short robe riding up on her thighs beneath the tabletop and wished we were back on the couch.

As I poured water in my cup I said, "What did Brandon tell you about Laurie's disappearance?"

"He said she left Thursday with some script material and Mackenzie was frantic to get it back. Laurie's run away before but not for more than a few hours. She's never gone far—just around the neighborhood. She must have been pretty upset at Mackenzie. I should tell you, I know all about my husband's little dalliances; I've known for years, I suppose. But I wanted to protect Laurie as long as I could. His video setup here I didn't know about until today. Pathetic, isn't it? Poor Mackenzie, collecting his conquests on tape so he can look at them again and again. Or show them to his buddies in the locker room at Hillcrest. I suppose that's what Laurie really took when she ran away, isn't it? Volume nine or whatever of Mackenzie's conquests. No wonder he wanted it back."

"To keep it from you?" I asked.

She nodded and sipped at her tea. "To keep it from me and the banks. Mackenzie's little production company was a shell, you know; the only assets it had were its past films, and they weren't bringing in anything to talk about now. The company was technically bankrupt. Mackenzie had been trying to raise money, a hundred million at first, but he decided to cut back to something more reasonable. He was full of ideas and hoping to find investors to back him. Mackenzie was always better at raising money than making movies. He expected me to kick in a bundle, too. We were going to talk about any investment of mine when I got back from England."

A little uneasily I said, "Brandon Stiles told me you two were thinking about marriage when you got back."

She held her cup near her mouth and looked at me a moment, trying to read something into my words that wasn't there. Finally she said, "Mackenzie had absolutely no idea Brandon and I were planning to get married. We had just decided ourselves. But Mackenzie wouldn't have given a damn *what* I did as long as I poured some money into his production company first. He was desperate. He needed as much money as he could get, mine or anyone's; it didn't matter. We had a prenuptial agreement that kept our assets separate, so he would have gotten nothing from a divorce settlement."

"In other words, he couldn't afford to upset you."

"Exactly." She put the cup down and glanced out to sea. A day-cruise fishing boat had anchored off a kelp bed three hundred yards offshore; with the hazy, obscured sun moving behind it, the boat appeared to be suspended between sky and sea like a surrealistic painting or a vision in a dream. Catherine seemed to be staring at it for a long time, studying it as it shimmered in gray-blue space. Then, softly, looking away from me, she said, "His little video would definitely have upset me. As would Laurie's disappearance."

"The cassette Laurie took has shown up. That's a good sign, I guess; it means she's probably still somewhere near Hollywood or Beverly Hills. Unfortunately the film's ended up in the possession of Howie Wiltz at *Hollywood X-T-C*."

She turned back to me with a mixture of disbelief and resignation. "Howie Wiltz! That's just great, isn't it? Is he going to put some stills in his trashy magazine or sell the video to the home market so everyone can have the same fun as Mackenzie and his golfing buddies?"

"I don't know what he'll do. But my guess is, he'll use it for whatever publicity value it has."

She got up, holding her cup of tea, walked to the far end of the wall of glass and stood staring out again. One hand rested on a large floor-mounted globe, her fingertips unconsciously pressing against it as if it were all that held her up. After a moment, in a low voice, she said, "I guess I don't really care about those pictures. Mackenzie's life was his own; perhaps it's fitting that it reach its culmination as a publicity gimmick for a sleazy mens' magazine." She turned and looked at me. "Do you know Kerry Daniels?"

The abruptness of the question caught me off-balance again. "I've met her," I said with what I hoped was nonchalance.

"What's she like?"

"Don't you know her?"

She shook her head. "She was in the Beverly Hills house with Mackenzie a few times doing paperwork while I was there. She came to dinner once. But I didn't pay much attention. What's she like?"

"Nice," I said. "Competent. Businesslike."

"Was she screwing Mackenzie?"

"I wouldn't know."

"I guess she sort of works for me now. The usurers at the bank put her in charge of the film Mackenzie was working on. They own half of it, but I own the production company. I guess if she's any good she'll be making movies for me in the future. I suppose we'll have a thing or two in common—something to talk about in the dull moments."

I didn't say anything. Catherine was still staring out the window; after a few seconds, she finished off her tea in a gulp and put the cup down on a low coffee table. When she came back her eyes were red. "Why can't anyone find Laurie?"

So we talked about what I had done to find her daughter. It had been tough, I said, without anything tangible to go on. And in a city as big as Los Angeles, it was tough under any circumstances. But now with the LA and Beverly Hills police looking, the television coverage, as well as the fliers I had put out, something was bound to happen. I tried to put a good face on it, tried to sound optimistic. There was nothing else to do now but wait, I added.

"There *is* something," she said. "I'm going to offer a reward. The police are going to announce it at a press conference later today: one hundred thousand dollars. No questions asked. All I want is my daughter back." She paused. "They think it'll turn up someone who's seen her."

I said I thought they were probably right. For that kind of money, she'd have the street people on her side rather than making a show of their indifference. If Laurie was in Hollywood, we should hear something as soon as the word got out. But if she wasn't . . .

"Do you think there's someplace else she might try to run to, someplace special for her?"

Catherine shook her head. "No. I've tried to think, but there's no place. Just her school."

"What about Richard Ravich's?"

She looked over at me, her eyes softening, and smiled. "Laurie told me about her boyfriend just before I went to London. I was so thrilled for her. Every time I called her, she'd start talking about Richard, having lunch with him at school, talking to him about toys and games and TV shows. She'd get so excited, telling me about him, that I would have to ask her to calm down. Once she started rattling, there was no understanding her."

Catherine was thinking about the two of them, Richard and Laurie, a faint smile still on her lips. I said, "Do you think Laurie might
have tried to see him?"

Her eyes blinked as her thoughts shifted again to the present, and
she slowly shook her head. "I think she'd want to but I don't know
how she could. Laurie couldn't go anywhere by herself except to
school. Did you ask Richard's mother?"

"I'm seeing her later this afternoon. How much do you know
about her?"

She seemed surprised at the question. "She's quite nice, I think.
She doesn't teach, of course, but she and Mrs. Stevens have been
very good for Laurie. I'm quite happy with Holstead."

"When I talked to her earlier, she didn't mention anything about
Richard and Laurie. I wonder why?"

"Maybe she didn't think it important. But it is important, isn't
it?" Her expression turned quizzical. "Anything about Laurie could
be important. I can't imagine why she wouldn't mention it." She fell
silent for a second, then said, "How did you find out about Richard
if Mrs. Ravich didn't tell you?"

"I broke into your Beverly Hills house. I found a picture of
Richard in Laurie's room."

She held my gaze. "I guess I should be angry but I'm not. I don't
feel anything; I won't until Laurie's found."

Again she fell silent. I was beginning to feel restless. My tea was
gone and I began to wish I had a drink. I definitely *did* believe in it.
Gingerly, because I didn't want Catherine to turn hostile or suspicious again, I asked, "What time did you get into LA?"

She stared at me. "Three o'clock in the morning. Why?"

"And you called your lawyer at 4:30 but didn't actually see anyone
during that ninety minutes or so?"

"No. I drove by the house like I told you and saw someone's car in
front, so I went out to Malibu. What difference does it make?"

"Did the police question you about this?"

"They took a statement. That was it. What are you getting at?"

"Your husband was killed during that time. You might have to
explain what you were doing."

She looked at me without emotion. "Look, I'm not worried about
having an alibi. I didn't kill Mackenzie and I'm not going to have to

prove it. The only thing I'm worried about is finding my daughter. Then I'm going to take a long vacation with her, take her to Switzerland for a while and relax." She glanced around the house. "And sell Mackenzie's little playground. No wonder he spent so much time out here. I suppose you know all about the camera setup in the guest bedroom."

"I heard something about it."

She came to her feet and let out a deep breath, her face drawn and pale. "Let me show you. You won't believe it."

"No, I really don't think—" Gordon was dead, I thought to myself; why peer into his dirty little secrets now?

But Catherine insisted, as if it were somehow important to her. "I want you to see it: it says something about Mackenzie's arid mentality. And why no one will mourn his death."

Obediently, I followed her down a long hallway—watching her lovely little rump as it struggled against the short robe—to a bedroom that was down three steps. A massive waterbed took up much of the room; there were mirrors on the walls and mirrors on the ceiling. The few furnishings were French and feminine, someone's notion of sensuousness. It reminded me of Mackenzie's Beverly Hills bedroom: garish, childish, and a little sad. Instead of going in she took me around the side.

"This used to be a linen closet. Look—" She yanked open the door to expose a jumble of wires and a video camera on a tripod aimed through a mirror at the bed.

"There's another in the attic, directly over the bed. They're hooked to a switch underneath the bed so all he had to do was drop his arm and presto. . . . What do you think of someone with a setup like this?"

"A man with an ego problem."

"More problems than that. Come over to the video room and I'll show you the results."

She led me back up the steps and around a corner to a smallish room with two love seats in front of a large-screen TV.

"Mackenzie was his middle name, you know. His first name was Robin. Robin Mackenzie Gordon. Here, this is the film I was watching when you got here.

She took a cassette from where it was resting on top of the projection screen and bent to pop it into the VCR, pleasantly ending my speculation about what was under the robe. Straightening, she flipped off the light and came back to where I was standing. "Sit." I did, like a good Rover and she took the other love seat.

"Cock Robin, he liked to call himself for reasons I have yet to fathom. But it was typical of his adolescent humor. The great Cock Robin and his conquests. Now all we need do is find a sparrow, I suppose, and we know who the villain is. Let me fast-forward through this a minute." She took the remote and zapped through to the point she wanted. "Mackenzie's little videos have a surprising political coloration as you'll see. Wait . . . here it is." She rewound a few seconds, then pushed the play button and sagged back in the chair. "Recognize her?"

"Oh, God, yeah!" I said instantly. "She's on that new show about lady lawyers in New Orleans." Recognized her right away, although I'd never seen her stark naked on TV; must be my detective's eagle eye, I decided.

"Watch this. I guess it's why they're always referring to her as 'up and coming.'"

"Ah, yes . . . " I murmured. I would have to start paying more attention to that show.

She hit the fast-forward and raced through the tape to a new spot. "Here's something you don't see everyday."

No indeed. Jesus! After a moment I said, "How do you think she does that?"

"She's double-jointed."

"At least."

We watched for a while, and I was reminded of Howie Wiltz's gypsy bareback riders. Catherine was staring at the screen. "Pay close attention to the subtext in this film. What appears to be sexual in content is really a question of dominance. The message with Mackenzie is always one of control, power."

Subtext?

She went on in her lecture-hall voice as if the spirit of Pauline Kael had suddenly inhabited her body. "He seems to be having a problem here until his resolve stiffens. But poor Mackenzie never understood pacing in his films. You'll notice in a moment he didn't in real life either."

"Oh . . . Well it happens to everyone at times I suppose."

She hit the off button. "You get the idea. Let's go back in the living room."

I stood up, feeling a little uneasy, as if I had suddenly learned more about Mackenzie Gordon than I wanted to know. "I think I'd better be going," I said and looked at my watch. "There's a few things to take care of. . . ." My appointment with Anna Ravich in the Wilshire District mainly. I was going to have to hurry.

"Of course."

She walked me through the house and out to where my car was parked. A chill wind had begun to blow; the storm I had seen out at sea was starting to move in on us. I opened the door and looked at Catherine and was reminded again that I was standing here with a legend, someone I had admired since she had sat on Gregory Peck's lap and read a Christmas list a foot long. I had been seven the first time I'd seen that film, and instantly in love. As she looked at me, her eyes seemed as big and blue as the Pacific stretched out behind her, her skin as soft as a summer cloud. And when she smiled I could see a perfect line of small, even teeth that couldn't ever have known a cavity. You're star-struck, I told myself; you're infatuated like you were twenty-five years ago.

She said, "I suppose the news about Brandon and myself will cause the usual Hollywood tittering: older woman, younger man, and all that. And it's easy for people to disparage Brandon: he's young, he's made mistakes, he has a temper. But that could have described Orson Welles when he was starting out, too. I won't use that overworked word 'genius,' but Brandon's something special. Don't write him off."

As I climbed behind the wheel and shut the door, she smiled at me through the open window, the meager autumn sunlight backlighting the soft lines of her hair, and the sparkling chrome of the window framing her marvelous face.

"You'll call me the moment you hear anything about Laurie?"

"Of course." For a moment I didn't move, the need-to-know vying with the burden of bad manners in my mind as I wrestled over whether or not to ask. But need triumphed, as I knew it would, and the words blurted out.

"Tell me something, Catherine. What's it been like knowing all your life that every man you've met has wanted to hop in the sack with you?"

Her expression didn't change as she held my gaze. "Have they? I never gave it a thought."

# 15

"THIS IS VERY DIFFICULT FOR ME. . . ."

Anna Ravich slowly turned a scotch and soda on the table in front of her and stared into its depths as though the murky liquid would suddenly resolve into words, revealing the phrases it seemed impossible for her to find on her own.

I fiddled with my draft, tilting the glass this way and that and trying not to drink it in a single gulp, since this promised to take some time.

"It's about Laurie," she went on, her accent more pronounced than it had seemed in her office.

"Do you have any idea where she might be?" I prodded.

"No, no. Nothing like that." She stared around the Gold Rush bar as if it were the most alien and exotic place she had ever found herself in. Small and dark to the point of obscurity even at five o'clock, it had probably opened for business the day prohibition was repealed and hadn't been redecorated since. In LA that would qualify it for historic landmark status. There was a bar with a brass rail and a dozen stools where five young men in baseball caps sat with longneck Buds, and a scattering of tiny tables, all but one of them empty, the exception occupied by three well-dressed Chinese businessmen from Hong Kong talking mid-Wilshire real estate.

"I wanted to tell you when you were at the school earlier but . . ." She started fiddling with her hands. I had the sense that if I didn't help her we'd be here all night, and I didn't want to be here all night: I wanted to be looking for Laurie. I smiled weakly across the table and tried to give her a little shove.

"Because Mrs. Stevens was there?"

"Oh, partly that, I suppose, but I could have talked to you alone if I really wanted to. But I was worried about . . . the school."

"It's not your fault if a student disappears," I said, although I didn't really believe that that was what was bothering her and had led to this somewhat furtive and insistent meeting. Somehow, I thought, she was going to work around to Richard—Richard and Laurie. Consolingly, I added, "After all, Laurie disappeared from home, not school."

"No, no," she said quickly: I wasn't getting it and it was beginning to annoy her, as though the fault lay in my comprehension and not her communication. She picked up her drink and finished what was left of it, and I signaled the only waitress for two more.

"Mackenzie—Mr. Gordon—and I had become friends," she blurted out. "Very good friends. . . ."

I looked at her dully, trying not to show my surprise, and thought, Of course! Mackenzie and his sexual frenzy again. I should have known: it was getting to be a common refrain, maybe the only common refrain in this case.

A sudden burst of laughter from the businessmen seemed to shake Anna Ravich from her stupor. She glanced over at them and quickly returned her gaze to me. "We had a . . . a relationship—" and her eyes fell to the tabletop again.

"When did all this begin?" I found myself asking after a moment, as if there were some real significance to the answer.

She blinked and looked past me toward the wall where an ancient dart board hung. "Last year Mackenzie came to the school to talk about Laurie's progress. He was very interested in Holstead, in what we are doing. And very pleased with the improvement in Laurie."

"I didn't get that impression from Mrs. Stevens."

"Yes, well—"

She broke off as the middle-aged waitress arrived and put the drinks down and smiled at us.

Anna Ravich picked up her glass and sipped. "Mackenzie did not go around to the classrooms, but he was very interested in the school as a whole. We often talked about it. At one time he was going to make a major contribution, but then his company started having problems with financing. When he died, he was making plans for a celebrity tennis tournament to raise funds for us. He had been talking to some of his entertainment industry friends. Quite a few of them had promised. Very famous people."

"Do you know that for a fact? Or because he told you?"

Anna Ravich's eyes snapped toward mine; like a wolf, I thought, surprised on the frozen tundra, and for a moment she stared at me. "Mr. Eton," she said, finally, "I am not an idiot. Mr. Gordon was not always a nice man. I know what he wanted from me; I know precisely what he wanted from me. But he could be very understanding, very helpful. He hoped to assist the Holstead School. It was not what you call a 'scam.'"

Back off, in other words. OK, shift things around just a little, make Anna Ravich feel a bit less defensive about her "relationship" with Mackenzie. "When I talked to Gordon, I didn't get the impression that he was very concerned about his daughter's disappearance. It seemed more an inconvenience to him."

"Oh, but he was! He called me almost immediately. He thought I might be able to help find her. And then he came out to the school to question the other children. We already told you that."

"It wasn't Laurie he was worried about. Not primarily. He was concerned about a videotape she took with her."

"Yes, yes, the video. He mentioned it."

"Do you know what's on it?"

"Something from his film, I think. The one he's working on."

I shook my head. "Home movies. Mackenzie and his girlfriends romping in bed."

She looked at me, startled. "What do you mean, Mackenzie and his girlfriends?"

"He never told you about his toy? That's probably a compliment."

"No, what is it? What are you talking about?"

I sat back and studied her, the long thin face, the sharp cheek bones and deep-set eyes. Except for the dusky complexion she looked like a young Garbo, the Garbo of silent films, of *Wild Orchids* and *Flesh and the Devil*. Exotic. Sexy. Dangerous. Around us, ice tinkled in glasses, the businessmen murmured in the dark, and candles in tabletop bowls glowed like votive offerings in a grotto.

"Gordon was a voyeur," I said finally. "He liked to film his sex acts with his partners. He had a camera hidden at his Malibu house that he could activate from bed."

She stared at me, speechless.

"He never told you?"

Her voice was distant, her mind working it out. "No. . . ." Then her eyes darted to mine. "You have seen these films? You are sure they exist?"

"They exist."

She became alarmed. "Do you think I'm in one? Do you think he filmed me?"

It was almost certain, but I said, "Probably not. Or he would have told you. He liked watching his partner's reaction when she found out. My guess is he had too much respect for you to add you to his collection. Most of his partners were young actresses, people he had some power over."

"Most? How many were there?"

"I don't know. A lot."

She fell silent a moment. Someone dropped a coin in the jukebox and an Asian song started playing softly, a soulful female voice, probably singing of love. Or betrayal. Or both. I said, "Why are you telling me about you and Mackenzie now? Why is it suddenly so important that I know?"

She took another drink and then set the glass down and gazed aimlessly around the bar. The fingers of one hand began to toy with the wet cocktail napkin under her glass, pulling tiny pieces away, which she unconsciously collected in a pile. "I'm afraid," she said finally.

"Of what. Your husband?"

She nodded slowly. "That. And for my school. I can't allow anything to happen to Holstead. It's too important to me, we've accomplished too much with the children to let it be destroyed because of a stupid indiscretion on my part. My son is a student there also, you know." She lifted her eyes from the tabletop and stared again into mine. Her face had gone blank: We're getting to it now, I thought—why we're here.

"Richard was born retarded. He is in Laurie's class with Mrs. Stevens—" She pushed the drink aside and crumbled up the remaining napkin in her fist. "When you came to Holstead you mentioned checking through Mackenzie's past, digging around, you said—reading his mail. . . . I was afraid you'd see my name somewhere or hear something—you'd find out." She finished off her drink but I sat silently and waited rather than ordering another.

"I didn't know what to do. I couldn't tell you about Mackenzie and me, but I was terrified that you'd find something and then it would become public. Finally I decided to do nothing. I would wait; maybe nothing would turn up, no name on a scrap of paper, no witnesses."

Her voice suddenly cracked. "Then I saw that girl—"

"At the Bowl?"

She nodded and started crying. "I couldn't believe what someone had done to her. I've never seen anything like that before. I was so *scared*. So scared for Laurie. I don't want her to end up like that. After the policeman took me home I couldn't sleep. I kept seeing that poor little girl's body, the stab marks, the blood; it was so brutal. . . ."

She started rummaging in her purse for a Kleenex, and I called the waitress over and this time ordered two scotch and sodas. The drinks arrived a couple of minutes later along with new cocktail napkins. When the waitress put the drinks down, she scowled at me as if I personified all that was evil about men, then tried a little smile with Anna.

Anna looked at me through her tears. "I'm sorry for how this must look."

I waved it aside.

"I want you to know," she went on, "that Mackenzie and I were not seeing each other when he was killed."

"When did it stop?"

"A month ago. I told him it had to stop. If my husband had found out—"

"I really hate to pry into your private life like this, Mrs. Ravich, but how long did this relationship last?"

She stared at her glass, thinking about it, then looked up at me with a slightly exasperated expression. "Oh, I don't know. Off and on, less than a year. It was all so stupid!"

"And you met at his Malibu house?"

"Mostly. Sometimes in Beverly Hills. He lives over on Atherton, not far from the school."

"Do you think Laurie might have found out about the two of you?"

She looked at me with stricken eyes, horrified by the idea. "Oh, my God! No! I mean, I never thought about it. My God! You don't think that's why she ran away, do you? She saw me and her father?"

"Laurie left because she was being disciplined," I said in a soothing tone. "She was mad at Gordon because he wouldn't let her watch a cartoon. But that doesn't mean she never saw you two together."

Her mind went back in time as she tried to work it out. "I don't think she ever saw us together. I usually went out to Malibu in the afternoon. Laurie would still be in school, sometimes at a friend's house."

"Stephanie Chauk?"

"Yes, Stephanie's. I don't think Laurie was ever at home. Once when I got to his Beverly Hills house there were some movie people, a young man and a woman. The man was Brandon Stiles. I remember being very impressed because he's so well-known. We didn't . . . " She made an annoyed gesture with her hand. "They were busy that day so I drove back to school. That was the last time I actually saw Mackenzie until he came looking for Laurie. I called him later that night and told him we'd have to stop. It was too dangerous. It was just stupid."

She looked at me with an embarrassed little smile which she tried bravely to keep on her face. Did Garbo ever smile? I wondered idly and seemed to recall a few feeble attempts that flitted quickly across the screen, little accidental cracks in the grand façade. Anna Ravich's smile finally faded, but the face left behind was beautiful in a mature and darkly haunting way not usually seen in sun-worshiping, youth-enthralled Hollywood. She was studying me across the table, the candlelight making two little dots dance in her black eyes. At length, I said, "Is it possible your son might have seen the two of you?"

"*Richard?* No . . . "

The alarm in her voice was like a flag semaphoring secrets. She was off guard: Time to make something happen. "Why didn't you tell me about your son and Laurie?"

"*Tell you?* Tell you what?"

"That they had become boy- and girlfriend."

"But that has nothing to do with Laurie's disappearance. Why are you talking about this? Richard is not involved with this."

"Richard is her boyfriend. Maybe he knows where she is. Or maybe she tried to see him when she ran away."

"No, no, that is not possible. Richard and Laurie—they became friends, that is true. But they never saw each other outside of school. Never!"

"How do you know that?"

"I know! I am his mother."

"Perhaps when you were with her father?"

For an instant I thought she might hit me. Then her face drained of anger and her gaze fell to the tabletop. For several seconds she was silent, thinking something out. Then, in an angry whisper, she said, "You do not understand what it is like for these children."

"I'm sure I don't," I agreed softly. I sat back in my chair. "Their lives must be very difficult."

Her eyes lifted to mine and a thin smile came and went on her gaunt face. "Not always difficult." Suddenly, it seemed, she wanted me to understand, and life came back to her expression. "Sometimes they are quite happy. When they are working, for instance. We have had very good luck placing our graduating students in jobs in restaurants. They do quite well, cleaning tables and washing dishes. It makes them feel wanted.

"But even more important to them is when they have a boyfriend, or girlfriend. It is maybe the happiest time of their lives. For so many years they've seen other people their age with lovers; they've seen their parents, and, of course, they see it endlessly on television, lovers—men and women, boys and girls. And all this time it seems to accentuate their own 'specialness'; their sense of being 'different.' But when Laurie had a boyfriend and Richard had a girlfriend—" she smiled warmly—"now, at last, they are like everyone else. Laurie especially was transformed. She was so *in love*. And Richard, too. It was very nice. But sometimes it is very sad for me."

"Sad?"

"Because they will never be able to marry. They will never be able to cope on their own. They will be little children forever, in need of care."

For a moment neither of us said anything, then I tried the same question again. "Do you think Laurie could have contacted Richard when she ran away?"

Anna Ravich shook her head, sighed, but changed her story also. "I did bring Laurie to our house two times after school. But just for a half-hour or so. Then I drove her home. But she would never be able to find us. We live in Benedict Canyon. It is very far, very complicated."

"But surely you asked Richard if he had any idea where she might be."

Her jaw tightened. "Of course I asked him! But he knows nothing. He has been very upset since she left. Every day he asks me when she is coming back. What can I tell him? Soon, I say: Laurie will be back soon."

"Did Gordon know about Laurie and Richard?"

"He would not have had any interest, I'm sorry to say."

Her frown gave me a little opening and I wiggled in. "I know this is none of my business, but how did you and Gordon happen to take up together in the first place? He doesn't seem like your type, if you'll pardon me for saying so."

She ducked her head toward the table, then looked up at me without emotion. Or perhaps the emotion was one of dazed wonderment. "It is something of a mystery even to me. I don't know. I have never done such a thing, not since Nicholas and I were married. That was eight years ago. Nicholas is my second husband. My first husband was a—" She searched for a word, found it, and dismissed him with a contemptuous toss of her head: "An animal, a filthy animal. He was without morals, without intelligence, and without spirituality. We were married when I was but seventeen and I did not know better. I could hardly speak English. Very soon I became pregnant with Richard. He left me as soon as he found out. Later I met Nicky and . . ." She paused and glanced around before continuing. "How did I take up with Mackenzie? I don't know. It just happened. He came to school, we talked of Laurie, he said it's getting late, would I like a drink at the Beverly Wilshire, and I said yes. That's how these things happen, I guess. I don't know. He was not a handsome man. But he was fun, and funny sometimes, and nice sometimes, but not always. And he liked me, maybe, and that made me feel good.

"And you," she added abruptly, smiling coyly across the little table: "How about your secrets? You have learned all about poor Anna. How did you end up as a private detective, meeting strange women in even stranger bars?"

The question surprised me but I went along with it. "Well . . . it's not much of a story," I said after a moment, relaxing back in my chair. "My family—aunts, uncles, cousins, parents—were all on the periphery of the movie business: wardrobe, electricians, bit players, and so on. Some of them go back three generations in the industry. But my mother wanted me to go to college, so I did, and majored in English lit. But it didn't work out. The first year I had trouble with Chaucer, the second I was baffled by Joyce. I saw in the college catalog that the next year I was going to have to take something called Deconstructionism—"

"What's that?"

"No one knows. So I bailed out. I was in the LAPD for a few years, then I opened my own office. I don't take off-the-street stuff, just jobs through the studios."

"You are single?"

"A widower. With a thirteen-year-old daughter who's as obscure to me as James Joyce."

The bar door burst open in an unwelcome flash of sunlight and smog, and at least ten Korean businessmen bustled in and noisily moved some tables together so they could sit as a group.

"You have a girlfriend?"

"They come and they go," I said, thinking with some ambivalence of Judy Chen.

"No one special?"

"Well, maybe. There are some areas of disagreement between us."

"Po-ta-to, po-tah-to?"

"More or less. Little things mostly, but they irritate."

Another burst of sunlight and another group of four businessmen came in. Japanese, I thought, as they ignored the others and commandeered a table in the rear. The bar was beginning to arrange itself in an analogue of worldwide trading blocks. We needed some OPEC countries, though; they could blockade the bar, take hostages, and jack up the price of bourbon.

Anna Ravich darted a surreptitious glance at her watch when she thought I wasn't looking. But she made no attempt to leave. There was evidently something else besides her brief encounter with Mackenzie Gordon that she had wanted to see me about. Her little foray into Vic's romantic history had likely been meant to soften me for the main event by forging a link of shared experiences: my love life, your love life, and we're all brothers under the skin.

When our eyes met suddenly, I could see her working on her courage, trying to remember the speech she had probably prepared for this moment. I decided to offer her a transition and gather some needed information at the same time. "How did Gordon act when you broke it off with him? Was he upset with you?"

From the look on her face I could tell that it hadn't been a transition at all but the main event. Her gaze dropped to the table again, and after a false start she said, "He did not ask me to change my mind." She made an angry, dismissive gesture with her hand and tears began to swim at the edges of her eyes. "He was very much *not* upset. But he wanted me to do something for him. Something I did not want to do."

I waited as the bar sounds mingled around us.

"Nicholas—my husband—is an investment banker at Payne-Stanley in Beverly Hills. He deals in mergers and acquisitions, leveraged buyouts—mostly things I don't understand. They also have a venture capital side; they invest other people's money in small businesses—usually new firms, high tech firms, mostly."

She shook her head and took a deep breath. "I need another drink, but if I do, I'll never be able to drive home. My God, what have I gotten myself into?"

The fun and games of the "entertainment" industry is what you've gotten yourself into, just like a thousand other innocents, I thought with some asperity, but kept my silence.

She looked up at me and a half-hearted smile appeared suddenly, tiny wrinkles showing attractively at the edges of her mouth. "Bear with me, please. I'm getting there."

She took a deep breath again and pushed on. "Mackenzie wanted me to talk to Nicholas about helping to finance his production company. He wanted Nicholas to put up a lot of money. Not his own, of course, but through the firm. Investment money."

"How much is a lot?"

"Twenty million. Or more."

"What did he expect you to do?"

"I was to 'convince' Nicholas."

"Maybe I'm not following this. Why didn't he approach Payne-Stanley on his own? He could have done this up front without his relationship to you becoming known."

"Because he knew he'd be turned down. He had been all over town. Everyone was afraid of him. They thought his films didn't do well enough to warrant taking a chance. And the financing of films is a gamble anyway—not an investment. So I was supposed to convince Nicholas for him."

"What did you say?"

"I told him I couldn't possibly do that! I don't interfere with Nicholas's work and he doesn't bother me about the school. My God, the school needed money more than his movie company did. He was married to Catherine Wilbourne. All he had to do was ask *her* for money. But he wouldn't do it."

"That's when he got nasty." She paused a moment. "He told me he'd go to Nicholas if I didn't help him. He'd tell him about our relationship . . . "

"How would that help Gordon? He didn't expect your husband to invest with him after that, did he?"

"Of course not. It wouldn't help him at all. He would do it out of spite, out of hatred, because I would not help. He would do it to hurt me." She sat back in her chair and gave me a glassy-eyed stare. "That is the kind of man he was—who would hurt if he didn't get his way."

"What did you do?"

"What *could* I do? I talked to Nicholas. I told him about this parent who had a film company and who had a sure hit on his hands. He said he'd have his people look into it.

"What else could I have done? I didn't want to lose Nicholas. And if it had gotten out about Mackenzie and myself, the school would have been hurt. Our parents just wouldn't stand for scandal. And there's the state licensing board to think about: We can't operate without a license. So I did what I had to do."

"Did Nicholas look into it?"

She hung her head. "Yes."

"And?"

"He said putting money into a Mackenzie Gordon film was like going to Las Vegas: Some people come out very much ahead but most lose everything. He wouldn't commit his clients to such a deal."

"Did you tell that to Gordon?"

She was silent a moment. "No. I didn't have a chance. He died."

"Lucky for you," I said and immediately regretted it and added, "Sorry."

"No, no. It's all right. It *was* lucky for me."

The five guys sitting at the bar plunked down some change and walked out into the sunlight, tilting the balance of trade toward Asia. Anna Ravich looked at her watch again and then glanced around the dark room. "I don't much go to bars. Normally I don't much drink. Just a little wine at dinner."

"What time does your husband get home?"

"Seven, seven-thirty. We have a housekeeper who watches Richard."

"You have some time," I said and signaled the waitress. Shift-change must have already come and gone because the waitress that appeared was a bubbly, petite black woman. I ordered two coffees and they came quickly.

"How do you think your husband went about checking up on Gordon?"

"Oh, the usual ways, I imagine. It wouldn't be at all unusual for him; he does this all the time. They call banks, talk to people who have invested in the past, look at their product, look at their expenses."

"Would he have talked to Gordon?"

She looked startled. "I don't know. Usually he would interview the president of a firm before investing, but I don't know. He didn't mention it to me. Maybe he didn't need to."

And maybe he did, I thought, and asked, "What are the chances he found out about you and Gordon?"

Her eyes flickered. "None! Nicholas did not know. I'm sure of it."

I gave a silent sigh again at the self-delusional certainty that seemed to envelop everyone I met: Brandon was positive Mackenzie Gordon didn't know about Catherine and himself; Kerry insisted Catherine didn't know about her and Mackenzie; and Anna Ravich was convinced her husband didn't know about Gordon. The mind reels.

"What would Nicholas have done if he did find out," I asked and added, "Hypothetically . . . "

"What would he have done?" She repeated the question as if it perplexed her. "I don't know. I don't know what he would have done."

"Is he the violent type? Does he throw things and yell and scream?"

"Certainly not. Nicholas is very refined, very cultured."

"Hitler and Mussolini listened to opera. Stalin liked Tolstoy. Lizzie Borden probably read poetry the day she chopped up her parents."

"But Nicholas would never do anything violent." Her voice soared; she was beginning to lose control again.

I gave her another shove, a little harder this time. "You knew about Mackenzie's nasty little films all along. You were out at Malibu and he filmed the two of you and then he told you about it. Or showed it to you."

Her voice rose uncontrollably; she thought we had gone beyond the question of the films and she wasn't ready to face it again. "No! Of course not."

"Gordon's playmates—you probably saw them all: young and old, black and white, the whole stable—"

"No—"

"Gordon *always* showed them to his girlfriends. That was part of the fun. He liked to watch their reaction. How did you react?"

She sat back suddenly in her chair and looked at me with a mixture of defiance and shame. "I hit him!" she snapped in heavily accented English.

"But you didn't stop seeing him."

"You wouldn't understand."

"He showed you the film of yourself? And others?"

"Some others. A few. Some actresses."

"So your little show of indignation a few minutes ago when I told you about the films was—"

"Exactly that. A show!"

"That was what Gordon threatened you with, wasn't it? Those films. He wouldn't just show them to your husband—he probably told you he'd send pictures to the parents of your students. Anonymously, of course. Pictures without him but where Mrs. Anna Ravich, grand mistress of the Holstead Special Day School, would be clearly visible. What would all the mommies and daddies say?"

Her eyes glittered with hatred. "He would have, too. So, of course, I talked to Nicholas, encouraged him to help Mackenzie with his stupid little movie."

"And Nicholas never found out why?"

"Never! I am certain of that."

*Maybe*, I thought. But what would the betrayed husband have done if he *had* found out? Strike out at his wandering wife? Or at the man who was preparing to ruin her? Maybe I should visit Nicholas Ravich, see what sort of man this refined and cultured captain of finance was.

Anna Ravich suddenly leaned across the table, grasping my hand. "I want to hire you."

"I have a client," I lied.

"This will not conflict. I want you to keep my name out of the police investigations. I don't want them to find out about my meetings with Mackenzie. And I want that tape destroyed—the one with me on it. I want it burned."

"You don't have to worry about me or the police dragging you into anything," I said. "As far as the tape goes, you're probably on the one Laurie took."

"Laurie?"

"It wasn't a cartoon. It was a sex tape. Mackenzie probably didn't tell you because he wanted you to believe he still had it. He sure didn't want you to get hold of it. For all we know, it could be in a trash can or the bottom of the lake at MacArthur Park." No sense telling her about Howie Wiltz, I thought; I'd wait and see what he planned for it.

"You mean Mackenzie *didn't* have it?" Her voice bordered on hysteria.

"It doesn't make any difference now, does it?"

She shook her head slowly, as if a great weight were dangling from it. "No . . . no, it doesn't. Unless it turns up."

"If it does," I said, "it'll never be made public. At least, not your part. Believe me." Even Wiltz wouldn't want photos of Mackenzie Gordon with a schoolteacher no one had ever heard of, I thought.

Anna Ravich was not totally convinced. "If you find it, the film, I want it. I will buy it, I will pay you for it."

"If I find it, I'll destroy it."

She looked at me, half-gratified, half still concerned that the video would end up in the wrong hands. But she had done what she could; now she could only wait. I said, "When you said you knew precisely what Mackenzie wanted from you, it wasn't sex, was it?"

She slumped back in her chair; her eyes darkened and her body went slack. "Money. Investments."

"Unless you come to the attention of the police they won't be bothering you. But if they run across your name they might start investigating."

She looked at me hopelessly. She had been thinking the same thing for days.

I said, "They're going to want to know where you were when Mackenzie died."

Her eyes went wide. "Where I was? But I didn't kill him. I was in bed."

Three-thirty in the morning, I thought. Everyone involved in this case was in bed. Someone's.

"And your husband?"

Her face drained of color and her mouth dropped open. "Nicholas was on business in San Francisco. You can't possibly think—"

"Of course not." I stood up and dropped some bills on the table. "It's getting late. You're going to have to get home."

We walked out onto Wilshire together, leaving the bar to the Pacific Rim. Another analogue of modern life, I thought.

# 16

AT DINNER I TOLD TRACY I HAD MET CATHERINE WILBOURNE. SHE was impressed. Hell, I was still impressed.

"What was she like?" Her eyes grew large and she leaned excitedly over her dinner of microwaved enchiladas, frijoles, and rice.

"Complex," I said. "It wasn't always easy to read the subtext."

She sank back in her chair. "I have the same trouble with Jason."

Rudy arrived as I was putting away the dishes; his own reaction to Catherine was somewhat more basic. "Yum yum."

I brought him a Miller's from the fridge and plopped down on the couch, listening to it sigh like a final death gasp as my body hit the cushions. "I tried to return your call before going out to Malibu, but you were out."

"They named another building after the mayor. I had to help with crowd control." He twisted the top off the bottle and hooked it into a waste basket, where it rattled like a BB in a bucket. "I wanted to let you know that Catherine had finally surfaced," he said. "But you knew that anyway, didn't you, you little rascal?" Tiny droplets of foam hung precariously from his lavish black mustache as he plunked the bottle down, already three-quarters empty.

"Nothing on Laurie yet?"

He shook his head and stretched out his legs, resting his feet on this week's *Sports Illustrated* on the coffee table. "*Nada.* I talked to a captain in Missing Persons; he told me they've turned up the heat as far as they can. They're getting worried now. If she was out there she should have turned up. We all know that. They're hoping the reward will help."

"They let Catherine think Laurie will turn up in a matter of hours once the word gets out."

He gave me a look. "That's distraught-mother talk—get her out of everyone's hair. The department hasn't got diddly, Vic. All they can do is wait. And wait."

I thought about my appointment with Howie Wiltz later tonight. It was time to put some pressure on him: whoever he bought that film from was the key to Laurie's whereabouts. Assuming he knew who he bought the film from: with porno publishers, business can be transacted at midnight with cash in envelopes.

Rudy swilled the remainder of his beer, then put the bottle down carefully on the coffee table. Too carefully, I thought. His face was studiously calm as he relaxed back and clasped his hands behind his head. But he wasn't looking at me.

Uh oh.

Wait him out, I thought.

Calmly, he said, "So Catherine Wilbourne has her own production company? Think you'll be going out there again?"

Not after my parting question to her, I thought. But I knew instantly what he was getting at and sighed inwardly. How was I going to get out of this?

"She doesn't read scripts, Rudy. She's an actress."

He waved a large hand in the air, brushing my objection aside as a meaningless technicality, and sat up straight, putting his feet on the floor. Getting down to business now. "Give me her address, then. I'll drive out and drop it on her doorstep; won't even bother her. Raquel Welch bought a script that way, you know, that roller derby thing. Catherine'll love it, Vic, really. It was *made* for her. Christ, I had her in mind the minute I started working on it."

"I thought it was a cop story, a homicide dick, a Rudy Cruz sort of guy."

He gave me an annoyed frown and blinked rapidly. "Look, Vic, I can always change the *sex* of the star. It doesn't *have* to be a man!"

Catherine Wilbourne as a cop. Maybe. . . .

"All right, Rudy," I sighed, giving in to the inevitable. "But be careful of the subtext."

He looked stung and brushed nervously at his mustache. "I always am!"

Rudy went home shortly after seven. I had almost another two hours until my appointment with Wiltz. Not a lot of time, but I had an urge to check out Gordon's house again. It wasn't likely that Laurie would be there, but it was worth another look. Once again I began to sense that she was not a runaway after all: Whoever sold that video to Wiltz almost certainly had gotten it from Laurie. Or had he? Christ, I hadn't thought about that before: why couldn't whoever it was have gotten the tape the same way we all supposed Laurie had—by picking it up from Gordon's desk. A videotape isn't so big you couldn't secret it somehow while in the house—stick it in your pants or in a purse. But who would have had access? Kerry? Brandon? Catherine? Or any of dozens of film company people who might have been at Gordon's house for one reason or another. Again I thought Wiltz was the key, since only he presumably knew who he bought the film from.

Leaving Tracy to her homework, I drove west toward Beverly Hills. The storm I had noticed earlier out at sea had picked up in intensity and was bending thirty-foot palms and twisting branches from smaller trees as I headed up the now-familiar canyon road. This early in the evening there was a steady stream of traffic, most of it flowing toward me down the hill, heading like moths in the direction of the city lights stretched out on the plain below. It began to rain and I flicked on the wipers. Crummy goddamn night . . . Five minutes later I was at Gordon's, and I swung a sharp left onto the driveway, then coasted through the gate and up to the large house, darkened now and without a sign of life. Catherine must still be in Malibu. I switched off the engine and stepped out into the chill and the rain and darkness, taking my large five-cell flashlight. For a long moment I stood and gazed around, shivering in my jacket as the wind whipped the rain in my face, stinging my eyes and cheeks. It was as dead as an abandoned movie set, no sign of life anywhere, no sign that there had been life recently. I flicked on the light and swung the beam in a long slow arc through the grounds, trying to orient myself. The house was on a slight, grassy ridge that declined ten feet or so to the pool area. Trees and underbrush ringed the property on all sides; I might as well start there and work my way back to the car.

As the rain pelted down, I tramped out to the rear of the property where clumps of pines and oleanders created a forestlike barrier between Gordon's property and his neighbors behind. The grass was long and the underbrush thick, and it was obvious that a child—or an adult for that matter—could have hidden here for some time without observation. There was no point to subtlety, so I plunged into the middle of it, shining my light into the bushes and up in the trees. Twenty feet back, I found a twelve foot chain link fence and a similar jungle on the other side. Obviously the property line, and probably too much for Laurie to climb.

Moving slowly, I made a complete circuit of the property, keeping the light dancing into bushes and trees, jumping around when the storm sent branches crashing to the ground. But no Laurie, and no sign she had been here. By the time I reached the front again, I was sopping wet and my shoes were caked with mud.

The house was easier. I started in the front, rattling doors and pointing my light through windows. Nothing.

Walking out to the pool area, I stood on the concrete deck as the wind made whitecaps skip across the water. I flicked off the light and listened in the darkness. Nothing but the wind, drowning out even the noise of cars on the street. After a moment I called Laurie's name, shouting above the storm. Then again and again, but there was no response.

Above me a cloud moved in front of the moon, casting a shadow on the darkness and sending a little shudder of uneasiness through my body, like a fingernail scraped along the spine. Snapping the light back on, I tried the pool house. The metal door opened with a groan, and I flipped on a weak overhead light that barely illuminated a jumble of pool equipment and chemicals and lawn furniture; everything seemed layered with grime, and there was no sign of anyone having been in here since summer. I flicked off the light and shut the door.

A flagstone path led around to the five-car garage. The large, metal overhead doors were locked. I glanced through the old-fashioned, small-paned windows: two nondescript autos squatted in the darkness; some lawn equipment, a work bench, gardening tools. No place for anyone to hide except inside the cars, but also no way to get in and then relock the garage doors. I walked up the outside stairway to the apartment on top and peered through the uncurtained window as rain water trickled down the collar of my shirt. It didn't appear as if anyone had lived there for years. The door was locked.

Laurie wasn't here.

Back in my car I flipped on the interior light and looked at my watch. Ten minutes after eight. Taking a map out of the glove compartment I checked the bus route Laurie followed every day: down Doheny to within half a block of Chauk's. Maybe I'd try that, then check out the small park two blocks away before going on to Howie Wiltz's office in Hollywood. Or if I had time, hurry home and change into something dry.

I started the car and headed down the hill, driving slowly and watching the sidewalks, peering into the darkness between houses and behind parked cars. Nothing appeared to be out of the ordinary, certainly no kids visible anywhere, no adults for that matter except a slightly mad-looking man with a plaid umbrella walking his Irish setter in the rain. When I got down to Chester, I turned south and drifted slowly up to Chauk's house; the Toyota was gone, but I drove into the driveway and tried the doorbell anyway. No answer. I yanked open the car door and was about to slip behind the wheel again when a terrifying noise screeched from somewhere above me, and a cat leapt from a tall wooden fence, landing at my feet with a plop and a scattering of mud. I whirled around instinctively, my heart pounding, and gave an embarrassed little laugh when I saw what it was. Then I heard another short laugh and I froze.

I waited for a long moment, then said, "*Laurie?*"

I was guessing. It was completely still except for the rain drumming down, and the wind swirling around me and rustling bushes and trees. Maybe I imagined it. Then I heard it again on the other side of the fence, and my heart sped up a notch. I had to force myself not to run toward the sound. Taking a deep breath, I slowly turned toward the gate I had seen Chauk's daughter disappear through chasing this same cat just two days ago. Raising my voice only slightly, I said, "Laurie? I'm a friend. Your mother sent me. She wants me to bring you to her."

"Mommy?" The voice sounded small and confused, then said, "Ginger!" in a scolding tone, and the cat stopped momentarily and glanced back at the sound.

The fence was made of wooden grape stakes six feet tall. I could see the thin white fingers of one hand grasping the top of it as she steadied herself on the other side and peered through the irregular slats.

The cat had brushed up against me. I reached down carefully and picked it up, shielding it from the rain with my arm. "Do you want Ginger, Laurie?"

She made no response, but I could hear her moving behind the fence as the wind whipped leaves and pine needles and the pages of a newspaper around us.

"Laurie, your mother wants me to bring you to her. Do you want to see your mother?"

This time the gate tentatively opened with a squeak, and she stood there in bare feet, wearing purple jeans and a Lakers T-shirt. She was sopping wet and shivering with cold.

"Laurie, I'm a friend of your mother's. I'm your friend, too. Do you want to see your mother?"

She put her fists on her hips and stared at me defiantly as the rain pelted down on us. "Mommy's away!"

"Mommy's home, Laurie. She wants to see you. Do you want to see Mommy?"

She squinted, blinking her eyes several times and frowning. Then, as if the idea had just registered, said, "I don't know you. You're a stranger!"

"I'm a friend, Laurie. And I have a little girl your age. Her name is Tracy."

"Tracy's at my school," she said angrily, as if she had caught me out in a lie.

"We'll go see Mommy," I said, trying to make up her mind for her. I patted the cat on its head. "We'll take Ginger too, if you want." I came slowly toward her. "Do you want to take Ginger to Mommy?"

She looked at me with grave seriousness and shook her head. "Ginger lives with Stephanie."

I put the cat gently at her feet and she leaned down just inches from its face and hissed loudly, "Shoo!" The cat twisted suddenly around and escaped through a hedge. Laurie straightened up and began to giggle.

"We'll go see Mommy," I said again. "She's in Malibu. Do you know where Malibu is?"

"Of course, silly. Malibu's the ocean." Her gaze bounced randomly around the yard before suddenly coming back to me. "Mommy's in England!"

"Mommy came home just to see you, Laurie. You had her very worried because she didn't know where you were. Were you living here with Mr. Chauk?"

"Stephanie, silly! Look!"

She pulled my hand, leading me through the gate to the rear of the house. The yard was bare except for two thirty-year-old citrus trees and an aging, prefabricated sheet-metal tool shack about eight feet by six feet, huddled indifferently against the rear fence.

"Is that were you stayed?" I asked disbelievingly. "In that little house?" It must have been freezing in there, I thought as I stared at it.

"Of course!" She giggled and led me over to the door and pulled it open with excitement. "Barbie's house!"

Barbie's house. A little-used, uninsulated shed with a lawn mower and garden tools just visible in the darkness. It had the smell of earth and moisture and rotting grass.

I put my hands on Laurie's shoulders and looked into her face. Kerry had been right: she was at that age where she wasn't a little girl anymore. At least five feet tall, there was a striking, almost age-less movie-star quality to her smooth, even features, a beauty that promised someday to transcend the ordinary. I recalled what others had said about her: spiritual, ethereal, gorgeous. And I thought: of course, Catherine Wilbourne's little girl. I could see it in her eyes and cheekbones and perfect lips. Catherine as a girl; a bouncy, cheerful, and incredibly beautiful child—who would probably always have the mind of a five-year-old.

I saw some dolls and half a loaf of white bread on the bare dirt floor. "Who gave you the bread, Laurie?"

"Steph, silly! Steph's bread."

"Did Mr. Chauk know you were here? Did Steph's father know?"

She put her fists on her hips again and began to tap one foot impatiently on the ground. "Of course not! I ran away. I'm hiding." Then she added confidentially, "Daddy can't see me."

The wind was whipping frigid eddys around us and pelting us with rain. "Let's go see Mommy, Laurie. We'll drive out to Malibu."

Leading her by the hand, we went out to my car. Laurie stopped as I opened the passenger door and screamed, "Goodbye Ginger," at the top of her voice.

I found a towel in the trunk and made her dry off as well as she could. Then we headed toward Sunset. At the first gas station, I stopped and called Catherine at Malibu. Her answering machine came on, anonymously announced the number I had reached and said I could leave a message if I wanted to. I did, telling her to call me at home immediately.

Now what? Take Laurie to the police? I didn't particularly want to abandon her to Juvie without her mother present. After Juvie and Missing Persons, Homicide would get involved. I didn't think Laurie would handle that very well by herself; none of these departments were noted for their compassion or tact.

I had twenty minutes before my meeting with Wiltz. I was going to be late as it was, but I didn't want to miss him altogether. I decided to take her to my apartment and leave her with Tracy until Catherine could pick her up.

On the way, we stopped at a video store, and I took Laurie inside and let her pick three cartoon videos. When we got to my apartment Tracy was gone—at the library, I supposed. I asked Laurie if she knew how to work the VCR, and she looked at me as if I were mad. "Everyone knows how to do that."

"I'm going to let you watch these cartoons, then. My daughter Tracy will be home in just a few minutes and you can talk with her. You'll like her. She's about your age."

Her eyes narrowed. "Tracy's at school!"

"This is a different Tracy, Laurie. She lives here. You'll like her. I have to leave for a while. When I get back we'll go get your mom."

But by this time Laurie was ensconced on the couch, watching Elmer Fudd waving a shotgun at Bugs Bunny. I brought her some slippers and a robe from Tracy's room and gave her a Coke and a bag of chips. "You'll stay here now, won't you? Tracy'll be here soon."

She picked up a video cassette and gave me a heartbreaking smile. "Road Runner next!"

I scribbled a quick note to Tracy, telling her to keep an eye on Laurie until I got back. I didn't feel happy about leaving her alone, but it wasn't going to be for long—probably a half-hour or so—until Tracy got home. Still, I'd have felt better if someone was with her. The only person I knew in the building well enough to trust was Mrs. Macdonald, an eightyish widow who lived next door. Maybe it would be best if she came over.

After telling Laurie good-bye, I carefully shut the door behind me and stepped over to Mrs. Macdonald's and rang the bell.

"Won't do any good," a raspy female voice announced from behind me.

It was a heavyset woman about sixty, ambling down the hall with a bag of groceries. "Won't do any good," she repeated when she got even with me. Her eyes bored into mine as if she were trying to gauge why I was ringing the bell. She must have decided I could be trusted with her confidences. "Fell and broke her hip yesterday," she continued in a schoolmarmish voice. "They took her to the hospital. Saw it myself, ambulance pulling up outside with its sirens blaring like kingdom come during 'Wheel of Fortune.' Think she'd know better, trying to change a light bulb at her age. Imagine: up on a chair and reaching like that. Serves her right, not that I'd wish bad to come to anybody, specially Clara, sweet soul that she is."

She started moving down the hall to her own apartment. "You can see her at Hollywood Pres if you want to. Suppose they got her in a cast now. She sure as blazes won't be back here for a while."

Well, that was that. I went back to my apartment, slipped the key silently in the dead bolt from outside and locked the door. I stood for a moment and listened but heard nothing except the cartoon. Laurie had turned up the volume as soon as I had left.

I hurried out to the rear lot and retrieved the Buick for my trip to Wiltz's. I had forgotten my jacket and shivered uncomfortably until the heater finally took hold about a mile down Vine. The rain had eased into a fine light mist, cold and clear and sharp as glass as it pressed against the windshield. By the time I got to Santa Monica Boulevard, this part of the city was just coming alive for the evening; prostitutes—mostly male—grouped on every corner, bending and speaking into car windows, reciting their prices, and displaying their charms as customers blandly sized them up. I drove up and down for ten minutes looking for a parking spot before leaving my car in a lot three blocks west of Wiltz's office; a kid in thick, round glasses accepted my keys with a blank look on his face, then jammed my car in behind a BMW, missing its rear bumper by a paper-thin margin and grinning at me as he strolled back to his little unheated shack. As soon as he got inside, he bumped up the sound on his radio so I could enjoy it too.

But it wasn't just him, I realized, as I headed down the street: music seemed to engulf me, as if everyone out here were afraid of being left alone with their thoughts. A block from Wiltz's, half a dozen teenagers with a giant portable were joking with three hookers freezing in miniskirts; the kids weren't buying, though, and they glared at me as the hookers struck a pose and smiled and asked if I wanted a date as I walked by, everyone making me feel very old and very alien. One of the kids said, "He couldn't afford you no-how, Tanya," and the whole group howled with laughter.

The bookstore on the ground floor of Wiltz's building was as busy as an IRS office at tax time, men in raincoats entering and leaving with the same furtive glances they probably gave tax auditors, and clutching brown paper bags of literary and cultural materials destined for future close reading. I checked my watch as I mounted the outside stairway to *Hollywood X-T-C*. Almost ten o'clock; I was later than I had expected, but I could see lights inside; Wiltz had waited.

The door to the outer office was unlocked, but the room was empty, only a night-light burning on his secretary's desk. There was a band of yellow light stretched under the door to Wiltz's office and I could hear voices inside. Not wanting to burst in, I called his name. No response. I walked over to the door and rapped on it. Nothing. So I opened it. The room was lit up and exactly as I had last seen it, paper and trash scattered everywhere with a sort of to-hell-with-it-all happy abandon. But no Howie Wiltz. No anyone, just a television tuned to a local newscast.

My spine began to tingle, a primitive warning system left over from when our cavemen ancestors huddled around fires to keep the terrors of night at bay. Something was very wrong. I called Wiltz's name once more, then walked over and flipped off the television. On a hunch, I laid a hand on top of the VCR above the TV. It was warm; maybe Howie had been entertaining himself with home movies again.

His desk was littered with photos and page mock-ups and copies of other mens' magazines. Sex seemed to hang in the air in here like music did outside. Did Howie and his minions go through the day in a state of constant priapic excitement, I wondered, or had it all lost its meaning to them and become like numbers to an accountant? All these questions again. Maybe I'd ask him. Maybe I'd have Catherine ask him.

The top drawer of the desk where I had last seen him put Gordon's video was locked. I looked around for something I could use to manipulate the lock and found a letter opener shaped like a medieval sword. It was probably the only thing in here without obvious sexual symbolism. Then again . . . I inserted it in the narrow opening and recalled the old Freudian joke: sometimes a cucumber is only a cucumber. I moved it around a bit, but it was too thick. I needed something thinner and more flexible. None of the other desks turned up what I was looking for, so I tried what was obviously a closet; as I pulled the door open, Howie Wiltz tumbled out, just missing me and landing on his face at my feet. My heart thumping, I nudged his body with the toe of my shoe. Still pliable, no rigor; I reached down and felt his cheek; probably not dead fifteen minutes.

With effort, I rolled him over with my foot. One clear wound in the middle of his forehead like a Hindu caste mark. And a look on his face as if he had always expected it to end exactly like this.

No reason for finesse now. I grabbed a steel ruler from a tabletop and went back to Wiltz's desk and pried the drawer open. Inside, there were check stubs and more papers and photos but no video cassette. Knowing it was probably useless, I patted Wiltz down, but the tape was not on him either.

Time to go, I told myself; this wasn't the sort of thing I wanted to have to explain to Captain Reddig and Don't-Call-Me-Geraldo. Using a piece of paper to prevent fingerprints, I picked up the phone and punched out the number for the Beverly Hills police. When a woman's voice came on the line I gave her the address and told her she'd better write it down because there was a very famous person very dead there. When she asked me automatically for my name I hung up. This wasn't within the jurisdiction of the Beverly Hills PD, so they'd have to call Los Angeles, all of which would give me time to be miles away when they showed up. On the way out I locked the door behind me and wondered, as I walked to my car, how many people knew Wiltz had that tape. And how many of those would kill to get it.

# 17

I WAS SPEEDING ALONG VINE A MILE FROM HOME BEFORE I MADE THE
connection. And by then it was too late. I had spent so much time
looking for Laurie that I had been blinded by my luck at finding her.
But finding her had been only the beginning, I now realized, not the
end. Laurie had unwittingly become the key to two murders, the
only person who tied everyone together in a web of relationships
that only now became clear. And when that pattern, like the slowly
turning pieces of an old-fashioned kaleidoscope, suddenly resolved
into clarity, it was obvious there was only one person with both the
motive and the opportunity to want Gordon and Wiltz, and now
Laurie, dead.

I double-parked on Rossmore and raced up the stairs to my apartment. Tracy was cooking something in the microwave.

"Where's Laurie?"

"Laurie?"

"Didn't you see my note? When did you get here?" I was almost
screaming.

She looked at the clock and shrugged. "Ten minutes ago. Why
are you—"

"Laurie wasn't here?"

"No. What's going on?"

I rushed into the living room. The television was flickering, a
played-out cassette in the VCR.

"Call Hollywood PD. Tell them Laurie Gordon was kidnapped from here tonight. She's with Gregory Chauk in a white Toyota. I'm going out there now but it's probably too late."

"But why—"

"Just do it!" I shouted at her. "And lock the door and don't let anyone in. Anyone!"

I grabbed my jacket, slamming the door behind me, and raced down to the car.

Tracy's hunch the first night that Laurie might be at Chauk's was probably correct. Not in the house but in the backyard, where Chauk must have discovered her and the video that he instantly recognized as the gold mine it proved to be. The notion of selling it to someone like Howie Wiltz must have hit him immediately: to Chauk it was like turning over a rock and finding an unexpected cache of money; to Wiltz, though, it held a more primitive but equally irresistible appeal—as a way to get back at Mackenzie Gordon and make a few bucks at the same time. So Chauk sold it to Wiltz for sixty thousand dollars. But why did Gordon take a hundred thousand out of the bank? Wiltz had bigger plans for it. Much bigger. And why were Gordon and Wiltz killed?

I raced along Sunset to Doheny, then to Chester, cutting my speed and cruising slowly past the darkened house and yard. No car. But if he wasn't here . . .

What the hell was Chauk up to? He snatched the girl when he realized I had her. He could have taken whatever money he'd gotten out of this and run instead. With a murder rap or two hanging over him that would have been the logical thing to do at this point. But he didn't. Which meant he felt he could beat it. And the only way to do that would be to eliminate the only two people who saw the link between him and Gordon and Wiltz: Laurie and myself. So Chauk was playing and not running. . . .

I parked four houses up the street and got out of the car. From a spot under the spare tire I extricated my 9-mm service revolver, checked to see it was loaded, shoved it in the waistband under my jacket, and dropped a spare magazine in my pocket. Then I walked toward Chauk's in the rain and darkness.

The gate to the backyard was still open, the garage closed and locked with a clasp lock. The porch light was out, but a streetlight next door caught the house in its dim vaporous arc, and I could see it clearly. The rain had come up again, and I drew the revolver from my waistband and shoved both it and my hands in my jacket pockets as I approached the house. If Chauk was inside he could see me. There was no point in stealth but no point in making myself a target either. I crossed over to the garage and jerked on the padlock, but it didn't give. Wondering if Chauk's car was inside, I moved around to the side where I had seen a small double-hung window. But a cabinet or piece of wood inside had been shoved up against it, and I couldn't see in.

As the rain continued to drum down, I moved through the gate to the backyard. A bicycle and a wagon were sitting half-on, half-off a narrow concrete strip adjacent to the rear of the garage. There was a small door giving access to the garage from the yard. I pulled on it, but it was locked with a dead bolt. Gregory Chauk was a careful man.

I moved under the overhang of a citrus tree and stared at the house a moment. It looked dead. Chauk must have taken Laurie elsewhere, but I was going to have to check it out. I held the revolver with the barrel pointed down, and crossed over to the uncovered back patio. It was typical California: an umbrella table and five chairs, built-in barbecue, planters of impatiens and pansies. A sliding glass door led to the rear of the house. Locked. Of course.

Cupping my hands around my eyes, I peered through the kitchen window. The house was dark, but I could see all the way through to a corner of the living room and the entrance hall. Nothing. With the rain pouring down, I moved toward the other side of the house and looked through the windows of two bedrooms, but there was no sign of life. Another gate led to the front yard. I walked around to the front porch.

Now what? I stood on the porch, protected from the rain, and thought about it. Although I couldn't be certain, Chauk probably wasn't inside. It had been a gamble anyway. Why would he have come back here when he was sure to know I would follow him? Unless he wanted me to follow him. But if that had been the case, he could have taken me anytime in the last five minutes as I trudged around the yard.

I could still go in through a window, but I wasn't feeling quite that foolhardy. And what would I do if Chauk was inside with a gun on Laurie? The LAPD should be here any minute; let them handle it. If Chauk *was* inside they would need the hostage team.

Then I remembered the small metal shed in the backyard where Laurie had been hiding. It was worth a look, anyway. Going back into the rain, I sloshed through the puddles on the front steps and onto the narrow cement pathway that led through the side gate to the rear.

The wind had slammed the gate shut, and I pushed it open and let it swing closed behind me. As I came around the corner of the house, I could see the tiny shed huddled alone in the rear of the yard as rain pelted down noisily on its dull metallic surface. I tightened my grip on the wet revolver as I edged my way forward. And then a blinding white light exploded in my brain, and I was half-aware of landing facedown in a puddle as the conscious world abruptly came to an end.


How much later was it?

I woke up in the rear seat of my car to the sound of muffled sobbing. I was stretched sideways on the seat like a rolled-up carpet, and I could see the back and top of Laurie's head in the passenger seat bobbing up and down as she sobbed through a gag that had been twisted around her head. Chauk's right hand flung out, striking her in the face. "Shut up, goddamn it, or I'll kill you right here."

I shifted on the seat, trying to lean up on my arm, and Chauk caught my eye in the rearview mirror. He smiled at me without turning his head. "That's electrical cord on your wrists and ankles; that way there won't be any telltale rope fibers on your skin or clothes. The rag under it is to keep it from tearing or burning your flesh. We want everything to look like an accident, of course, and rope burns wouldn't do at all. Frankly, I hadn't expected you to come back to consciousness. It's a testament, I suppose, to your Spartan life-style and thick skull."

Thick skull or not, my head was splitting with a jackhammer pain that ran down my spine to my legs; my eyes were having trouble focusing, giving Gregory Chauk a curious, faded look like the dream sequence in a second-rate film. "What did you hit me with?" I asked after a moment, vaguely aware that it was a mostly irrelevant question.

"A simple two-by-four—making do with what was handy. But it worked, didn't it?"

I tried sitting, but the cord wound around my feet had been tied to the front seat belt anchor on the floor of the car.

Chauk held up my revolver. "Don't even think about moving, or I'll stop right here and kill you *and* the girl. Much messier, but I'll do it if I have to and worry about explanations later."

I sank back on the seat and Chauk said, "When I discovered Laurie was missing from the shed tonight, I had a momentary worry. Then I thought, where is it likely she went if not with the nosy detective? How nice of you to be listed in the phone book."

Laurie started sobbing again, and I tried moving my hands to see if I could twist out of the electrical cords while Chauk was distracted, but he had done too methodical and careful a job. His hand shot out again, slapping Laurie across the mouth and nose. "Self-centered little rich-bitch," he muttered to himself. Laurie's head snapped to the side, and I could see a trickle of blood on her face as her nose began to bleed.

Where the hell was he going? I couldn't see anything in the darkness, but it was obvious that we were climbing through hilly, rural terrain. Assuming that I hadn't been unconscious for more than ten or fifteen minutes, there were only a couple of places we could have been. I tried the obvious. "Griffith Park."

"Bravo," Chauk said. "Give the man a serious accident." And he held up the revolver again.

"You weren't worried about making it look like an accident with Gordon," I said, and another pain raced down my spine and legs.

Chauk accelerated quickly around a turn, tossing me momentarily against the back of the front seat. The mention of Gordon seemed to infuriate him.

"That disgusting fat little man with his Rolex and gold neck chains and sexual obsessions. An ostentatious obscenity getting rich from pandering to the lowest tastes of the public. He actually offered me the grand amount of five thousand dollars—less than the cost of his watch, I might add—if I found his daughter; he had a feeling she was with Stephanie. Of course, what he really wanted was that video of him and his not-so-innocent playmates. I found the girl that very night as it turned out: he was so convinced she might have come to see Stephanie that I went out back and found her asleep in the shed. As simple as that. When I saw the unlabeled videotape, my curiosity was piqued; I took it inside and popped it in the machine and instantly knew what I had. That was when I decided Gordon was going to pay for it, and pay handsomely."

"A hundred thousand," I said.

He waved his right arm in the air. "Only a bit more than that automobile of his cost. But not so much, perhaps, that it would cause suspicion if he withdrew it from the bank. He had no idea it was I who had the video until we met at the airport." Chauk chuckled under his breath. "I told him our little meeting had more drama than his films were said to have, but he failed to see the humor."

"Since you got what you were after, why did you kill him?"

Chauk looked at me in the rearview mirror, his thick eyebrows knitting together. "You're the detective. You tell me." He twisted up another sharp curve and snapped off his headlights.

I said, "You figured, why stop at a hundred thousand? You'd sold a copy to Howie Wiltz, too. You're probably making plans now to contact some of the actresses on the film. And you couldn't let Gordon live once he knew you were the one doing the blackmailing."

Chauk shrugged. "Essentially correct. Very deductive of you. Except, perhaps also, I just wanted Gordon dead—my contribution to a civilized world. Selling the film to Wiltz was a major mistake, I saw quite soon. But I had anticipated just the two sales, one to Gordon and one to Wiltz. Then Wiltz demanded his money back, which I obviously wasn't prepared to do. He also figured out who did in poor Mackenzie, of course; it wasn't exactly hard to do, was it? He wasn't upset by it at all, rather pleased, I imagine, but he said he'd go to the authorities if I didn't return his sixty thousand dollars. He was afraid of being implicated in the murder; rightly so, given the circumstances. That sixty thousand was just the beginning, however: I'm sure most of the young ladies in that film will be delighted to buy their way out of the sort of unseemly publicity that would result in making their little romps with Gordon public. Do you know that film has already returned twice my annual salary at UCLA? Twenty-five years I've taught chemistry to the ignorant and rapacious offspring of LA's elite, and what have I got to show for it? While scum like Gordon and Wiltz own solid gold Cadillacs—metaphorically speaking, of course. I have a perfect right to be upset, don't you think? I mean, who has made a greater contribution to the world—those two idiots with their filth, or people like me who struggle for a lifetime to make things better for humanity?"

I didn't respond; I also didn't bother to tell Chauk that Kerry thought few if any of those actresses would pay to keep the film secret. Why disturb his visions of moral retribution and sudden wealth?

"The money will also help Stephanie," Chauk continued, his tone more reasonable now. Evidently he felt a need to justify—or at least explain—himself: "I'm fifty-six years old. What's going to happen to Stephanie when I'm no longer here to take care of her? With no money of her own, she'd end up in one of those horrible group homes for the adult retarded. With a trust fund, however, she can continue to live in the same house she always has, with a paid companion to look after her. Until I found that film, that was just a dream—not really possible. Now it is."

The car began to slow, and we turned again and began to rumble along what was obviously an unpaved road, a fire road probably, rutted with mud and potholes. Griffith Park, unlike most urban parks, is not a vast expanse of smooth, golf-course-like lawn but a mostly wild and mountainous forty-one hundred acres where people have lived for years among the coyotes and ravens without being discovered by the authorities. Access to the entrance roads is blocked at night and the park closed, but Chauk had managed to circumvent—or break through—one of the flimsy gates.

We traveled for several minutes on the road before the car finally stopped. Chauk leaned over the front seat and pointed the revolver at me, his jaw set with determination. "Pardon my triteness but one funny move and . . . well, you know."

He climbed out into the total darkness of our surroundings and crossed behind the car to the passenger side, where he yanked open the door. "Get out," he ordered, and Laurie, still sobbing, stepped unsteadily onto the road, looking as though she expected him to hit her any second. The rain had subsided, and the only sounds I could hear were the wind and Laurie's muted sobs. Her wrists were tied tightly with cord behind her back. Chauk grabbed her forearm, jerked her savagely away from the car, and yelled at her to sit on the soggy ground while he pushed the front seat forward and took out a pocket knife to cut the cord that held my feet to the floor. But the moment his back was turned, Laurie struggled unsteadily to her feet and began to run into the darkness as fast as she could.

Chauk swore loudly and raced after her, still holding the knife. From my position on the back seat I could see only that we were in a steep rocky area of thick underbrush and trees. Because of the storm there was no moon or stars, and the night swallowed up everything beyond fifty feet. Chauk and Laurie were out of sight, but I could hear Chauk grunting and swearing, and his feet splashing through the mud. A moment later he reappeared, holding Laurie by her bound wrists and pulling her along beside him. When they got to the car he gave her a furious shove, and she slammed against the fender and slumped to the ground, sobbing. Chauk bent in front of her, pressing the knife against the skin of her cheek. "You try to run away again and I'll cut your goddamn head off." Then he reached behind the front seat and quickly cut the cord holding me to the floor.

Waving my revolver, he said, "Very, very slowly, back out and stand next to the door."

It wasn't easy to do with my hands tied behind my back and my feet tied together, but I managed to wiggle out. Chauk kicked the seat back into an upright position. "We're going to have an automobile accident, Mr. Eton. You and the rich kid. But if you even *think* about running or trying to get away, I'll kill the both of you right here. An accident would be neater but—"

I was trying to judge my surroundings, but it was useless: somewhere in Griffith Park, but it might as well have been Montana from all I could see. Chauk looked down at Laurie. "Get up. *Now!*"

Laurie squirmed on the ground, her head and arms sprawled in a shallow puddle, and moaned loudly. Chauk nudged her angrily with his foot, and she rolled away and sobbed through her gag and kicked at the ground.

"Idiot!" Chauk mumbled to himself and reached down with his knife and sliced through the cords on her wrists, carefully picking up the cut pieces and putting them in his pocket. Then he bent and grabbed Laurie's arm and pulled her to her feet. Holding the gun on me with his right hand, he yanked her over to the open car door, shoving her onto the passenger seat.

He was too far away for me to risk trying anything. Without Laurie, I might have been able to run for it, since we were at the edge of a ravine that descended eighty or a hundred yards into darkness below. If his attention were diverted I might, somersaulting and hopping and tumbling, have been halfway down before he could react. Maybe. But it was obvious if I tried it now he'd put a bullet in Laurie first, then look for me.

When he got Laurie into the front seat, he checked her ankles and then rubbed her wrists to restore circulation where the cords had been too tight. I had to admire the way he had thought of everything. When our bodies were pulled from the wreckage of my automobile, he didn't want any suspicious marks on them to give cause for an investigation. As Chauk finished with Laurie, he took a two-gallon plastic container from the floor of the car and placed it on the ground.

"How are you going to explain my being at Griffith Park with Laurie in the middle of the night?" I asked.

Chauk smiled. "I don't have to explain it. I'm not involved in this at all. But it should be clear to the police that you found Laurie somewhere and took her off for whatever devious purpose of your own. Maybe you were hoping for ransom money, or, more likely, had some sexual need in mind and had to get rid of her after enjoying the obvious pleasures of her young body. You did bring her to your home tonight, didn't you? Perhaps someone saw that, also. If they didn't, an anonymous telephone call will send them to your apartment, where dear Laurie's prints abound. In the meantime you're going to the bottom of that canyon. Stand very still."

He approached with the knife in his left hand and quickly sawed through the cords on my feet, then stood up and pointed the gun directly in my face, moving cautiously forward until the cold metal of the barrel pressed against my lips. "I am not very good at this sort of thing," he said. "If you do anything to make me any more nervous than I already am, I'll shoot. I don't have the option of thinking about it: I'll just shoot. Understood?" With the gun still pointed at me, he moved slowly to the rear of the car, popped the trunk, and lifted out a metal five-gallon gas can. Holding it with his left hand, he crossed to the open door and placed it at my feet next to the plastic container he had removed from the front of the car. "Turn around and face the door."

I did as he said, and Chauk cut the electrical cords on my wrists, then quickly stepped back several steps. "Throw the cords over here."

I grabbed them from the ground and flung them at his feet. Chauk bent, retrieved the pieces, and shoved them in his pocket. I was wondering why he hadn't closed Laurie's door, when he pointed to the plastic container. "Pick it up."

It was a cheap picnic jug, I saw now, about ten inches across with a spigot and a tight-fitting press-on lid. I lifted it to my waist.

Chauk half-smiled at me. "I thought it unwise to risk leaving a can in the wreckage so I siphoned gas from my Toyota into this. Come the fire, it'll burn to nothing. A well-thought-out plan, though on reflection a gallon or two didn't seem quite enough. Therefore the can: insurance, we could call it. I want to make absolutely certain about this so it's better to error on the side of excess. I'll have to find a place to dispose of the container, of course, perhaps back up the hill somewhere." His voice rose abruptly, as if it were important that I recognized the attention he had given to all of this. "It's really quite clever, don't you think? An explosive device would leave traces, but with an auto accident, you'd *expect* to find a residue of gasoline. Even so, I imagine most of it will burn off."

I held the jug in my hands. Chauk took a step forward and waved his gun at me. "Take off the top and pour the gasoline on the floor. Be sure to get the passenger side too. Then throw the container inside."

I could hear a pack of coyotes yelping in the darkness, a distant high-pitched accompaniment to Laurie's continued moaning. She was watching me with undisguised fear through the windshield, not at all certain of what I was doing but terrified beyond belief.

Chauk's eyes were on both me and Laurie as I pried open the lid, the trapped fumes floating up around my head. Holding the jug in two hands, I knelt by the front door to move Laurie's legs away from the floor where I was to pour the gasoline. Then I turned, springing suddenly up at Chauk a half-dozen feet distant, and dousing him with the full two gallons of gasoline.

"*Run Laurie, run!*" I screamed.

# 18

CHAUK INSTANTLY SENSED WHAT I HAD DONE TO DISARM HIM: IF HE pulled the trigger now, the spark would set off an explosion that would immolate him.

Swearing violently, he ripped at his shirt, tearing it and an undershirt off. Laurie had disappeared into the darkness, and I did the same, racing down the steep ravine where Chauk had intended to push the car. The rain had unsettled the hillside, and I slipped on wet grass and loose rocks and tumbled forward, landing on my shoulder and the side of my head, careening downward. I scrambled to my feet and again toppled forward; this time I let gravity take over and wrapped my arms around me and rolled until I stopped. And then there was silence. I lay completely still and listened: the wind, and coyotes, now sounding far away. I could feel blood coming from my cheek, and I was caked with mud. Where was Laurie?

I had landed at the bottom of the narrow, steep-sided canyon, in what looked like an old riverbed, not more than twenty feet wide here. The undergrowth was thick and tall and extended into the darkness on either side of me as far as I could see. But above the riverbed along the canyon walls there was only rock and mud and an occasional bush too small to use as cover. I was OK as long as I didn't leave the bottom and as long as the storm clouds didn't move out, leaving the moon and stars to illuminate my hiding place. For several moments all was quiet. Then I heard a sound near me, like a small animal stirring.

"Laurie?" I whispered.

There was no response. It *couldn't* be Laurie; she had gone off in the opposite direction. Hadn't she?

Afraid to move, I held my breath and listened. Then I heard it again. But this time I knew what it was: Chauk, somewhere far above me, throwing rocks into the darkness, trying to spook me into revealing myself.

Rocks landed to both sides of me for several minutes. Then abruptly he changed tack.

"Eton!"

I didn't respond; I couldn't even see him, a voice from the darkness, echoing into the canyon from everywhere like the voice of God. I carefully pushed into a sitting position and tried to blink the mud from my eyes. Chauk's voice again boomed down.

"I have the girl, Eton," he yelled. "Either you come up now or she's going to die a very painful and very slow death. Do you hear me? I'll do it right here so you can watch if you want."

Then the headlights of the car far above me on the ridge snapped on, sending a double beam of moist white light shooting over my head.

A moment later Chauk's form appeared indistinctly in the glare, a bearded and bare-chested giant, his hair wet and disheveled, holding Laurie by the arm with his huge fist. She was soaked through and trembling. "Either you come up or she dies now," he yelled again.

Chauk was bluffing: he needed her dead, but he needed her dead in an accident that ended the investigation, not with a bullet. Or so I hoped.

Chauk spun Laurie around in the light so she was facing the ravine. "What's your daughter going to think when they find you dead with the fourteen-year-old retarded girl you were supposed to be searching for? Dear old Dad had a few perversions of his own, huh?"

I was looking around me, figuring how I could get out of the ravine and up to the top without Chauk seeing me, when his voice boomed out again, this time full of the hatred and futility and envy that seemed to have driven him these last few days. "Goddamn it, talk to me . . . " And then my five-cell flashlight snapped on, and a shaft of light hit the ground in front of me and swept off to the left. I flattened backwards onto the mud as the light swung again in my direction, tracing an erratic pattern all around me. "Eton . . . "

And then a popping sound and another and another as he shot wildly into the darkness.

"Then we'll wait!" Chauk yelled, sounding suddenly calmer, as if he had reconsidered his options. "It'll start getting light about five and the park doesn't open until after six. I can *afford* to wait. You're not going anywhere. Neither is she."

He flipped off the flashlight and pushed Laurie out of the beam of the headlights. A moment later I heard the car start and back up a few feet so Chauk could reposition it at the edge of the ravine, its front wheels off the road and over the side so the headlights shone down into the canyon, completely lighting up one end. In a little while I heard his voice coming down from a hundred yards away on the other side of me.

"We'll wait until it gets light. Have a good night." And for a few seconds he aimed a beam of light from my flashlight down into the canyon bottom.

He had me trapped now and he knew it: the automobile headlights on one side lit up the whole end of the small canyon, making escape from that side impossible. And Chauk guarded the other side. He was right; he could wait until morning.

For ten minutes I did nothing. Every once in a while the flashlight snapped on and sent a sudden beam of light racing through the bushes, then just as abruptly shut off. I tried to gauge how far away he was from me: I seemed to be just about equidistant from where he sat on an outcropping of rock eighty yards above, and the lighted end of the canyon where my car was. I had to do something, I couldn't wait for Chauk to make the first move. And morning would be too late. Slowly, I began moving away from his end of the canyon toward where the headlights shone down. I crawled on my hands and knees, through mud and rock, carefully bending aside underbrush and letting it settle back in place. The mist had thickened again, but it wasn't heavy enough to clean the mud that clung to my hands and face like clay.

After what must have been half an hour I had worked my way down to a cluster of hawthorn and manzanita at the point where darkness gave way gradually to the light from my headlights. Now what? Chauk hadn't shown his light into the ravine since I had moved off, I realized. What the hell was he doing? I turned back and stared up to where he had been, but I was too far away to see. I wiped mud from my eyes and hair; I was soaked through to my skin, and my suede jacket felt as heavy as an army overcoat. I wanted to take it off, but I had a light-colored shirt underneath that would have shown up too easily in the dark.

Somewhere in the distance I heard a twig break and my heart jumped. Chauk! Or was it? Maybe it wasn't, maybe it was the wind or an animal, a coyote that had come over to see what all the commotion was about. Seconds later I heard it again, louder. No doubt about it, this time. Chauk was coming after me; he'd decided not to wait after all. Impatience seemed out of character but he probably wanted to get it over with so he could disappear before it turned light.

Then I heard a bush move as a body brushed against it. I had to get out of here. I stared around, trying not to panic. I couldn't go forward because of the lights. How far away was he? There was no way to judge but it didn't matter; I had to get on the other side of him, toward the dark end of the ravine. And I had to do it now. Moving with what felt like agonizing slowness, I set off at an angle toward the rising wall of the canyon to my rear, dragging mud with me as I slipped between growths of manzanita and sagebrush and knee-high grass.

When I heard him again, I flattened against the ground. Bushes moved suddenly twenty feet away; twigs cracked and broke; I could hear more branches being pushed aside. I took a breath and held my body rigid against the ground.

He was coming closer, but moving slowly, not knowing where I was and wary of being jumped. *Do it!* I told myself: find a stick, a rock, wait and come up behind him. Then I saw his shoes, caked and heavy, and his legs, as he came within ten feet and stopped. I didn't dare move my head, and my heart pounded against the wet earth as I focused on his feet. I could hear him breathing, a quick, shallow, gasping sound. For a long time he stood stationary, looking around. Then he began walking again.

I let my breath out as he disappeared. Wait! Let him get farther away. I lay still. Three minutes . . . five minutes . . . Long enough? I couldn't tell. But I had to get out of here. Pushing onto my knees, I began to crawl in the direction Chauk had come from. After half a minute I stopped and listened. Nothing. I moved off again, staying on my hands and knees, halting when I heard something.

In five minutes I couldn't have covered thirty yards. Again I stopped and listened briefly. The wind, icy and wet, rustling the grass and bushes, making me shiver with cold . . . an airliner droning far overhead in the darkness, disappearing to the north. *Move!* A moment later my hand came down in a puddle and I fell forward, my arm slipping out and my face dropping into the muddy water. I pulled my body through it and listened again. Still no Chauk. Turning back, I gazed along the beam of light shining down from above. Where the hell was he? What was he doing?

I had to move faster. Chauk would soon realize I'd gotten around him. Keeping low to the ground, I began to scramble through the mud. Five minutes later I was at the darkened end of the ravine, below the spot where Chauk had been waiting earlier. I sat on my knees and caught my breath. Where could he be? At the other end, I guessed, wondering where I was. Probably panicky that he couldn't find me. I was going to have to get Laurie.

I took a breath, then started climbing the canyon wall. Halfway to the top I turned and gazed below me into the dry riverbed. Except for the faint outline of bushes and trees I could see nothing. I began to hurry. Two minutes later I was at the top, my car coming into view at the far end of the clearing, its front end and headlights pointing down the cliff.

Standing behind a scrub oak, I caught my breath again, and watched. Was he there? On the other side of the Buick, maybe? I'd have to chance it: I couldn't wait any longer. Moving as quietly as I could through the mud and grass, I raced to the car. Panting, my legs trembling, I looked in the back seat. Laurie was on her side, hands and feet bound and a gag in her mouth.

I opened the car door, jamming my finger on the door button so the interior light didn't come on. Chauk had taken the keys out of the ignition. Pulling forward on the seat, I whispered, "Laurie." She moaned and turned and gaped at me with fear.

"Laurie. Try to get out of the car. We're going away."

She stared wildly, her eyes widening and full of tears.

"Get out, Laurie!"

Her head shook furiously back and forth.

With an effort I made my voice go calm. "Laurie, we'll go see your mother." Using my free hand, I tugged gently on her foot. "We're going away from Mr. Chauk. He won't hurt you. We'll go see Mommy."

She moaned again through the gag and tried to say something.

"Come on," I whispered urgently, and pulled again at her feet.

"Please, Laurie. Mommy—"

She looked at me and blinked her eyes, then nodded slowly, as though recognizing me vaguely as a friend, someone who knew Mommy. Abruptly she began squirming on the seat. "Hurry—" I said.

With slow, clumsy movements she managed to push her feet out the door. Keeping my left hand on the button, I reached for her bound arm and pulled her through the opening. I shut the door instantly, lifted her in my arms, and ran as fast as I could to the edge of the clearing. There was no way she could be quiet enough for us to sneak away, and the terrain was too hilly and unstable for me to carry her out. I was going to have to deal with Chauk. Thirty feet up the incline I found an overgrown hawthorn, hurried to the far side of it, and laid her carefully on the ground.

Kneeling down, I said, "Don't move, Laurie! Don't try to leave. I'll come back and get you in just a minute. Do you understand?"

She nodded her head, up and down, up and down, up and down. Deciding she was safer with her gag on, I patted her firmly on the shoulder. "Don't move!" I whispered again and smiled at her.

Coming back around the bush, I could see that Chauk still hadn't returned. I hurried back to the Buick. Slipping the door open, I again placed a finger on the light button, and got into the driver's seat, letting the door close softly. Quickly, I climbed into the rear of the car and, using both hands, pulled as hard as I could on the seat back. Within seconds it sprang free. A thick fabric and cardboard liner formed the back wall of the trunk. I hit it with my fist, stuck my hand through, and rummaged around blindly for my toolbox and a shop rag. When my fingers touched a box of 9-mm ammunition, I pulled it out, too.

Outside the car, I dropped to one knee and grabbed a small Phillips head screwdriver from the toolbox along with a disposable lighter I keep for road flares. Then I flattened on the ground, scrunched underneath the car, and rolled over on my back. Placing the tip of the screwdriver on the underside of the gas tank I hit the handle with the heel of my palm. It clunked dully. Quickly, I hit it again and made a small indentation on the rusted surface of the tank. Two more hits deepened it. Then pushing as if I were driving a screw, I twisted the screwdriver into the metal until a thin stream of gasoline began to fall. Perfect! I thought: only a trickle, make it last. . . .

I scampered out from under the car, hurriedly grabbed the box of shells, and reached under, placing it next to the dripping gasoline. I didn't really need it, I supposed, but every little bit helped. Then I shoved the toolbox out of the way under the car, also.

Now Chauk's gas can, the added insurance, he called it. It was still next to the car, where he had set it. I twisted off the cap, hefted it up, and began to pour a trail from under the rear of the car to a cluster of bushes thirty feet away. It didn't matter if the grass was wet—it was the gasoline that was going to burn. There was another gallon or so left, so I put a ring around the front of the car, too. With the smell of gasoline on his torso and pants, I was counting on Chauk not noticing; he wasn't going to be there long enough to think about it anyway. With the final half-pint or so, I soaked a strip I had ripped from the shop rag, then put the can back next to the car.

I needed a rock. When Chauk returned to the car I wanted a diversion. I could tie the rag to a rock, light it, and throw it over the cliff or into the woods, then torch the trail when he was facing away to see what had happened. Two seconds! I thought: That's all I need. The whole thing wouldn't take two seconds.

Hurrying to the edge of the woods, I quickly found a baseball-sized stone and was tying the rag to it when Chauk's angry voice rumbled up behind me. "Going somewhere?"

With a sinking feeling I turned around. He was standing twenty feet distant, breathing hard, the gun in his hand. His hair and beard were caked with mud, and his hand trembled as he pointed the gun at me.

"Where's the girl?" he demanded.

"Gone," I said. "Ran off. You'll never find her."

"Where could she go?" he said derisively, his eyes darting around the clearing. "I'll find her! It might take some time, but she won't get far." He waved the gun angrily at me. "First things first." Carefully backing up, he moved to the car, keeping the gun on me, and yanked open the passenger door.

"You've proven to be a great deal of trouble," he said loudly. "It all comes to a satisfactory end, however, if somewhat more tardily than I would have wished."

He bent to retrieve the plastic picnic jug from the ground, and I slipped the lighter from my pocket. Two seconds—I repeated to myself and let my hands hang at my sides. As Chauk straightened, our eyes met across the darkness and my heart speeded up. *He knows*, I thought: Christ, he saw me. But Chauk seemed too intent on his self-congratulations to notice. His voice again rose. "There was nothing wrong with the plan. Only the execution. We will continue as before with the removal of the evidence." He tossed the jug carelessly into the car and smiled grimly, catching my eye again and savoring the moment. "This time *I'll* handle the gasoline. Do not move—" With the gun in one hand he knelt by the hood to unscrew the top of the five-gallon can that he had planned to use to immolate Laurie and myself. The instant his eyes left me I touched the lighter to the gas-soaked rag and flung it underhand at the rear of the car.

Bending down, Chauk lifted the surprisingly light can, and in that second he knew, in that seemingly infinite speck of time, holding the can in his hand, his mind working, he knew, he *knew*, and his mind worked, and he looked at me but it was too late and the fire leapt up all around him and he gazed and gazed and his face turned toward me in rage and astonishment and then fire reached the ammo and dripping gas.

# 19

CIVILIZED LIVING REQUIRES CERTAIN COMPROMISES, TRACY AND I HAD discovered after a few years of father-daughter disagreements. So we came up with a list of rules which we would try to abide by: neither of us would hog the telephone; we should have breakfast and dinner together every day if possible; and—most important—civilized people do not give surprise parties.

So I was ready when Tracy brought Kerry, Moses, Rudy, and Eddy Baskerville into the living room where I was mending from my wounds. Rudy was carrying a six-pack of Bud in longneck bottles, and I accepted one gratefully. Then he relaxed back on the couch and explained to me the strange memory I had of flying.

"The police helicopter saw the explosion and thought it was a fire in the park. When their spotlight picked you out they figured you started it and had gotten hurt. They kept you in their light until a patrol car could find you. Then they saw Laurie and figured you for a kidnapper or rapist."

Unconsciously I rubbed at my wrists, which had been handcuffed behind my back before I had been helicoptered out to the jail ward at County General. I guess the cops thought I had wounded myself in the side, too: shrapnel from the Buick, some of it catching me as I was flung to the ground from the force of the blast. I hadn't been too injured to retrieve Laurie, but as I was carrying her back to the clearing I sank into unconsciousness. Two days in the jail ward followed before being transferred to a regular room, where Pakistani doctors and Spanish-speaking nurses trooped by and told me I was very lucky. For being alive, I asked, or for no longer being shackled to the bed? I'd come home yesterday.

"It took a couple of days before Laurie could explain it all," Rudy went on. "She was pretty upset."

I took another beer from the six-pack and felt the stitches where they had sewn me up. I'd been pretty upset, too. Kerry twisted the top off the beer for me and smiled as I took it from her hand. She was looking good, I thought, in wintry rose-colored slacks and a ski sweater. She and Tracy had visited me in the hospital once the cops had allowed it, and we'd spent a lot of time talking. I was happy to see how well the two of them got on together, since Tracy and I didn't always see eye-to-eye on my women friends. Before Kerry left that night she had wondered if I might like to spend a week recuperating in Maui with her, once Jason Esserton started actual production on the film. Just as I'd been about to answer, the phone had rung, and Tracy picked it up and said, "It's Judy Chen." "Who's that?" Kerry asked and when I said, "A friend," she turned to Tracy and said, "Tell her he's busy."

"Recuperating," I'd added.

Now to Kerry, I said, "How's Laurie holding up?"

"Catherine took her to Switzerland for a month. She took Stephanie, too. Catherine said she'll probably enroll them both in a private school there. I felt so bad for Laurie when I heard she'd been living in that awful shed in the back of Chauk's house."

"I guess Chauk didn't want her in the house where Gordon might find her, and there was no reason to kill her until he realized I had her and probably knew who had found the film and was using it for blackmail. How's Esserton coming along, by the way?"

Kerry smiled. "Shooting starts Monday. There shouldn't be any problems. . . ."

"Now that you've got the storyboards," I said and she smiled again. "I do feel a strong need to recuperate," I added as I finished off the beer.

Kerry dropped an envelope on the coffee table. "Airplane tickets. For medicinal purposes only."

"Pure greed," Moses said, abruptly changing the subject. "Poor old Chauk should have been satisfied with selling that film once, if he had to sell it at all. But he tried to choke every penny he could possibly get from it. He should have known there'd be trouble. Good heavens, he was a *scientist*."

"I think he got tired of seeing all the wealth in that part of town," I said. "He'd worked for years at the university and had nothing to show for it, while people like Gordon flaunted their jewelry and bad taste at the same time."

"Still," Moses said. "The film was certainly good luck for him, but if he had been thinking rationally he'd have seen that it wasn't quite the gold mine he dreamed. And blackmail is the most dangerous of crimes—"

"He *wasn't* thinking rationally," I said. "It was the frustrations of a lifetime hitting all at once. When he saw a chance to make some money he took it; when he saw how eager Wiltz was to get the film, he figured he could sell it over and over."

"We should've thought of Chauk from the first," Eddy said. "Because of the bomb. Whoever made it knew what he was doing; not many people would. But Chauk was a chemist."

Moses looked abashed. "Of course . . . "

"Hindsight," I said.

One thing was still bothering me. "What happened to the video—the one everyone was so anxious to get their hands on?" The one with Kerry and Anna; the one that could still destroy both their careers if it got out. Presumably it would have turned up at Chauk's house in the police search. Then we'd start hearing things in the gossip columns.

Kerry looked at Rudy and Rudy looked at Moses and Eddy. Everyone shrugged. A mystery.

Rudy said, "It seems to have disappeared. When I searched Chauk's house—"

"Wait a minute," I said. "*You* searched his house? You weren't even on the team."

"I volunteered to help out with the search. Captain Reddig took me along. If there was any video there it must have walked out under some guy's shirt."

I looked at him. "That would be obstruction of justice."

Rudy shook his head. "Obstruction of the law. It's not the same thing."

Kerry smiled. "I videotaped the Lakers game you missed when you were in surgery. It's the oddest thing—someone threw an old cassette in my car. I just taped the game on top of it. Why don't you come over tonight and watch it? Start recuperating early—"